NOSTRADAMUS

NOSTRADAMUS

KNUT BOESER

Translated by John Brownjohn

HarperSanFrancisco
A Division of HarperCollins*Publishers*

Originally published in Great Britain by Bloomsbury Publishing.

FIRST EDITION

Library of Congress Cataloging-in-Publication Data

Boeser, Knut.
    Nostradamus : a novel by Knut Boeser, based on his screenplay / Knut Boeser. — 1st ed.
      p. cm.
    ISBN 0–06–251245–5 (pbk.)
    1. Nostradamus, 1503–1566—Fiction.
    2. Prophets—France—Fiction.
    I. Title
PS3552.O425N67   1994   94–22761
813'.54—dc20   CIP

---

94 95 96 97 98 HAD 10 9 8 7 6 5 4 3 2 1

This edition is printed on acid-free paper that meets the American National Standards Institute Z39.48 Standard.

PART ONE

Sophie

Storm-driven flames swept the face of the earth once more. The conflagration spread, avidly seeking nourishment. The heavens darkened, the turbulent clouds were rent by shafts of lightning, the earth's crust split open. Colossal buildings of steel, glass and stone collapsed and fell into yawning fissures and chasms. A tidal wave engulfed the land. Boiling magma gushed from the bowels of the earth, so hot that the inrushing water evaporated in an instant. It was dark now – dark and cold, desolate and deserted. Not a sound broke the silence. Death, nothing but death reigned supreme far and wide.

Michel cried out and sat up with a start, trembling in every limb. His forehead was beaded with cold sweat. He peered around in a daze, not knowing where he was. The little room: the bed, the table, the chair, the closet, the books, the celestial maps on the wall. Outside, the sunlight that was streaming through the open window shone brightly on the familiar roofs of Montpellier.

He could hear street traders and craftsmen at their work, hear the iron-rimmed wheels of heavy wagons rumbling over the cobblestones. A bell was tolling in the church across the way.

He had fallen asleep over the books that littered his desk, having worked throughout the night yet again. Unrefreshed by his brief nap, he rubbed his eyes and stretched. He ached all over, every muscle contorted by his uncomfortable position at the desk and the physical tension induced by his nightmare. It was always such an effort to withstand the horrors that kept crowding in on him.

He slowly pointed to every object in the room and spoke its name. "Table," he said, and rested his hand on it. Book, quill, ink, cupboard, chair — he named them all in turn and, by so doing, knitted the world together again. Everything was in its accustomed place. Nothing had happened, thank God. He breathed a prayer that all might remain as it was, familiar and dependable. All was well, nothing must ever change.

Lucille, his landlady, knocked and entered. She was his own age, twenty-two. Guessing what had happened, she gently stroked his brow.

"It was only a dream," she said. "A bad dream, monsieur, nothing more. You have them so often."

He nodded. "What's the time?"

"Not far short of ten o'clock. You'll be late for your lecture again."

"Why on earth didn't you warn me?"

She sighed. "I didn't dare knock before. You're always so angry when I interrupt your work."

"But I wasn't working. I fell asleep."

"How was I to know? I don't have second sight."

Lucille clicked her tongue at him and made for the door, where she turned for a parting shot. "Next time, you'd do better to sleep in your bed."

Michel made an impatient gesture as the door closed behind her. At length he stood up, took his coat from the hook and put his hat on. He surveyed the room once more. Everything was as it should be. All was well – yes, but why was he haunted by these terrible visions? What was this curse that weighed upon him so heavily? It had always been the same, ever since his childhood. He would start up in bed and run screaming from the room. He had just turned eight the first time he saw such visions of disaster. He dashed downstairs to the kitchen, where his father sat at breakfast with his grandfather, who was paying them a brief visit. "It's the end of the world!" he shouted. "Everything's on fire!"

Father had taken him in his arms, stroked his hair, and talked to him soothingly.

"You had a nightmare. It's nothing. You're too fanciful, that's all."

"High time his mother returned," said Grandfather.

Michel had taken a piece of bread from the plate and was making for the stairs again. "Aunt won't die for another ten days," he said without thinking, "so Mother won't be back till after the funeral."

Grandfather stared at him. "What was that you said?"

Michel turned. "I don't remember."

"You said your aunt won't die for another ten days."

"If I did, it must be true." So saying, Michel left the kitchen and climbed the stairs to his room again.

"Does he often do that?" his grandfather asked.

"What?"

"Well, make predictions."

"Oh come! It was childish nonsense, nothing more."

"You must beware of that."

"Why? You don't think he has second sight, do you?"

"Let us hope not. Those who know what the future holds in store suffer twice over. It's a terrible affliction to be singled out by God in that way."

"An affliction?" Michel's father raised his eyebrows. "Wouldn't it be more accurate to call it a blessing?"

"God exalts the prophet above common mortals," the old man said solemnly, "and they exact a terrible revenge."

Michel overheard those words. He was too sleepy to think about them at the time, but he never forgot them.

He took some paper and two books from the table and stowed them in the small leather scrip he had inherited from his grandfather. There was a loaf of bread on the table. He broke off a piece and wolfed it as he went. In the hallway he almost tripped over Lucille, who was down on her knees scrubbing the floorboards with a stiff brush. She looked up at him and smiled.

"You're always late."

"I don't know why I go at all," Michel said grumpily. "I already know everything they tell me."

Looking at her, he was reminded of Sophie – yes, buxom, rosy-cheeked, fair-haired Sophie. Lucille had the same big, blue, alert eyes, the same almost imperceptible squint, the same spirit of mischief, the same vigour – even the same dimple. When she laughed, baring her white teeth, it might have been Sophie laughing. Her full breasts threatened to overflow her linen dress. The buttons always came undone when she was working, but Lucille didn't care. It had been the same with Sophie. Michel shook his head to banish the recollection . . .

Sophie had been his parents' chambermaid. She was just putting a big pot on the stove when he entered the kitchen. He was nine now – it was a year since that first, terrible dream. He sat down at the table, helped himself to a slice of bread, took a bite, and opened the book he had brought downstairs with him. Sophie bent over him, sniffed, and pulled a face.

"Ugh, you grubby little beast, you haven't washed again. Shame on you!" She made a vulgar noise and held her nose.

Michel laughed. "No time. Besides, washing is bad for you."

"Not washing, you mean. People who don't wash make themselves ill." Sophie took his book away. "And don't read at table. You behave well enough when you eat with your parents, so why not with me? I may only be a maidservant, but I wasn't born in a pigsty." Guessing what would happen, she darted around to the other side of the table, laughing gaily, and held the book above her head. Michel jumped up, climbed on the table, and tried to snatch it away. He hurled himself at her, clung to her, tried to pull her arm down, but she was far too strong for him.

"Too much reading makes a person soft in the head," she said, glancing at the title of the book. "Anyway, this isn't the book you're supposed to be reading. Ovid's *Art of Love* isn't for little children." She flicked him lightly on the nose. "Mind your grandfather doesn't catch you."

Michel stared at her in surprise. "I didn't know you could read."

Sophie laughed and shook her head. "You're meant to be reading Plutarch — that's what your grandfather said. I'll tell him you disobeyed his orders."

"And I'll tell him you sneak out into the woods at night and gather herbs with Gabrille from the smithy." He put his arms around her neck.

"I only gather them for your grandfather. He needs them for his medicines."

"So why do you dance around the fire with Gabrille and old Jacqueline? Why in the middle of the night? Why at a crossroads? Do you do *that* for Grandfather's medicines?"

Sophie turned pale. She set him down, put her hands on his shoulders, and looked at him earnestly. "How did you know all that?"

"I followed you one night without being seen. I wanted to know who your lover was."

Sophie kneeled before him. "Michel, if anyone finds out — "

"I know," he broke in. "You'll be burned as a witch. That's because your lover" — he laughed and prodded her bosom with the tip of his forefinger — "is the Devil."

Sophie was speechless. Michel took advantage of this momentary opportunity to snatch the book from her hand and scamper out of the kitchen.

"Michel!" Sophie called after him. All at once, there was a note of panic in her voice.

Michel stopped short and retraced his steps. "Don't be afraid, Sophie," he told her reassuringly, "I won't

give you away. Tell me, though, how is it you learned
to read?"

She shrugged. "Before I came to you, while I was
still living at home with my parents, I often cooked
for a priest whose housekeeper had died. It was he
that taught me."

Michel quickly grabbed another slice of bread from
the table and ran upstairs to his room. He sat beside
the open window, reading his beloved Ovid, nibbling
the crusty bread, and thinking of Sophie. He loved his
games with her – loved frolicking with her. She thought
nothing of it when he hugged and kissed her or forced
her to the ground and sat on top of her. To Sophie
he was just a little shrimp – well, she was welcome
to think so – but to him she was sheer delight. When
they rolled around on the floor, or when she was
making his bed and he romped with her among the
pillows, or when he saw the beginnings of her breasts,
or when he inhaled the scent of her, or when he buried
his face in her skirt, or when he caught a glimpse of
her thighs, or when he quickly fondled her - all those
things excited him. He sometimes suspected that she
had long ago grasped what was really going on, and
that she pretended not to only because she enjoyed
such frolics as much as he did – frolics which were,
of course, permissible only for as long as she thought
him an innocent, affectionate, playful, exuberant child.
On the occasions when he became too boisterous she
would laugh and say, "What ever will become of you!
You're going to drive the womenfolk mad some day."
And when he looked at her inquiringly, as he did each
time, she would ruffle his hair. "You don't understand
that yet, you little rascal. Come on now, back to your
books. I've also got work to do."

Some friends playing ball in the street spotted Michel at the upstairs window and called to him. He laid his book aside, climbed out, and nimbly descended the trelliswork. Once safely down he trapped the ball, kicked it across the street and raced after it, feinting and dribbling as he went. Ovid and Sophie, Grandfather and Plutarch were forgotten in a trice.

Sophie emerged from the house soon afterwards. She was angry – his grandfather had been looking for him everywhere – but she had no chance to scold him because he merely laughed and ran off. Let her catch him if she could! He sprinted down the street but tripped and fell, grazing his knee on the gravelly surface. Blood oozed from the lacerations, which hurt like the devil. Michel sat down on a doorstep and fought back the tears that welled from his eyes. He blew on the graze to take the sting out of it, gingerly plucked off shreds of skin, extracted fragments of grit from the raw flesh. Sophie, panting hard, caught him up. She examined his knee and shook her head a little. Then she knelt down, bent over, and applied her tongue to the wound. Michel watched her open-mouthed.

"What are you doing?"

"Licking it clean."

"Why?"

"Because that's what animals do. It'll heal quicker that way. Always watch what animals do – see what herbs or flowers they eat when they're sick. Animals are the finest physicians of all."

Michel preserved a vivid memory of Sophie down on her knees before him, of her cherry-red lips and the pale pink tongue that was slowly, deliberately licking his wound clean, of the hands that were clasping his knee. He could see down the front of her dress – see her smooth, milk-white breasts. He put out his hand, hesitated for a moment, then gently buried his fingers in her hair.

She stared at him in astonishment. The little fellow was actually looking down her dress! She wagged her head in disapproval, but she couldn't help laughing at his effrontery.

"You're beautiful, Sophie." He said it very softly, very seriously.

"Nonsense, you rascal. Your mother's beautiful. I'm just a country girl. Country girls are strong and healthy, not beautiful."

"Yes, you are. You're very beautiful."

"What's come over you, you naughty boy? You're far too young for such talk!" She wagged her head again, looking thoroughly embarrassed.

Michel remembered that day as if it were yesterday. It was late summer, the sun was shining, and he was gazing into Sophie's big, blue eyes. He could see and hear nothing but her. With a final shake of the head she bent over his knee and continued to lick the wound clean. He shut his eyes and pleasurably surrendered to her ministrations.

And then, without warning, Sophie was jerked to her feet. Four black-clad figures, servants of the Holy Inquisition, had caught her by the arms and were holding her fast. Frightened townsfolk steered clear of the group and hurried past on the other side of the street. None of them wanted anything to do with such an incident.

"Sophie Bertrand," the leader of the four proclaimed in a sepulchral voice, "I arrest you in the name of the Holy Inquisition. You stand accused of lycanthropy: of having, at the full moon, transformed yourself into a she-wolf and fornicated with the Devil in that bestial guise; of having kissed his hind quarters and licked his privy parts, in return for which he thrice insinuated himself into your lascivious body and entrusted you with poisonous herbs whose traces no one can detect; of having used the said poison to kill the blacksmith's honourable and late-lamented wife so that his maid-servant, Gabrille, could bend him to her will and lay hands on his worldly goods."

Sophie shook her head. She even laughed. "This is absurd," she said.

Michel was amazed that she should show so little fear of such men. Had she no notion of the danger she was in? She looked them straight in the eye, and he saw the three underlings avert their gaze. Only the inquisitor himself remained unmoved.

"Do not seek to deny it," he said. "Gabrille has confessed all. How the two of you prepared the poison at dead of night and did secretly administer it to the blacksmith's wife in her soup. How you fornicated with the Devil, devoured his dung and drank his urine. She has sworn by the Holy Virgin that you bewitched her with all manner of herbs and juices, with dark conjurations and obscene caresses. It was thus that you put her under your spell."

The inquisitor nodded to his henchmen, who started to drag Sophie away.

Michel hurled himself between them. "Let her go!" he shouted. Desperately, he caught hold of Sophie's dress and tried to wrest her away from the men. "Let her go this instant!" he shouted again. The inquisitor grabbed him by the collar and lifted him off the ground. Holding the boy so tightly that it hurt, he told him, in a voice like the hiss of a serpent, to hold his peace. But

Michel continued to shout with all his might, calling for his father and grandfather. Sophie just had time to tell him to go home before the men dragged her away.

Grandfather came hurrying up. "Come with me, boy," was all he said, holding out his hand. The inquisitor put Michel down.

Michel shouted to Grandfather to help Sophie. He ran after her, embraced her with tears streaming down his cheeks. He was in despair. One of her captors wrenched him away and brought him back to the inquisitor. He lashed out with his feet, pummelled the man with his fists, bit, scratched, kicked. The inquisitor shook his head. Looking at Sophie, he murmured, "Have you bewitched this child, too, that he should behave like a besotted fool?" He turned to Grandfather and added, in a low, ominous voice, "This matter needs further investigation. We shall return."

Grandfather took Michel's hand and drew him towards the house. "Come home, boy."

"But we must help her!"

"There's nothing we can do. Come home, please."

The servants of the Holy Inquisition marched Sophie off. She offered no resistance. The inquisitor looked round once more, pointed to Michel, and said menacingly, "We shall look into this matter."

Sophie made a full confession under torture and was burned in the market-place that same afternoon, watched by the many townsfolk who had gathered to watch the spectacle. Michel, determined to be with Sophie until the very end, was there too. Having stolen out of the house and wormed his way to the front of the crowd, he saw her lashed to a stake on top of the pyre. She scanned the spectators as though searching for someone. Then she caught sight of Michel, and a smile flickered across her tormented face. She said something he couldn't catch. Everyone around him was talking excitedly. The witch would soon be consumed by fire, they told each other. The angel of death would spread his wings over the square and bless them all, for all of them lived under the sign of death and craved his favour and mercy. He was now to receive his sacrifice. Would he be content with it?

Michel saw a man step forward with a blazing torch. The inquisitor, arms folded on his chest, was standing on a platform behind the pyre. He gave the man a little nod to signify that he should light it. The brushwood caught, the flames shot up, ignited Sophie's dress and ate into the flesh beneath. Sophie was ablaze in no time. The scorching updraft blew her fair hair skyward before the flames set fire to it, and for an instant she resembled a transfigured saint bathed in celestial radiance. Then Michel heard her cry out. A single, piercing cry of agony issued from deep inside her. Michel saw her open mouth and her staring eyes, now raised to heaven in entreaty. But the flawless blue sky remained mute and gave no sign. At last her head fell forward on her breast and she went limp, unable to feel the pain any more.

Grandfather had pushed his way to the front of the crowd. He took Michel by the hand and led him away. The last thing Michel saw was the inquisitor looking across at them. There was a malicious little smile on his thin lips, and Michel knew that he would never forget that face for as long as he lived – that it would haunt him for evermore.

The townsfolk, disappointed that the whole affair was over so quickly, lingered until the pyre had been reduced to a heap of ashes. Michel and his grandfather had withdrawn to the outskirts of the crowd and were standing in the lee of the church. The sweet, pungent scent of Sophie's roasted flesh hung heavy over the market-place. Flakes of ash were whirling through the air. Michel looked up at the sky, and all that was left of Sophie came drifting down on him like a dark snowstorm. He caught a flake of ash on his palm and put his tongue to it. Oh Sophie, so sweet in life, so bitter in death!

Since then his thoughts had been of her alone. No other girl or woman had interested him thereafter. He felt dead inside. Sometimes, though, Sophie would come to him in the night. She was ablaze, and everything around her was enveloped in glorious refulgence. She stretched out her hand to him. And when he went to her, torn between fear and desire, she would take him in her arms. He was always nine years old in these dreams. He would rest his head on her breast, and she would gently caress and console him, and then he, too, would catch fire.

Michel looked down at Lucille. "But you're not on fire," he muttered.

Lucille looked puzzled. She tossed the scrubbing brush into the bucket and stood up. "What's wrong with you? You look so strange – as if you've seen a ghost. It really frightens me when you look like that."

Michel shook his head and made no reply. He walked quickly past her to the front door.

Lucille followed him, drying her hands on her apron. "Will you be home late?"

"No, why do you ask?"

She straightened his collar. He always looked so untidy, never paid attention to his clothes, was forever day-dreaming, forgot things unless she jogged his memory, needed looking after the whole time, even forgot to eat.

"I've just baked a cake," she said. "You must have a nice big slice of it, otherwise you'll fade away to nothing. Always reading, always looking at the stars when there are plenty of good things down here on earth." She stroked his face. "You're all pale. I shall have to think of something that will put some colour back into your handsome face."

Michel stared at her. "I must go," he said.

"Very well," she said, with her hand still resting on his chest. "Then go, monsieur."

He nodded, but he continued to stand there, gazing at her. He knew what she wanted and he wanted it too, but he was too diffident. He didn't dare, wasn't sufficiently sure of himself. Did she really desire him? He knew so little about women. Was she merely teasing him? Was she making fun of him? No, there was a kind of veil over the eyes that were gazing deep, infinitely deep, into his, and her squint was a trifle more pronounced than usual. No, he wasn't mistaken. Or was he? Perhaps it was all a figment of his overheated imagination. After all, he could scarcely distinguish between dreams and reality at the best of times. He was forever being assailed by mental images, and not only in his sleep – in the daytime, too. They were frightful scenes of destruction and desolation for the most part. He seldom had cheerful, happy dreams.

What would happen if he simply took her in his arms? Wasn't that what she wanted? On the other hand, she might be outraged – furious and offended. She might scream and push him away and lash out and scratch and bite him and cry for help to her ugly husband. A surly, boorish, brutal, vulgar fellow, always drunk and ill-humoured, Louis worked in the tannery along the street. His wrinkled skin was as ingrained with filth as his behaviour was mean and vindictive. Why in heaven's name had she married him? Michel found it incomprehensible. She was young and pretty, sturdy and intelligent. What could she see in the man? Michel had been watching her for weeks now, ever since the day he moved in. It was two months since he had come to Montpellier from Avignon and enrolled at the university as a medical student. He was forever inventing pretexts to watch Lucille: in the kitchen, when her strong hands kneaded dough on the wooden table; at the stove, when she stirred a pot of soup with her wooden ladle; when she scattered the soup with herbs by bruising them between her palms; when she bent over the tub to do the laundry, rubbing the sheets and hard soap against the ribbed wooden washboard; when she stooped and the skirt drew tight over her haunches; when she wiped the sweat from her brow with the back of her hand. He could have watched her for hours on end, and was always devising some excuse to be near her. He chopped firewood, kindled the stove, carried water into the house. Then he would stand in the doorway, gazing at her. As for Lucille, she never seemed to notice him, always concentrated on her work. He liked to watch her when she knelt on the floor, scrubbing the boards with her skirt and her sleeves hitched up, brushing the odd stray curl out of her eyes. Her movements were so straightforward, so purposeful and sensible, so useful and good – that was what made her so infinitely desirable to him. Why didn't he simply grab her and kiss her the way his fellow students would have done? They were always boasting of their conquests. If they were to be believed, a woman actually liked it when you overcame her resistance and took her by force. If she struggled, never fear, it was only to whet the appetite, her own and yours. But perhaps that was merely foolish braggadocio. Michel couldn't tell. He was so ignorant, so filled with longing and trepidation. Abruptly, he turned to go.

"Why trouble to attend that lecture at all?" Lucille asked. "If you already know everything they tell you, it's a waste of time."

Michel laughed. "True, but without a diploma from those idiots I'll be nothing."

All at once she took his head in her hands and kissed him. "Come," she said, "my cake is still warm. That's when it tastes the best."

"What about your husband?"

"He's a fool and a drunkard."

She laughed and led him into her bedroom, kicking the door shut behind them. They stood facing each other. She put her arms around his neck. "Kiss me," she said. "Or don't you fancy me?"

"Of course I want to kiss you. I've wanted to do so all this time."

"Well, why didn't you?"

"I was afraid you wouldn't like it."

"But it's what I've been waiting for ever since you came here, couldn't you tell?" She kissed him softly on the lips. "There, was that so difficult?"

Michel was trembling all over. Lucille unbuttoned his coat.

"You're all atremble," she said.

Michel tried to undo the bow of her apron, but he was so clumsy that he got the ribbons in a knot. Everything seemed to be taking an inordinately long time. She freed the knot with a tug, stripped off her dress and let it fall. Naked now, she stood before him. Michel just gazed at her. Motionless, silent, spellbound. She removed his coat, his shirt, his trousers, then drew him down on the floor and lay beside him. Michel still couldn't take it all in: the scent of her skin, her hair, the sheer, sensual delight of her proximity. He felt faint.

"Take me," she said, "please take me!"

"Yes," he said, "yes!" And she pulled him on top of her, led him, guided him. He was overexcited and maladroit, but she reassured him. "Your skin is so soft," she whispered, caressing him. He couldn't have enough of her, he wanted more and more. And so did she.

A naked woman was laid out on the wheeled dissecting table. The professor inserted his knife beneath her clavicle and slowly drew it down through the flesh as far as the pubic bone. Then he opened the cadaver. Situated in the very centre of the oval auditorium, the table was overlooked by the ascending tiers of steps on which the professor's students sat to watch him at work. The professor coughed and wiped his perspiring brow on his sleeve just as Michel came panting in. He took a bite of Lucille's cake and stuffed the remainder into his mouth as he hurriedly made his way to a vacant place. The professor paused and turned to look at him.

"Ah! Monsieur de Nostradame has deigned to honour us with his presence after all," he said. "How gracious of him." He waited until Michel had sat down. Then, pointing to the dead woman in front of him, he turned to his students. "This woman poisoned herself. The poison heated her blood; the blood expanded and exerted inordinate pressure on her brain. That is what killed her, but it might yet have been possible to save her life." He levelled his gory knife at one of the students. "How, exactly?"

"By bleeding her in good time."

"Correct. That would have relieved the pressure on her brain." The professor coughed again and wiped some spittle from his mouth with the back of his hand. His forehead was beaded with sweat. Noticing this, Michel nudged the student seated beside him. "That man is ill," he whispered.

The professor surveyed the room. "Question: In what organ is poison to be found?" He pointed to a student.

"The heart."

The professor shook his head and pointed to another student.

"The feet."

The professor laughed, and everyone joined in. Coughing and wheezing, he pointed to Michel. "Monsieur de Nostradame, kindly enlighten your fellow students."

Michel nodded. "The answer you wish to hear is: The kidneys."

"Quite right, monsieur, but I detect an undesirable undertone in your reply."

"The latest research conducted in Paris by Doctor Rabelais indicates that high concentrations of poison may also be found in the liver."

"Paris!" the professor exclaimed scornfully. He reached into the woman's body, grasped the liver, and cut it out. Then, holding it up, he rotated on the spot so that all the students could see it. "The liver, messieurs. Very well, where's the poison? I see no evidence of any poison, do you?"

One or two students sniggered.

Michel was only too familiar with such stupid sallies at his expense. "Let me have that liver and I'll prove it to you."

"Nonsense."

"It can also be found in the heart."

"Rubbish!"

Michel wondered whether or not to dispute the point. Why should he? What purpose would it serve? There would only be another of those stupid altercations in which he was bound to be worsted by higher authority. Let the man say whatever he pleased . . . Then he changed his mind – he even rose to his feet, infuriated by the professor's pigheadedness and lack of discernment.

"The medical faculty of the University of Montpellier," he said coldly, "is the finest in Europe, thanks to the cadavers we're able to obtain for dissection. Why do you content yourself with information gleaned from old textbooks, Professor, instead of carrying out a thoroughgoing examination of the organs available to you?"

"Are you presuming to teach me my own business?"

"No."

"So you concur with my diagnosis? I'm flattered."

More sniggers.

"You're correct in asserting that the poison heated her blood."

"I'm grateful for your confirmation of that fact, Monsieur de Nostradame." The professor sketched a little bow in Michel's direction.

"But that's not what killed her."

"So what did – in your opinion?"

Michel kept his temper. "I'm convinced that her blood became heated as a result of poisoning because the body was endeavouring to heal itself. The function of the hot blood was to fight off the effects of the poison."

"Balderdash." The professor contemptuously tossed the liver on to the table and wiped his bloody hand on his apron.

"That being so," Michel went on, "bleeding the woman would have been the incorrect treatment. Venisection would actually have inhibited the healing process."

That really enraged the professor. He couldn't afford to tolerate such impertinence any longer, it undermined his authority. He could see the other students waiting for him to explode. They had no love for Michel, but they relished his clashes with the professor even though their outcome was never in doubt. This time he had gone too far. He would be cut down to size at last, the show-off whose omniscient manner had been getting on their nerves for so long; who always fell silent and walked off when bawdy jokes flew thick and fast; who never drank or swore or gambled with them; who had never yet been seen consorting with a woman and never had any amorous adventures to recount for their delectation. Michel had often provoked the professor before, but this time they hoped his goose was finally cooked. The professor could surely not stomach any more of his impertinence – he might even expel him from the university. Then they would be rid of him at last, the conceited, self-opinionated coxcomb.

"Monsieur de Nostradame," the professor said sharply. He coughed and fought for breath, loosening his collar a little. More beads of sweat erupted from his forehead. "If you are to qualify as a doctor of medicine, you must first learn what we try to teach you here."

"You may ask me any question you please," Michel said, "and I'll give you the answer you wish to hear. I'm fully acquainted with what it says in the old books."

"I tolerate your foolish chatter only because you're one of the most promising students here, but don't think you can take any liberties on that account."

"All I did was to cite the results of the latest research conducted by Doctor Rabelais."

"Be damned to your Doctor Rabelais! You aspire to play God, do you, like that sanctimonious bore? Rabelais is a renegade Franciscan, a renegade Benedictine, an apostate from the Church as a whole. He recklessly endangers his patients' lives for the sake of his own ludicrous self-esteem, depopulates whole districts for his own immortality's sake. Have a care, Monsieur de Nostradame! Your Doctor Rabelais is in league with the Devil. If he continues in this manner he'll doubtless have occasion to pay his lord and master a visit ere long. Then he can express his gratitude by kissing the Devil's anus!" The professor made a brusquely dismissive gesture and turned to the others. He aimed his knife at the woman's corpse. "Gentlemen, bleeding was the only treatment that would have helped this woman."

"Yes," said Michel, "helped her to die the sooner." He had no wish to listen to any more such nonsense. He had seen again and again in hospitals how venisection, which was employed as a cure-all, debilitated patients instead of benefiting them. It appalled him to think that this "proven remedy" was being drummed into all the dimwits around him, and that they would shortly be embarking on a medical career.

"Be quiet and sit down!" thundered the professor, quite beside himself.

"Your venisection would only have weakened her still further. She had a hot fever, not a cold one, you said so yourself. A cold fever is generally fatal. A hot fever is the beneficial manifestation of an ailing body's resistance to disease."

"Sit down, I said!" The professor's voice broke. "You dare to correct me? You dare to tell me what to do?"

Michel resumed his seat, only to stand up again. "I am simply anxious to assist the natural curative process which God, in his mercy, has permitted the human body to initiate of its own accord."

"Monsieur de Nostradame, you're free to quit this class at any time, but if you do, you need never return. I've no time to waste on students like you. I have other, more important . . ."

The professor got no further. He clutched his throat, coughing and gasping. He looked round wildly and put out his hand in search of support. The knife slipped through his fingers and fell to the floor. Then he slumped forwards on to the woman's corpse.

Nobody moved. Everyone stared down at the table in horror. The professor continued to lie there inert, draped over the gaping cadaver. Michel hurried down and dragged him off. Two other students helped to lay him carefully on the floor. Michel unbuttoned his shirt. That was when he saw the suppurating boils on the professor's chest and under his arms: bloated, moist and shiny, they ranged in colour from dark red to black, and some of them had already burst. The other students shrank back. "He has the plague!" yelled one.

That was enough to send the entire class fleeing from

the auditorium in blind panic. Michel alone remained at the professor's side.

"You're a very sick man," he said.

"I know," the professor whispered. "I'm dying."

"You shouldn't have come here. You'll have infected us all."

The professor gave a shrill laugh. "It's a divine punishment. I shall die and take you all with me, you fools!" He gave another cackle, sat up and gripped Michel's arm. His fingers dug into the flesh, his lips oozed dark froth. He stared at Michel wide-eyed. Then he fell back and breathed his last.

Michel detached the fingers that continued to cling to his arm, even in death. He got to his feet, wondering what to do. He had heard of a few cases of plague in recent days, but they had occurred some distance from Montpellier. Now the disease was here in their midst, and there was no telling how many people had already contracted it. The professor must have known of his condition for days, but he had said nothing and thereby endangered them all. Michel pushed the woman's cadaver to the edge of the dissecting table and seized the professor under the arms. With a supreme effort he managed to hoist the upper part of the dead man's body on to the tabletop, then his legs. That done, he wheeled both corpses out of the auditorium.

Leaving the table in the middle of the university quadrangle, he gathered some brushwood, logs and old rags, and stacked them beneath it. Then he lit his makeshift pyre. Flames leapt into the air, set fire to the table, and began to consume its burden. The air became filled with black, noisome smoke. Michel stripped off every last one of his clothes and threw them on the fire. A handful of students stood watching in the gateway that led to the street. They obviously thought he had gone mad, but he paid them no heed. Going to the well in the middle of the quadrangle, he hauled up a bucket from the depths and emptied the water over his head. He drew another bucketful and poured that over himself too, drew yet another and scrubbed himself from head to foot. Some sacks of corn had been dumped outside a store-room on the other side of the quadrangle. He tore one open, emptied out the corn, and tied the empty sack around his waist. Then he went over to the gateway and urged the watching students to take their final examination without delay – there might be no one left to examine them in a few days' time – but they merely recoiled from him and took to their heels. Michel shrugged and went out into the street. There would be corpses strewn everywhere before long – in every street, every square – and nobody alive to bury them.

Lucille was plucking a chicken in the kitchen when Michel returned. She was in the best of spirits. Her husband had come home from work and was stretched out on the bed in a drunken stupor, snoring. Lucille laughed when Michel walked into the kitchen, he looked so funny. Giggling and pointing to the sack around his waist, she asked what had happened. Had he fallen among thieves?

Michel peered through the bedroom door at her husband's recumbent form.

"He's drunk again," said Lucille.

Michel went in. The man's forehead was bathed in cold sweat. He wasn't drunk. Michel opened his shirt. Sure enough, his chest was covered in black, suppurating boils. Lucille screamed and clapped her hands to her mouth.

Michel asked her when the boils had first appeared.

"They weren't there yesterday," she said anxiously, "I'd stake my life on it. What are we to do, for God's sake? You're the physician – you must know."

Michel shrugged. "We neither know what causes the disease, nor can we predict its outcome. It's a mystery, the whole thing. Some people die within hours while others survive, no one knows why. There's no known remedy." He looked more closely at the man's skin. "Your husband will be dead before long."

He took her arm and shepherded her out of the room. If she had any relatives in the country, he said, she should go to them at once – now, this very minute. She must take only the barest essentials and go. Her husband was past saving in any case – he wouldn't survive. She mustn't touch him again, neither his person nor his things. Everything must be burned. Lucille wept, overcome with despair. Michel took her in his arms and comforted her.

Just then her husband emerged from his stupor and caught sight of her in Michel's arms. Laboriously, he struggled up off the bed and staggered towards her, bellowing abuse. She was a slut, an adulterous whore, and Michel was a randy young goat. He clenched his fist and raised his arm to strike Lucille, but his strength failed. He slumped to the floor at her feet. She made to lift him up, but Michel restrained her.

"No!" he said sharply.

"But we can't leave him lying here."

"There's nothing to be done. He won't last another hour."

"Then I shall stay with him until he's dead."

"If you do you'll infect yourself as well. Do you love him so much that you're willing to die with him?"

"No! No, he disgusts me."

"So why did you marry him?"

"You really want to know? Louis was our lodger – he rented an attic in my parents' house. One day, when no one else was about, he raped me. I was thirteen at the time. My father came home without warning and caught him in the act. He persuaded Louis to marry me rather than bring disgrace on the family. He even gave him some money when he proved reluctant. Louis didn't want a wife like me, fine gentleman that he was – not a girl who had already been deflowered! Can you imagine how I felt? I thought I would die on my wedding night, but a person can survive all manner of things."

Michel looked at her, shaking his head. "But why do you want to stay with him?"

"Because I'm a Christian. Because I think it my duty to be at his side when he dies. We were married in the house of God, after all. He's my husband. He may be a bad lot, but I'm not. That he never made of me."

"If you remain here you'll die too. Go and wait outside. I'll stay with him."

"Won't you catch the disease yourself?"

"No."

"How do you know?"

"I know, that's all. I won't infect myself."

"Are you in league with the Devil?"

"Please go. Wait for me outside."

"But he'll have to be buried."

"No one will bury him now."

"I'll go and fetch a priest."

"If you can still find one. If you do, and if you tell

him your husband is sick of the plague, will he come? I'll believe that when I see it!"

Lucille ran out of the house. Michel bent over the sick man and helped him up, but he was too weak to walk and had to be dragged back to the bed.

"What's the matter with me?" he muttered. He looked down at his chest, touched one of the boils that had burst, sniffed the viscous pus on his fingers, and vomited.

"Where's Lucille?" he whispered.

"She's fetching a priest."

"I won't do you the favour, the pair of you!" he yelled suddenly, sitting up. He laughed, retched, and choked on his own vomit. "I won't die, not I – not before you're both six feet under!" Dark blood gushed from his lips. There was a terrible stench of putrefaction. Then his strength failed and he fell back on the bed.

Michel went to the kitchen to fetch a damp cloth and laid it on the dying man's forehead. There was nothing more he could do, so he sat beside the bed and waited. Perhaps Lucille would find a priest willing to hear his confession and give him extreme unction. Time was running out fast. The man regained consciousness once more, caught sight of Michel, and uttered an obscene oath. Then he died.

Michel debated what to do. The university would now be closed. His only living relative was Paul, his elder brother, but why should he trouble him now? Paul had troubles enough of his own. Michel had seen him only twice since fleeing from the parental home, the last time when their mother died, and they had been very distant with each other. He had returned by night and stood beside his mother's grave till dawn.

Then, before sunrise, he had gone away again. The inquisitor was still in office and had since acquired a fearsome reputation. Greedier for victims than ever, he extracted confessions by any and every means available to him, and Michel was afraid he might still be on his list. The ecclesiastical authorities would esteem it a special pleasure, after so many years, to question a man whom they had once sought to interrogate as a child. It would prove that no one could hope to evade the long arm of the Holy Inquisition for ever.

Grandfather had hurried home with him that day. He too had glimpsed the look on the inquisitor's face and knew that there was no time to be lost. They stowed Michel's few clothes and books in a basket, carried everything out into the courtyard, and hid it in a wagon laden with a few empty barrels for appearance's sake. Michel hugged his father and his brother Paul. Then he climbed aboard the wagon and concealed himself beneath a big jute sack.

"His mother will be heart-broken," Father had said.

"But he must leave here at once," Grandfather replied. "They shrink from nothing, those people, not even from browbeating little children. If the inquisitor believes that Sophie bewitched the boy, they'll come to fetch him. They would question you and him both, and who knows what the outcome would be?"

Having embraced Michel's father and brother, Grandfather got up on the driver's box. He pulled an old, broad-brimmed hat down low over his eyes and wrapped himself in a tattered blanket. Then he ran his finger over the rim of the wheel beside him and smeared his face with grime. One crack of the whip, and the horse slowly set off across the courtyard. Father accompanied them as far as the gate. Michel peered out from under his sack.

"I'll come to visit you with Mother," Father said. "Work hard, give your grandfather no trouble, and don't be sad. It's better this way."

Michel nodded, then pulled the sack over his head and concealed himself behind a barrel. His brother opened the gate and the wagon emerged into the street. Michel's father pounded the gate with his fist in mute despair. Paul, standing beside him, was mystified by the whole proceeding.

One afternoon Grandfather received a summons from the local monastery and invited Michel to accompany him there. It was a sunny day, so Grandfather, being in no great hurry, stopped the wagon beside a field path. They alighted and went into the neighbouring field, where they sat down in the shade of the hedge and ate some fruit they had bought with them. The corn was already cut, and peasants were busy burning the stubble. Michel had now been lodging at his grandfather's house for two weeks, every day of which had been devoted to school work: Greek and Latin, for the most part, but astrology and mathematics too, likewise the rudiments of medicine, Grandfather being a noted physician.

"I'm very pleased with you," the old man said. "You learn fast – in fact you're making excellent progress." He produced a letter from his pocket. "Your poor aunt died, just as you said she would."

"She was very ill."

"Michel?"

"Yes, Grandfather?"

"Do you often know what is going to happen?"

"Sometimes."

"How do these presentiments manifest themselves?"

Michel shrugged. "I don't know, I just see pictures in my head." He paused. "Why did they burn Sophie at the stake?"

"We live in terrible times."

"But why didn't you do something? Why didn't you save her? You're an important person."

"I couldn't save her."

"I still don't see why not."

Grandfather abruptly changed the subject. "Do you believe in Our Lord Jesus Christ?" he asked.

"Of course."

"And in the immaculate conception of the Virgin Mary?"

Michel nodded. "Yes, Grandfather."

"Good."

"Why do you ask?"

"Because walls have ears. Even trees and flowers do." The old man took him by the shoulders and gazed at him earnestly. "Trust no one, my boy. You can never be sure that a person won't betray you to the Inquisition."

"Why should they?"

"Do you believe in the omnipotence of Our Lord?"

"Yes."

"And in the Holy Ghost?"

"Why do you want to know all these things?"

"As a good Christian you're safe, but still . . ." Grandfather scanned their surroundings. Then, although no one could possibly have overheard them, his voice sank to a whisper. "You're in grave danger. That's why I took you in."

"Why should I be in danger? I haven't done any-thing."

"It's time you were told – you're old enough to know: Michel, my boy, you're a Jew."

"How can I be? I was baptized."

"A baptized Jew is still a Jew. If they discover the truth, you'll be in even greater danger. My father came from Spain. We Sephardic Jews were hunted like wild beasts by Ferdinand and Isabella and the Inquisition, so some of us escaped to France. We were needed here then, but it soon became dangerous again to be a Jew, so I had myself baptized and did the same for your father later on. It was still possible to come to such an arrangement in those days." The old man laughed. "Twenty ducats, it cost. We were baptized in a church dedicated to Our Lady, so our name has been Nostradame ever since. But times have changed, Michel. If they ever found out that we had besmirched their holy water with our touch, they would burn us at the stake. You must remember that and be on your guard. And if it's really true that you possess this special gift – that you can foretell the future – beware, because you're doubly at risk. They would say you're in league with the Devil."

Michel nodded. He thought awhile, then he said, "You should have helped Sophie for all that."

"I couldn't, Michel, do try to understand."

"I shall help people when I grow up. I won't let innocent folk be burned to death on account of some silly superstition, not ever."

Grandfather stroked his head and sighed. "Oh, Michel," was all he said.

They drove on to the monastery and got down from the wagon, Michel carrying the physician's bag. A

monk greeted them at the gate and led them down
a long flight of steps to the cellar. A few candles were
smoking in sconces on the cold, dank walls. The monk
glanced at Michel and hesitated. When Grandfather
explained that his grandson would be assisting him,
the monk ushered them into a cell where another
monk was lying with nothing between him and the
flagstones but a thin mattress of straw. Naked save
for a loincloth, his body was emaciated in consequence
of much fasting and covered with open wounds. The
palliasse was soaked in blood. The monk, having asked
if Grandfather needed anything, was sent for a basin of
water and hurried from the cell. An eerie, monotonous
chanting could be heard in the distance. Michel gave his
grandfather a look of inquiry, but the old man merely
shrugged, opened his bag, and took out some herbs
and bandages. As soon as the monk returned with a
basin of water he began to bathe the wounds. The man
on the palliasse, unconscious though he was, twitched
convulsively. Michel added some linden blossoms and
camomile to the water. Grandfather, shaking his head,
turned to the monk. "This man's wounds are badly
infected," he said. "He has a high fever. You should
have sent for me sooner. How did he inflict such
injuries on himself?"

The monk picked up a rusty chain lying on the floor
beside the palliasse.

Grandfather nodded. "I thought as much," he said.
Then he gave a sudden laugh. "You must be more
careful of him, or another of your number will go to
meet his Maker before his time. Whether that would
be agreeable to the Almighty, I beg leave to doubt."

"Monsieur de Nostradame," the monk retorted
coldly, "I do not presume to tell you what medicines to

take. Kindly refrain from instructing us on our spiritual exercises."

Grandfather shrugged his shoulders. He had no wish to quarrel with the monk. Let them kill themselves, he thought, and got on with his work. Having lightly sprinkled the lacerations with herbs, he dipped soft cloths in the herb-laden water and, with Michel's assistance, applied them as a dressing. Last of all they wound some moist, cool rags around the sick man's ankles to reduce his fever. Grandfather prescribed that, as soon as he had recovered consciousness, he should be given some fortifying chicken broth.

The monk took leave of them at the gate. They settled themselves on the box and drove home at a leisurely pace. They had gone some way before Michel ventured to ask the question that was on the tip of his tongue.

"What had he done? Why did he hurt himself with that rusty chain?"

"They think the more they flog themselves, the greater their contrition and the sooner God will forgive their sins."

"But those are two different things. Why should they believe they'll be forgiven more quickly if they hurt themselves like that?"

"They aspire to be their own redeemers. When they engage in flagellation, they're doing to themselves what was done to Christ. They believe they're atoning for the sins of the world, but it's merely an excuse to indulge their perverted love of blood and pain. Well, it's better they inflict pain on themselves than on others. If the wind ever changes, the results will be terrible. Their first victims will be the Jews. They always are."

"But why, Grandfather?"

"As they see it, the Jews murdered Jesus Christ.

That's why we're damned to all eternity. To them we're the authors of all evil, and when disaster strikes – when no one knows where to turn and culprits are sought – we make convenient whipping-boys. That has always been the way of it. At such times we become devils incarnate. We poison wells, we dismember little children and drink their blood, we desecrate the Host as a means of crucifying the Saviour twice over. We're charged with every foul crime their sick, twisted minds can conceive of. And three hundred years ago, to enable people to recognize us from afar, Pope Innocent III ordained that we Jews should wear a badge, a circular patch cut from yellow felt. That made it easier to round us up and slaughter us. The Jews of Basle were forced to erect a large timber building in a field near the city and herded inside. The building was then set ablaze. That destroyed the entire community at a stroke. The Jews of Strasbourg, two thousand in number, were taken to a graveyard, where they had to dig pits and drive a stake into the ground beside each. They were then made to tie each other to those stakes. A few, who had become converts in mortal terror, were employed to tie up the last of their number and set fire to them. The ones who performed this frightful task believed that their lives would be spared: they were privileged to look on while the others burned to death. The stakes were ingeniously situated so that, after the Jews had burned awhile, they would topple into the pits. The converts were then made to shovel earth over the charred corpses. Finally, in recompense for their services, they themselves had to dig pits and climb into them, whereupon they were summarily buried alive. The witnesses of this spectacle, of whom there were many, were permitted to throw in the last few shovelfuls. Even women took part, believing that they were doing God's work, though many of the spectators felt cheated. After all, what pleasure did it give them if someone choked to death below ground – if there were no screams of agony, no charred or lacerated flesh, no broken bones or dislocated limbs, no teeth knocked out with clubs? For that reason they buried many of the remaining Jews neck-deep only. Then they smeared their protruding heads with honey and looked on while ants and beetles feasted on it before devouring the victims' eyes and creeping into their bodies by way of ears and mouths and nostrils. Ah, Michel, human nature is base and brutal, and human beings seize upon any excuse to torture and murder their fellow creatures with impunity – preferably in a good cause. That makes it twice as pleasurable. I've told you all this to show you how truly careful you must be."

The old man said no more, nor did Michel question him further. They drove home in silence.

Lucille returned. She had found only one priest – all the rest had fled – but he had refused to come with her.

"They're leaving people to die unshriven. How will they answer for that to Our Lord?"

"Your husband is already dead. The most I can do is to pray for him."

"But what good is that?"

"You really think God will be angry with either of us if I say a Christian prayer over his mortal remains?"

She stared at him in sudden consternation. "Are you a Protestant?"

"Two hundred years ago, Lucille, the plague was raging here as furiously as it does today. If no priest could be found, any man, or, in a pinch, any woman, could hear the confessions of the dying. Pope Clement VI granted a general absolution to all victims of the plague because there was no one left to help them. Now please let me pray for him – and leave the room. I don't want you to infect yourself."

She shivered. "What have we done that was so evil that God should punish us in this way? Does he mean to kill every last one of us?"

She left the room but remained standing in the doorway. Michel said a prayer, then covered the corpse with a blanket. He came out, shutting the door behind him, and proceeded to pack his belongings.

"What's to be done with him?" Lucille asked. "We can't just leave him lying there to rot."

"His body must be burned."

"I'll help you. He's too heavy for you to manage on your own."

She overrode Michel's protests and went back into the bedroom. Together, they spread a blanket beside the bed and rolled the corpse on to the floor, where it landed with a dull thud. Having covered it with the other blanket, they hauled it out of the room. They couldn't carry it – the dead man was too heavy, and the blanket would not have supported his weight. They dragged him out into the courtyard, where Lucille poured oil over the blanket and set fire to it. Flames shot into the air. Michel tried to pull her away, but she insisted on watching the body burn. She merely retreated a few steps when the terrible stench became too much for her. She continued to stand there until everything had been consumed by fire. Then she spat on the ashes.

Michel accompanied her to the outskirts of town.

The roads were already swarming with refugees. Any-one able to leave Montpellier was doing so, but Michel refused to follow suit. He bade Lucille farewell. He wasn't needed in the countryside, he told her. The country air was healthy, and no one there had died of the plague – not, at least, till now.

Lucille did her best to persuade him to come with her. "Please don't desert me," she implored him. "Everyone is leaving. Why stay here? Come with me, I need you. I can't live without you."

But he shook his head.

She pleaded and wept, vituperated and slapped him. Was he really so intent on dying? Why couldn't he be sensible?

"I'm a physician, Lucille. I'm needed here."

In that case, she said, she would stay and help him. She refused to leave without him.

"No," he told her, "I lost you once, Sophie. I couldn't endure to do so a second time." There were tears in her eyes as he embraced her. "And now, please go."

He turned on his heel and walked quickly back into town.

PART TWO

Marie

The huge field stretched away into the distance, further than the eye could see. It was a mass of roses in full bloom – millions of glorious, heavily-scented red roses – and the women at work among them were cutting the blooms and collecting them in baskets. In their midst, also gathering roses, stood Michel. All at once a horseman rode up and asked one of the women where he could find Doctor de Nostradame. She pointed to Michel. The messenger dismounted and hurried over to him.

"The plague has broken out in Laon – we already have a hundred dead or more. Will you come and help us? There are no physicians left."

Michel merely nodded and turned to the women around him.

"Work hard while I'm gone," he told them. "We shall need as many roses again by nightfall."

A spacious shed stood at the edge of the field. Raoul, an old man who had been assisting Michel for some

time, was at work there with several women. One of
them was crushing dried herbs in a mortar. Raoul
weighed out the powder and used a small wooden
shovel to transfer it to a cauldron suspended above
the fire. This contained a paste which he wearily
stirred with a wooden ladle from time to time. Once
the herbal paste had lost most of its moisture and
cooled, another two women stationed at a big table
fashioned pills out of it and placed them in a large
wooden bowl. Michel entered the shed, followed by
some field-workers bearing baskets of roses. Three of
them plucked the petals from the stems and tossed them
into a big sieve above the fireplace to dry.

Raoul rubbed his eyes. "What, more roses?"

"The plague has broken out again at Laon – and at
Chinon and Aix, too. We need more rose pills, Raoul.
Do we have enough calamus and aloes?"

"Yes, but our stocks of carnation and iris are
running low."

"I see, then replenish them as quickly as you can.
How do we stand for cypress oil?"

"There's still enough left."

Michel took the ladle from the old man's hand. "Go
and lie down for an hour. We shall have to work all
night, in any case, so get some sleep."

"No, no, I can manage."

"Don't work yourself to death, Raoul, I need you.
Get some sleep. You're coming with me and we leave
at daybreak, not a moment later."

Mounted on donkeys, they rode into Laon shortly
after sunrise. It might have been a city of the dead.
The streets were deserted, the houses shut up. The
doors bore crucifixes, the windows had boards nailed

over them. Michel was leading a third donkey laden with medicines. They made their way to the hospital, where they alighted and tethered their beasts to a post. Then, taking two bags of physic with them, they went inside.

They descended the stairs to the cellar, where the sick were lying in serried rows on the bare, cold flagstones. Many were already dead, and no one could muster the strength to drive away the rats that were gnawing at their corpses. There was a terrible stench of vomit and decay, pus and urine, excrement and putrefaction. Mildew was creeping up the dank, grimy walls.

Michel surveyed the cellar aghast. "They're all sure to die in such filth. Each will contaminate the other."

An old woman gripped his arm and drew him down to her. "A priest," she whispered, "a priest, quickly!"

Michel opened the neck of her dress and examined her skin. Then he patted her shoulder and smiled. "You need no priest."

She stared at him in horror. "Are you the Devil?" she cried, loudly enough for all to hear. "The Devil! Satan has come to fetch us all!" She burst out sobbing and crossed herself in mortal terror.

"Don't speak," Michel told her. "Conserve your strength. The swellings aren't black, don't you see? That's healthy blood fighting the infection. You have a fever, which is good." He gave her a pill. "Put that under your tongue and leave it there until it dissolves." And he patted her again.

The old woman eyed the pill suspiciously. "What's in it? Are you trying to poison me?"

"All it contains are herbs and dried, crushed rose petals. You now have the essence of a hundred roses in your mouth. Think of roses."

A physician approached, looking more than a little grotesque. Laced up in leather smock that reached from neck to ankles, he was wearing a bloody apron and a mask with a birdlike beak jutting from it. Countless amulets dangled from his neck, and he had a long cane in his hand. His assistant, who was similarly attired, was carrying a bucket and a cannula with a tube attached. Michel and Raoul were just administering pills to some more of the physician's patients when he struck Michel on the hand with his cane. The pill he was holding fell to the floor.

"What are you doing?"

"Endeavouring to save the sick."

The physician gave a scornful laugh. "You're wasting your time, everyone here is as good as dead." A sick man was lying on the flagstones at his feet, covered in boils. He prodded one of them with his cane, and the man screamed in anguish. "You see? Just stinking, gangrenous flesh."

"But what treatment do you administer?"

"I open their veins to draw off the contaminated blood, what else?" He took the cannula from his assistant and drove it brutally into the man's arm at the point where he assumed a vein to be. Blood trickled into the bucket.

Michel thrust the physician aside and carefully withdrew the cannula. "Stop this nonsense," he said. "You're robbing the sick of their last remaining strength."

Raoul proceeded to bandage up the wound.

The physician shook his head incredulously. "Who are you anyway, you fool?"

"My name is Michel de Nostradame."

"Ah, the young student who's causing such a stir

with his miraculous pills! People are gullible enough to cling to any straw. You ought to be locked up, monsieur. Shame on you for arousing false hopes in poor, sick folk with your promises!"

"I make no promises," Michel retorted. "I simply do the best I can. Their lives are in the hands of God."

"So God is to blame if they die, is that what you mean? Very interesting!"

Raoul's face darkened. "For one thing, monsieur, it's you who are to blame for making your patients even weaker by treating them as you do." He indicated the cannula, which had a quantity of dried blood adhering to it. "For another, you transmit the disease from one to another by using that instrument."

"And by compelling your patients to lie in this filth," Michel put in. "No wonder the plague is spreading like wildfire. They must all be removed from here without delay."

"If anyone is to be removed, monsieur, it's you and your companion. Kindly leave. This hospital is in my charge."

"So all must remain as it always has been? Nothing must change, everything is satisfactory as it is? A splendid prospect, to be sure! Why were you born at all, if not to change things for the better? You're superfluous, doctor. Your life has been altogether pointless. It was over before you uttered your first cry."

"I shall call the guards. You can prattle to them to your heart's content – in prison."

"Let me do my work in peace, I've no time to argue with you." Michel quickly climbed a couple of stairs so that everyone in the cellar could see him. "I'm a physician," he announced. "My name is Michel de Nostradame. What I want to tell you is this:

anyone who remains in this foul hole will die, that much is certain. Although I cannot guarantee to save you all, many of you will survive – but only if you leave here."

The physician laughed contemptuously. "What nonsense you talk! Everyone here would be better advised to pray, not cling to life. They're all doomed to die. Don't encourage the poor devils to hope in vain."

Michel continued to address the cellar at large. "If you remain here you'll die beyond a doubt. Make up your minds what you wish to do."

One of the sick men struggled to his feet. "I'll come."

Another followed his example. "So will I."

A third demanded to know if he really would survive. "Tell me! Promise me!"

"No promises, but I'll examine you all, every last one. Those who are strong enough will tend the weaker. Come, all of you. Come!"

Michel beckoned to them from his vantage-point on the second step. He himself took the old crone's arm and started up the stairs.

A babble of voices filled the air. All who were strong enough rose to their feet, ruthlessly jostling and shoving in their eagerness to be the first to quit this place of death.

Michel turned and raised both arms, appealed for calm, urged them not to push and jostle. They would all get out of the cellar in due course, he assured them, but few paid any heed. His voice rose to a shout, took on a note of menace. "I tell you this," he cried, "I shall only treat those that help the ones who cannot walk unaided. Only those who help others will be helped themselves. Those who think only of themselves can help themselves as well!"

The physician looked on impotently. "Very well, go!" he bellowed. "Go, and the Devil goes with you! If one of you should survive, you'll owe it to him. You'll all be reunited in Hell, for this man" — he pointed to Michel — "is in league with Satan. How else could he hope to cure you? Even if your miserable bodies survive, you'll have sold your souls!" But no one paid him any heed. They were all intent on leaving the cellar. His voice cracked. "You're all doomed!" he yelled. "He simply means to rob you! He has designs on your clothing, your money, your jewels. He's a thief, a murderer! He'll kill you all! You're accursed!" Still they refused to listen. He barred their path, only to be swept aside and pinned against the wall by stampeding bodies. His assistant hesitated for a moment. Then he, too, started up the stairs. Furiously, the physician hurled his cane after him.

Once outside in the street Michel announced that he needed a clean building. "Where can one be found?" he asked. "Fresh air and sunlight, those are the prime essentials."

"What about the church?" cried someone.

Michel nodded. "The church, so be it. We shall also need water. You must all wash yourselves and burn your clothes. We need a plentiful supply of linen sheets. You must steep them in boiling water and wrap yourselves in them."

The pews were carried out of the church into the square and scrubbed. Men and women scoured the floor of the church and sluiced it with water. Many of those who had been lying in the hospital, apathetic and long devoid of hope, were suddenly imbued with fresh strength and confidence. The massive double doors had been flung wide and a big bonfire was blazing in the church square. All the patients' clothing was being burned. Tubs of water stood everywhere. The sick were either washing themselves or, if they were too weak to do so, being sluiced down by others. Raoul went the rounds handing out pills. The pews were carried back into the church and arranged in pairs so that the sick could stretch out on them in comfort.

Just then the priest turned up with the physician, who had removed his beaked mask and was carrying it in his hand. He pointed to Michel, who was examining a patient, and the priest went over to him.

"Monsieur de Nostradame?"

"Ah, Reverend Father, I'm glad you came. We've been looking for you everywhere. We wanted to ask your permission to make use of the church, but you weren't to be found."

The priest indicated the bonfire outside the church door. "That fire is burning the wrong fuel, Monsieur de Nostradame."

"What do you mean?"

The priest smirked. "It would, I think, burn better and be more pleasing to God if the flames were consuming you instead of those old rags."

Michel shook his head. "I don't propose to argue with you, Reverend Father. Please give us your church. There can be no better place in which to tend the sick."

"How can I give you what you already have?"

"Please help us. We need sheets and blankets, and the sick need your words of comfort and good cheer. Those are quite as important as my medicines."

"Holy Mother Church concerns herself with people's souls, Monsieur de Nostradame, not with their sinful bodies. You will therefore understand why I demand that you quit this place of worship forthwith."

"And if we fail to do so?"

The priest smiled and pointed to something outside. Several figures in black were approaching the church. Accompanying these representatives of the Holy Inquisition were a number of soldiers armed with pikes, and at their head strode the city's chief inquisitor, a short, thick-set man. Far too warmly clad, he had a black cowl pulled down low over his face and was sweating profusely.

"Unless you leave this church of your own volition," said the parish priest, "you will be compelled to do so."

"Then compel me."

Many of the sick had stationed themselves outside the door. They linked arms and refused to let the inquisitor's men pass. Not a word was uttered. They calmly stood their ground, some of them armed with pitchforks.

"Stand aside," said the inquisitor. "Out of my way!"

Nobody stirred.

"Stand aside, I say!" the inquisitor roared. He tried to forge a path through the human wall, but still the men refused to give way. He stared at them, utterly at a loss. "This is rebellion!" he cried. "I'll have you all arrested. Be reasonable and stand aside. Nothing will happen to you. All we want is that charlatan in there. Let us pass or you die, every last one of you."

He signalled to the soldiers, who lowered their pikes and slowly advanced. The situation was becoming dangerous. The inquisitor sensed this but knew that he couldn't afford to yield. At that moment

Michel emerged from the church. He made his way through the ranks of the sick and walked up to the inquisitor.

"What do you want?"

"Monsieur de Nostradame, I arrest you in the name of the Holy Inquisition."

Michel, standing cheek by jowl with the inquisitor, peered into his face.

"Before I'm under lock and key, Your Eminence, you yourself will be struck down by the plague."

"A curse?" cried the inquisitor. "You all heard it! This man cursed me." He laughed uproariously. "You're very presumptuous, monsieur, to believe yourself capable of cursing a churchman under the protection of Almighty God."

"That was no curse." Michel pointed at the inquisitor's face. "You're infected, and it would be better for you to let me treat you than to arrest me. It would also be better, if you have this city's survival at heart, to burn down the hospital that harbours the infection instead of burning me."

The inquisitor hesitated for a moment. Then he turned to the soldiers. "Seize him."

Michel's patients interposed themselves between him and the soldiers. They raised their pitchforks. The soldiers wavered apprehensively.

Michel raised his hand. "Never fear, I'll not be gone for long. My assistant Raoul knows what to do. Obey his instructions to the letter." And he followed the inquisitor's men.

The air in the big, gloomy room was warm and stuffy, but despite this, or because of it, the curtains were drawn and a fire was burning on the hearth.

Several representatives of the Holy Inquisition were seated at a large table in the centre. The inquisitor himself occupied a massive armchair upholstered in red velvet. A smaller table was reserved for the two clerks who were making a written record of the proceedings. Michel was standing beside a column in front of it.

The inquisitor gestured to one of the clerks to read out what he had noted down so far: "Michel de Nostradame, born 14 December, 1503, in rue de Berry, Saint-Rémy. Father a notary, both grandfathers physicians. Studied at Avignon: literature, history, philosophy, grammar, rhetoric. Later, studied medicine at Montpellier."

The inquisitor had risen. He paced nervously up and down, loosened the collar of his habit. His forehead was beaded with sweat. All at once, more nimbly than anyone would have thought possible in view of his bulk, he strode up to Michel and looked him suspiciously in the eye.

"And astrology? Did you not study astrology too?

"That too, yes."

The inquisitor tapped the sheet of paper in front of the clerk. "Astrology too, make a note of that." His tone was almost triumphant. He turned to Michel again. "What of the hermetic branches of knowledge? Occultism? No? Black magic? Alchemy? Diabolism?"

"I'm a scholar and physician, Your Eminence, not a sorcerer."

The inquisitor wiped his perspiring face on a cloth. He was manifestly feverish. "We have numerous ways of extracting the truth," he went on. "Persist in your disavowals, and the consequences will not be pleasant."

Michel leaned forward and whispered in his ear. "You're a sick man, monsieur."

The inquisitor was finding it hard to breathe. Overcome with faintness, he leaned against a column. Two monks darted forward. They caught him before he could fall and helped him back to his armchair. Imperiously, he shook them off and whispered to a minion to fetch the physician. "Be quick! Hurry!"

Michel walked over to him and looked him in the eye. "The physician will bleed you, Your Eminence, and by so doing will kill you." He opened the inquisitor's shirt. The flesh was covered in swellings. "You'll die unless you permit me to treat you," he added quietly.

The inquisitor laughed. "And surrender my soul to the Devil in return?"

"Nonsense." Michel paused. "Well, the decision is yours. What is it to be?"

The inquisitor grasped his pectoral cross and held it out. "Take hold of this cross. If you hold it in your hand, I'll believe you."

Michel shrugged and took it.

"Now kiss it," whispered the inquisitor. "If you're the Devil it will scorch your lips."

Michel kissed the cross. The inquisitor scrutinized him closely, then nodded.

Michel turned to one of the monks. "We shall need a litter. His Eminence must be taken to the church."

The inquisitor gripped his arm. "I shall remain here," he whispered. "Attend to me here."

Michel shook his head.

"So that is how you would revenge yourself, is it, by compelling me to lie among all the rest?"

"Revenge?" Michel retorted. "I don't know what

it is. I've often marvelled at the ferocity it arouses in others, but I myself am a stranger to its delights."

One of the representatives of the Holy Inquisition, a tall, waxen-faced, ascetic-looking man, had risen to his feet. "Why must His Eminence join the others?" he demanded.

"Aren't all men equal in the sight of God?"

The inquisitor stared at him in horror. "You're a Lutheran!"

"Even if I were, would you rather die than let me treat you?"

"*Are* you a Lutheran?" the inquisitor asked anxiously.

"No, I'm a devout Catholic."

"Prove it."

"With pleasure, but you'll be dead before you've finished catechizing me."

"Treat me here."

Michel shook his head again.

"Why not?"

"I can tend you better in the church. Besides, if you allow me to treat you the others will have more faith in the efficacy of my treatment. That will help. Faith can move mountains, as you yourself know better than I." He turned to the attendant monk. "Undress him first and burn his clothing."

The inquisitor looked appalled. "Impossible! These are the robes of the Holy Inquisition."

"Then you'll die in the robes of the Holy Inquisition and burn in their company."

The inquisitor deliberated for a moment, then nodded feebly.

The square was wreathed in dense, dark smoke from the corpses that were being burned without delay on

Raoul's instructions. Meanwhile, the church had been cordoned off by a semicircle of soldiers. Pikes at the ready, they were slowly closing in to the sound of drummers beating a muffled tattoo. The men armed with pitchforks continued to stand guard outside the door. The noose steadily tightened as any patients still in the square were herded back inside the church. It had been decreed that all must be together when the massacre began. None must escape. What was at issue was more than just a handful of foolish recalcitrants who would soon be dead of the plague in any case. They must all be cut to ribbons, even those who had already expired. None of them, alive or dead, must escape punishment. A principle was at stake here. No one could be permitted to cross an inquisitor with impunity; it would dangerously undermine his authority and that of the Church. Now was no time to vacillate or procrastinate, no time to display weakness or indecision, still less compassion for the wretched poor. That way lay disaster, especially now that Holy Mother Church was menaced on all sides by Protestants, Calvinists and humanists, by all those babblers who had emblazoned the word "individual" on their banner. Yes, they were individuals right enough – criminal individuals who all belonged in the fire. They were threatening the good order of the world and the universe as a whole, destroying the substance that held everything together: the law of God as administered by Holy Mother Church and her representative, the inquisitor. Unless such people were given short shrift, all would be lost. Subjectivism and individualism were the new watchwords, the empty claptrap that bred anarchy and chaos.

It was then that Michel appeared with the inquisitor,

who was lying on a litter borne by four attendants. The soldiers stood aside to let them pass as they crossed the square and made for the church.

"Order your men to withdraw," Michel called to the officer in command. "Or do you mean to butcher the inquisitor as well?" The soldiers looked at each other uncertainly. Michel, who had hurried after the inquisitor, turned in the doorway. "You can make yourselves useful," he said. "You can help us to tend the sick. We need all the assistance we can get."

But the soldiers shrank back in terror. Quite clearly, they had failed to grasp until now that they were in the midst of people smitten with the plague. They had no wish to approach such people or become contaminated by them. The first few men turned tail. The officer yelled at them to stand fast and rejoin the ranks, but no one obeyed. Throwing away their pikes and sabres, they scattered in panic. Michel retired to the church, where he worked unceasingly, day and night. Many of his patients died, but many survived.

Julius Scaliger owned a magnificent mansion set in spacious grounds adorned with trees trimmed into elaborate shapes. Beside the house was a large conservatory filled with exotic plants, and on the lawn in front of it stood a long banqueting table. Every one of Scaliger's many invited guests had turned up, for it was a particular honour to be present when such a celebrated man held his annual party each summer. The strains of a small orchestra were superimposed on a lively hum of conversation. Young maidservants were pouring wine and serving sillabubs.

Madame Scaliger looked round nervously. The meal was almost over, but her husband had yet to put in an appearance. This time he was really carrying things too far. She knew that he detested most of those present. He thought them shallow and conceited, arrogant and stupid, and would have liked nothing better than to cancel the whole affair. It had even been the subject of an argument between the couple. Scaliger had grown very irate despite his wife's efforts to placate him. She begged him to be reasonable. He himself had always pronounced it necessary to give this one party a year, if only to retain the good will of the people in the neighbourhood. Although the citizens of Agen were proud to have a man of his calibre in their midst, a natural philosopher whose reputation extended the length and breadth of France and even beyond its borders, and who corresponded with the finest minds in Europe, they kept a wary eye on all he did. He was often too quick to meddle in local affairs and dispense advice. His moral rigour had got on too many people's nerves. They would secretly have preferred to see him dead and erect a monument in his honour, but he was too prominent a personage. No one could touch him.

Not yet, thought the inquisitor, but the day would assuredly dawn when Scaliger, too, would burn at the stake – and what a red-letter day *that* would be! He was sitting half-way down the table beside Madame Auberligne, a place of honour that afforded a splendid view of the lawns running down to the lake. Visible in the background were distant mountains veiled in a bluish haze.

The mayor was seated opposite. He and the inquisitor were at one in their dislike of Scaliger. His urbanity, his refinement, his eloquence, his courtly manners – all were repugnant to them and smacked of arrogance and condescension. The inquisitor yearned to interview

Scaliger in the house of the Holy Inquisition. He itched
to put him through the mill, ask him pointed questions
and prevent him from parrying them with his usual pol-
ite evasions. He would pin the man down and discover
what he really thought. He would tear the mask – that
ever smiling, ever amiable, ever so slightly blasé and
supercilious mask – from Scaliger's face. Behind it, he
was sure, lay the gargoyle visage of the Enlightenment,
of unbelief, heresy, and blasphemy. What a triumph it
would be, finally to convict such a man of godlessness!
One had only to look at his multitude of published
works. No one man could have written so many; he
would never have had the time. And what a range of
subjects they embraced; no single man could possess so
much knowledge. How had he contrived it? Who had
secretly written his books for him? Someone must have
dictated them to him – someone who had endowed
him with such superhuman energy that he never grew
weary. Did the man ever sleep? Did he eat? Did he
drink? What must he have surrendered in return for
so much knowledge, wealth, and vigour? It could only
be his soul, the one thing lacked by those who have,
and can do, everything! The inquisitor longed to search
Scaliger's house from attic to cellar. No door, however
secret, would escape him. He felt sure he would find
evidence enough to bring the man to trial.

He turned to Madame Auberligne, his table companion, and raised his glass. He looked into her eyes.
God, he thought, not for the first time, what a pretty
woman she was! They drank to one another. "Another
ten years," he said, "and that man Luther will be a dead
letter."

Madame Auberligne laughed. "But you'll have to
send a great many more people to the stake, Eminence –

more and more every day. They multiply like blow-flies on a dung-heap."

The inquisitor laughed too. It was a pleasantry wholly to his taste, like the lady herself. The wine was delicious, the sun shining, and the food excellent. It had been an admirable idea of Madame Scaliger's to seat him next to Madame Auberligne. He looked down the table. Her husband was lolling at the far end, fast asleep with his arms folded over his paunch. He leaned towards Madame Auberligne and rested a confidential hand on hers. "I've already thought of an ingenious way of combining pleasure with utility. We should stoke our stoves with Lutherans in the winter. Then at least they would serve some useful purpose."

Madame Auberligne laughed. "A truly brilliant notion." She took a handful of her hair, twisted it around her wrist, and held it on top of her head. "This is how the women are wearing their hair in Paris these days. What do you think, Eminence? Would it suit me? Do say."

"It would suit you admirably, madame."

"You really think so?"

"Indeed I do, but there's something missing. You should entwine a few flowers in your hair. I shall pick some for you."

"Blue ones?"

"Yes, the colour of your eyes." Looking at her all the while, he moved his chair a trifle closer to hers and insinuated his hand beneath the table. Pulling her skirt up, he slid his hand between her thighs and under her drawers. It was just as he thought: the lecherous bitch was hot, wet, soft, and wide open to his touch. "If Henry of England continues to insist on marrying that Boleyn woman, he'll be excommunicated," he murmured. "And damned to all eternity."

"Together with his beloved Anne?" inquired Madame Auberligne.

"But of course."

"Together to all eternity?" She sighed. "What bliss!"

The mayor stepped in. "You're not in earnest, madame?"

"Of course I am." She laughed. "Lovers are utterly blind to their surroundings. Heaven or hell – it's a matter of complete indifference to them as long as they're together." She looked down the table at her husband, who had woken up and was in the act of devouring yet another gargantuan slice of cake. "My husband, monsieur, would never go to hell for me." She treated the mayor to a coquettish smile. "Would you?"

The mayor half rose, took her hand, and gallantly kissed it. "Only if you undertook to accompany me there."

Madame Scaliger came over to them.

"A memorable festivity, madame," said the inquisitor.

"Made the more so by your presence, Eminence," she replied with a smile.

"But where's your husband?" demanded the mayor's table companion, Countess Gallaut. "How odd of him to invite us and neglect to appear himself. I sorely miss his entertaining conversation."

"Ah, Countess," sighed Madame Scaliger, "when he's working he forgets everything, as you know. I'll fetch him."

Madame Auberligne watched her go. "Speaking for myself," she remarked to the mayor, "I find his absence downright offensive."

"Thoroughly contemptuous," agreed the inquisitor. "He despises us all."

"And hasn't even the courtesy to conceal the fact," said the mayor.

"But gentlemen," Countess Gallaut protested, "why so severe? You mustn't judge Monsieur Scaliger by normal standards."

"Really?" Madame Auberligne said with a suggestive smile. "So normal standards don't apply to Monsieur Scaliger. How fascinating. Can you be more explicit?"

The mayor guffawed and the countess couldn't refrain from laughing. "I fear I must disappoint you there. All our wise host's vital energies flow directly into his head."

"In other words," said the mayor, barely able to contain his mirth, "all that ever spurts is the ink from his pen."

Madame Auberligne suddenly turned pale. She gave a little gasp and clamped her thighs together, drew a deep breath through her clenched teeth and held it. Her nostrils dilated and her fingers tightened convulsively, overturning a glass. She closed her eyes, compressed her lips, and shuddered. At last she breathed out again.

"What is it, madame?" the inquisitor asked solicitously.

"Can I be of assistance?"

"It's nothing. I'm perfectly well." She picked up her wine glass, drained it at a gulp, and held it out to one of the serving girls. "I'd like some more. Today I want more of all good things. I simply can't have enough of them."

"In that case," smiled the inquisitor, "I must quickly devise some means of fulfilling your wishes."

"You're always so wonderfully unselfish, Eminence.

I shall debate how best to repay you for your many acts of charity."

The inquisitor gave a little bow. "I feel sure you'll hit upon some admirable means of doing so, madame." He briefly sniffed his fingers before wiping them on his napkin.

Seated in the spacious working area at the rear of the conservatory was Marie, a girl of nineteen. She was a strange young creature. Not beautiful, or not, at least, in any conventional sense of the word, she was very slim and somewhat austere in appearance. Her nose erred on the large side and was slightly tip-tilted like a duck's beak. Her cheekbones were rather prominent, and the thick eyebrows above her bright, watchful eyes almost met in the middle, but surmounting them was a lofty, curving forehead of classical perfection. Her luxuriant hair was simply gathered on her neck by a ribbon, and she was wearing a plain linen gown with an apron over it.

Very shy and self-effacing, Marie tended to be awkward and maladroit in the company of others. She invariably blushed when someone addressed her. It annoyed her to be so easily intimidated. She had no small-talk, no gift for coquetry or brilliant conversation, nor did her ambitions lie in that direction. She was obsessed with her work, which she performed with the utmost conscientiousness. She had fulfilled her duties here as Scaliger's assistant every day for the past two years. On the table in front of her lay a plant. She scrutinized it repeatedly through a magnifying glass, then dipped the finest of paint brushes in ochre and carefully reproduced the stamens on a sheet of paper.

Scaliger was standing at a lectern not far away,

carefully endeavouring to slit the stalk of a plant from root to flower-head with the aid of a penknife. His hand, which trembled a little, slipped, and he cut himself. Angrily, he threw the penknife on the floor.

"I can't do it! It's enough to drive one to despair. Age, Marie – age is an evil prank on Nature's part. It's absolutely detestable!"

Scaliger would soon be sixty. He was a short, slim, wiry man, brimming with energy and always in a hurry. Excitable and quick-tempered, he sometimes exploded with such fury that everyone flinched in expectation of physical violence. But, as with most irascible people, his outbursts soon subsided and he never bore malice. No stranger who saw him in a rage would have credited the serenity that could radiate from this man when he was devoting himself wholeheartedly to some subject he deemed important or addressing some person who was truly eager to learn. Then, no time or trouble could be too much for him. All that angered him was trivial, irrelevant, vapid, idle chatter. When people wasted his time and frayed his nerves with inanities, he could be brusque and impatient to the point of rudeness. His most striking features were his long, slender fingers and big, fleshy nose. He was a mass of incongruities. His wrinkled face, with its sharply incised wrinkles, conveyed an impression of great age, but the eyes that looked out of it had the naïve simplicity and unremitting curiosity of a child. Maria had once produced a caricature of him. All it showed was a big nose, big eyes and hands, but all who saw it recognized Scaliger at once. He himself had been highly amused by the drawing.

Marie got up. She retrieved the penknife from the floor and replaced it on the lectern.

"My eyesight is failing." Scaliger pursued. "I'm becoming hard of hearing and my hands are shaking. It's so humiliating when one's mind is still youthful and abrim with plans, yet the simplest action defeats one. It's Nature's revenge on us for exalting ourselves over her and preening ourselves on our superior intelligence. We can think of anything, we can even conceive of infinity and deny God, but this" – he indicated the tremor in his fingers – "this demonstrates what our intellect really consists of: just decaying, putrefying flesh. Isn't that deplorable? We think ourselves so superior, but what becomes of all our pomp and circumstance in the end? The stalwart youth turns into a tremulous, slobbering, forgetful dotard incapable even of retaining his own excrement. My young friend Montaigne is absolutely right: philosophizing means learning not to die in the accepted sense. Dying is the simplest thing in the world. Everyone dies as cattle do, even the most imbecilic of mortals. What is there left to learn about it? Philosophizing means learning to live, in other words, accepting our own inexorable decay, remaining in good heart, and discerning some sense in all the nonsense around us."

Irritably, he tossed the mutilated plant into a garbage pail, took another from a dish, placed it carefully on a marble slab, and handed Marie the penknife. She slit the plant open with great dexterity while Scaliger looked on, smiling. Having laid the dissected plant on a sheet of paper, he went over to her workplace and deposited it beside the one she was painting. He examined her illustration intently.

"Where should I be without you, Marie? My work would grind to a halt." He gently stroked her hair.

She looked embarrassed. "I only delay you and waste

your time with all my questions. You're so very patient with me."

He shook his head. "You give an old man a great deal of pleasure. Since you've been with me I've felt young again. The future has suddenly stretched ahead of me once more. I'm grateful to you for that."

Marie caught sight of Madame Scaliger coming across the garden to the conservatory. "Your wife," she said, pointing through the window.

Scaliger groaned. "She'll want me to join those buffoons. How I hate that!"

Madame Scaliger entered the conservatory. "The sillabub has already been served, Julius. Your guests are asking for you. Your continued absence is becoming the height of discourtesy."

Scaliger flared up. "Let them go to hell! Why should I listen to their stupid chatter?"

"Why indeed, as long as I'm prepared to put up with it for hours on end – is that what you mean?"

"Yes, Blanche, and I love you for it. Hold them at bay, I implore you. My God, why do we keep doing this to ourselves?"

"Because we need them. That's to say, *you* need them. All of them – the inquisitor and the mayor and the rest. It's important for you to remain in their good books."

"Oh yes, I need them right enough! What an age we live in! To think I have to kiss those fools on the backside instead of getting on with my work in peace – and all because a man can be denounced and sent to the stake by the first scoundrel who comes along!"

"Do you imagine I enjoy their conversation?" sighed Madame Scaliger. "It doesn't amuse me in the least."

"Send them packing, then. They've crammed their

bellies with our fare long enough, now they can go. They're welcome to excrete it in their own homes."

His wife was unmoved. "Do come along."

Scaliger removed his apron, threw it angrily on the floor, and donned his coat, which was draped over a chair. Marie picked up the apron, but he took it from her and put it on the table. "Come, Marie, have a quick bite with me. We've a long night's work ahead of us. We shall have to make up for the time these nincompoops are going to cost us."

Marie shook her head. "I want to finish this first."

"As you please. Yes, you're right. Why should you listen to their blather? I'd sooner remain here myself, but I must keep them sweet. You heard my stern, shrewd, efficient, diplomatic, utterly sensible wife."

Madame Scaliger laughed. "One insult after another. Enough, Julius."

"No, Blanche, I meant it as a compliment. I should have been ruined long ago, but for your diplomatic skill. You keep them off my back, and I thank you sincerely for doing so."

He laughed and turned back to Marie. "I'll bring you back some food." So saying, he took his wife's arm and escorted her out into the garden.

Marie watched them go. She picked up her brush and dipped it in the paint but made no move to use it. Chewing the end of the brush and slowly shaking her head, she continued to watch Scaliger. No sooner was he outside than he underwent a transformation. Marie saw him do the honours, salute the ladies and kiss their hands. They clearly found his conversation entertaining, because they fluttered around him like so many butterflies, laughing delightedly.

*   *   *

Most of the guests had dispersed and were strolling in the gardens. The orchestra was still playing. Some couples were dancing, others playing at shuttlecock. Scaliger was surrounded by a gaggle of female guests. They were reluctant to let him go, after he had kept them waiting for so long, but he jocularly excused himself and went over to the table where the inquisitor was still sitting with Madame Auberligne, the mayor, and Countess Gallaut.

The countess raised her glass. "Ah, the sun has risen at last. So our celebrated recluse is honouring us with his presence after all."

Scaliger laughed and kissed her hand. "It is I who feel honoured, Countess, that you should have graced our modest repast with your presence."

"Your cook surpassed himself," the mayor observed.

"The tartlets were superb," said the countess. "You missed a culinary treat."

"I'm fortunate enough to enjoy the services of my cook every day, Countess, but not the company of such charming guests."

"You're a flatterer, Monsieur Scaliger. What are you working on at present?"

"Would it really interest you to know?"

"But of course. We've talked of stuff and nonsense long enough."

"We're investigating similarities between the cellular structure of plants and animals."

Madame Auberligne looked as if she'd bitten on a lemon. "So that's why I haven't seen my daughter for the past week."

"You must forgive me, madame, but your daughter is becoming an ever more indispensable assistant."

"And fading away to a shadow as well. She scarcely

eats or sleeps. She's becoming old and ugly before her time. Soon she'll be lucky to find herself a husband. She may be growing ever more knowledgeable in your company, but how many men want a know-it-all for a wife? The one thing she hasn't learned is how to make a man happy. I view her present way of life with the utmost concern, monsieur."

"The world must become inured to such things," Scaliger replied. "Ladies are beginning to interest themselves in scholarship and natural philosophy, and your daughter, madame, is in the vanguard. She's exceedingly gifted, if I may say so. Very industrious, too. She will undoubtedly add to the world's store of knowledge in our field."

Madame Auberligne angrily brushed this aside. "It would be better if she added to the population by presenting some good, caring husband with a brood of children. Where is she, anyway? I was hoping at least to catch a glimpse of her."

"She preferred to remain at her work."

Madame Auberligne shook her head disapprovingly.

"She's in the conservatory, madame. If you would care to see her, I'll gladly escort you there."

Madame Auberligne made to rise, but the inquisitor, whose hand was lying on her lap, gently restrained her. She offered no resistance.

The mayor was peeling an apple. "You've taken on a great responsibility by employing the girl."

The inquisitor nodded. "I, too, view her activities with concern."

"Don't be such sourpusses," the countess interposed. "It's no business of yours. I find it wonderful that the girl should devote her time to such things." She turned to Scaliger. "But tell me, I'm interested: what of these similarities you mentioned – I mean, between plants and animals?"

"We suspect that they both originated in the same manner. Plants may be descended from the first, primeval water worms."

"You really think so?"

"We still know too little. However, the most primitive of living creatures, the coral-like products of the sea, are half-animal, half-vegetable in character. Interesting transitions are observable, to worms on the one hand, and, by way of gelatinous marine plants, to the ferns that grow on land. If we're correct in our assumptions, there must be structural similarities between them all, and I'm convinced that their structure resembles our own. Ours is the same, though very much more highly developed."

The countess giggled. "You mean I may be descended from a water worm?"

"An exceptionally beautiful one," the mayor said with a laugh.

Madame Scaliger came over with a basket of sweetmeats and deposited it on the table. The inquisitor helped himself to a bon-bon.

The countess took a piece of the apple which the mayor had peeled and quartered. She studied it thoughtfully. "If all things share the same structure, they must all have nerves and fibres. If so, an apple must feel as much pain when I sink my teeth in it as you would experience if I bit your arm."

"It's probable." Scaliger nodded. "Fortunately, however, an apple has no mouth or vocal chords with which to complain of the wrong inflicted on it."

"Are you so sure that an apple considers itself

wronged when I eat it?" the countess inquired coquettishly, taking a bite.

Scaliger laughed. "No, Countess, that applies only to us common mortals. I'm sure that any apple devoured by you would utter a cry of delight, if only it were able, for it would thereby have fulfilled its supreme natural function."

The countess smiled, looking flattered. "Your compliments are even sweeter than your tartlets."

"You're treading on dangerous ground there," said the inquisitor. He surreptitiously slid the hand holding the bon-bon beneath the tablecloth. Madame Auberligne glanced at him with a hint of curiosity.

"How so?" asked Scaliger.

"Well, the biblical story of creation furnishes us with an account of the origin of the species altogether different from your own."

"Everything in existence was created by God," said Scaliger. "All we are seeking to do is to fathom the marvellous secret that underlies the inexhaustible abundance of his handiwork."

"Why?"

Scaliger stared at the inquisitor. "Why?"

"Yes, why? Will it make people any less sinful? More pleasing to God? More industrious?"

"That I cannot tell, but I believe we should try to – "

The inquisitor cut him short. "Why do it if you don't know? You're a philosopher, are you not? The purpose of philosophy – as I understand it, at least – should be to improve the morals of mankind. Or am I in error?"

He withdrew his hand from under the cloth and rested it on the table. The bon-bon was now coated in a thin, viscous film. He contemplated it. A little droplet was forming at the base. Before it could detach itself and land on his plate, the inquisitor popped the bon-bon into his mouth and chewed with gusto.

Madame Auberligne shook her head, but she could not repress a smile. She picked up the basket of bon-bons and offered them to the inquisitor. He took one but, to her disappointment, put it straight into his mouth. He looked at Scaliger expectantly, eager to hear him dissent.

"If I understand you rightly," he pursued, "your work has only one end. You wish to undermine the authority of Holy Mother Church. For what reason? Do you truly believe that it would promote morality and decency if people knew themselves to be descended from a worm? Answer me that."

The inquisitor, who had suddenly gone puce in the face, uttered the last words in a loud voice. Heads swivelled in his direction.

Madame Scaliger realized that the conversation had taken an ominous turn, that the inquisitor was in earnest and her husband unwilling to let the matter rest. Scaliger was hesitating, but she knew him too well. He was in no doubt as to what he should say; he was merely debating whether to say it. Looking into his eyes, she guessed what would happen. There was a devil egging him on. Why couldn't he hold his peace? What possessed him? Why didn't he simply let the inquisitor have his say?

"May I bring the gentlemen a glass of cool champagne?" she asked quickly. "I have a feeling that all this talk is overheating you. Wouldn't you care for a glass, Julius?"

The mayor gently clapped his hands. "An admirable

suggestion. I fear our man of God may soon go up in flames, his cheeks are such a deep shade of crimson. You should be mindful of your heart, Eminence."

"You still haven't answered my question, monsieur," the inquisitor persisted.

"Leave him be," said the mayor. "Monsieur Scaliger is a God-fearing man. He does many good works on behalf of our community, you know that as well as I do."

"When the author of good works is suspect, I spurn them. What's more, if you'll pardon my plain speaking, I've never been entirely sure of the source from which our host derives the wealth with which he so often dazzles and impresses us."

Scaliger's face darkened. "Whatever I do, I do because it may be of use."

"To whom?"

"Why, Eminence, even to you. If you fall ill, a physician can truly help you only if he has an accurate knowledge of the composition of your body – the nature of its various humours, for example. Only then will he know which physic will be likely to combat which infection. If a herb is good for a certain disease, what is its effect on the body? If it eradicates the disease and promotes recovery, there must be something in the substance of the plant that corresponds to the substance of our bodies. That is what we natural philosophers term 'sympathy' – fellow feeling, if you wish. The beneficial effects of the herb in question would be inexplicable without it, would they not?"

The countess had been listening intently. "This Monsieur Nostradame of whom everyone has lately been talking – he also conducts such experiments. They say he worked wonders against the plague with his pills made of rose petals."

"The man's a fraud, a trickster!" exclaimed the inquisitor.

"I question that," said Scaliger. His voice was controlled, almost cool.

"He qualified with distinction," the countess went on, "and his treatments have resulted in cures that should give even you pause for thought, Eminence."

"You believe in such hocus-pocus?"

"Indeed I do."

"How ready people are to be impressed by charlatans! A handful of penitent sinners survive the plague by God's grace, and, merely because someone happens to have distributed a few pills among them, they all abase themselves before him and kiss his feet."

"Well," said Scaliger, "you'll soon have a chance to meet the man and form your own opinion. I've invited him here today."

"What!" The inquisitor looked startled.

"I'm curious to learn more about his work. If only half of what people say is true, the man must be a genius."

"I assume you know that the Holy Inquisition is also interested in his activities?" said the inquisitor.

"Yes," the countess observed drily, "the more so since his remedies saved the life of the inquisitor who had arrested him."

Scaliger smiled despite himself. "Apropos of your question, Eminence," he said. "In so far as I seek to fathom the mystery of life, I most certainly help my fellow men to please the Almighty – by living longer. A dead man can hardly perform good works, can he?"

The mayor laughed heartily. "Well said! You're a

shrewd fellow, Scaliger." He refilled the inquisitor's glass. "Drink up, Eminence. You shouldn't take such a narrow view of matters. Let the man do his work. He doesn't meddle in yours."

Madame Scaliger breathed a covert sigh of relief. Not for the first time, her husband had neatly averted disaster with a quip. The inquisitor had joined in the general laughter, but she could tell that he was dissatisfied none the less. He would never abandon so tempting a quarry. Having once picked up the scent, he would be reluctant to lose it.

Michel disembarked from the rowing-boat in which he had crossed the lake, that being the quickest way to Scaliger's residence. The servant who had helped him ashore took his bag, and they made their way across the lawn to the house.

Madame Scaliger caught sight of Michel and gave her husband an unobtrusive signal. Scaliger rose, excused himself, and went to meet the new arrival.

"Monsieur de Nostradame?"

"Monsieur Scaliger?"

"I'm delighted you could come. Are you weary after your long journey? Would you care to rest?"

"How could I be weary? I'm too excited to see you at last. Many thanks indeed for the invitation."

"Are you hungry, by any chance?"

"Only for a talk with you."

Scaliger took his arm. "You won't find my conversation too filling, I fear." He turned to the manservant who was following them. "Bring us some food, Lambert." And to Michel, "We'll eat in the library. We can talk better there."

The inquisitor caught sight of Scaliger making for

the conservatory with Michel. "Is that the famous Monsieur de Nostradame?"

The countess turned to look. "So wise yet so young? I hope he'll stay awhile, then we can all make his acquaintance."

Marie was just painting the delicate roots of her plant when Scaliger entered the conservatory with Michel. "May I present Mademoiselle Marie Auberligne? She's my eye and my hand. Without her, I'm nothing any more."

"Good evening, mademoiselle." Michel gave a little bow.

"Good evening, monsieur."

"This is Monsieur de Nostradame."

Marie eyed him with covert interest. "We've heard a great deal about you, monsieur."

"People exaggerate, but exaggeration has its advantages." Michel laughed. "If they hadn't exaggerated, you mightn't have invited me here."

"Come," said Scaliger, "we'll go to the library. We can get to it from here. I had a door inserted in the wall last year. It exempts me from having to see anyone when I leave here, my favourite place of work, and repair to the library or my laboratory."

He went over to the door, held it open for Michel, and showed him into the library. Marie rose and started to follow, but Scaliger unheedingly shut the door behind him. Disappointed, she stood staring at the door for a moment, then returned to the table and settled down to work. She dipped her brush in the paint but put it down almost at once. Rising once more, she went over to the window and looked out across the garden, where servants were busy lighting

Chinese lanterns and torches. She listened idly to the music, lost in thought. A few couples were dancing.

Books lined all four walls from floor to ceiling. The room was two storeys high and contained a gallery accessible by way of a spiral staircase. In the centre stood a large refectory table with a number of books and maps lying open on it. Beneath the gallery was Scaliger's massive desk. He and Michel had seated themselves at a small table near the window over-looking the conservatory, where Marie had by now resumed work. Michel was tucking into a plate of cold meat while Scaliger sipped a glass of water. He examined the pills Michel administered to the sick. He sniffed them, crumbled them, tasted them. Then he said, "Tell me, do you truly believe these pills contain the property that cures your patients?"

"I don't know, I can't be sure. I lack the requisite equipment. My method is primitive: trial and error. Cattle are my teachers." He paused for a moment. "Sophie taught me that."

"Who is Sophie?"

"She was our maidservant. I was very much in love with her as a youngster. She knew all about herbs. That's why they burned her at the stake."

"We live in evil times."

"So my grandfather used to say."

"Do you think they're getting worse?"

"I can't judge. I'm a physician, not a historian – nor a philosopher."

Scaliger looked at him. "Is it possible to be a physician without being a philosopher?"

"I've yet to become a good physician, still less a philosopher, that's why I'm here. I have great hopes."

"The world has awakened from its sleep," said Scaliger. "Many centuries of darkness and superstition, stupidity and gullibility lie behind us. We have much work to do. First, we must relearn all that was known before our time and has since been forgotten. You are versed in the Latin tongue?"

"Yes, and Greek."

"Excellent, that will save time. We must acquaint ourselves with all that was thought of in the ancient world. That's the foundation on which we must build. Shall I tell you what never ceases to fascinate me? How much people used to know and were able to do, once upon a time, and how they forgot it all and relapsed into the depths of barbarism from which we are laboriously extricating ourselves only now. When I read the plays of Euripides or the Homeric epics, or when I look at Myron's statues, his discus throwers and runners, I'm reminded of how much knowledge the ancients possessed! I do not speak only of their art, which I merely admire. They constructed dwellings that were taller than our tallest churches, did you know that? Their industry was highly developed, their economy well planned. They were bold, free spirits eager to know everything about everything." Scaliger chuckled. "They weren't exactly modest in their aspirations! We of today are still far removed from all that was taken for granted in their day. How much we have lost! Many more will have to die before we acquire even a modicum of their wonderful freedom of thought. Tell me, what put you in mind of roses in particular?"

Michel leaned back in his chair. "I experimented. I let sick animals choose from among various plants, and I found that rose petals must contain a mysterious substance that enhances the body's natural resistance. But I believe that my pills are less important than hygiene, cleanliness, light, fresh air, clean clothing, clean bed-linen. People tend to live in sewers of their own making."

"And you're not afraid of infecting yourself?"

"No. Diet is important too. No fat, no pork."

"Are you a Jew?"

Michel looked startled.

Scaliger laid a reassuring hand on his arm. "Never mind that. I'm glad you're here. When were you born?"

"You mean to cast my horoscope?"

Scaliger nodded. "If I may."

"I was born at Saint-Rémy at three minutes past midnight on the fourteenth of December 1503. The sun and Mercury were in conjunction under the sign of Capricorn, Mercury declining, likewise Jupiter, Saturn and Mars, all in conjunction under the sign of Cancer."

"So you also study astrology?"

"I do."

Scaliger went to the refectory table, produced some maps and tables, and spread them out. He traced numerous lines with his forefinger. "The great water trigon of five planets is strong, the moon anchored in Scorpio. You're a survivor, and that's essential, for you have a strong inclination to probe the secrets of preternatural phenomena. For that you have an ideal instrument in the conjunction of the declining planets Jupiter-Saturn-Mars. The trigon is completed by Uranus in Pisces. You're no stranger to ecstatic visions, but you also possess great scholarly curiosity. Fortunately, Uranus in Pisces prevents you from lapsing into irrational enthusiasms. You test everything with precision, yourself first and foremost. You're easily excited, sensual, passionate, sensitive. That makes you susceptible." Scaliger looked up with a smile. "Susceptible to worldly temptations, too. Take care, that's a lurking danger. You must concentrate your strength and energy on essentials, not expend and squander them. Passion is like a horse: good and useful when curbed but wild and capable of inflicting harm when given free rein. Without passion we achieve nothing; all depends on the direction it takes. Only that determines whether it is a virtue or a vice. The decision is yours, monsieur. In any event, you're a very exceptional person." He rolled up the celestial maps. "Tonight I shall cast you an accurate horoscope — it would interest me very much — but you must be tired and I still have work to do. My guests have wasted too much of my time. We breakfast at half-past seven." He escorted Michel to the door. "Marie will show you to your room. How long can you stay?"

"I don't know, I hadn't — "

"I hope you have a little time to spare." Scaliger opened the door and called, "Marie, please show Monsieur de Nostradame to his room, then come straight back." On that note he nodded to Michel and shut the door behind him.

Marie led the way upstairs and showed Michel to his bedroom on the first floor. She drew back the curtains. Michel went to the window, which overlooked the conservatory, and opened it.

"Have you worked with him long?"

"Two years."

"It's most exceptional for a woman to be interested in such things."

"You think I should tend pots and pans instead?"

Michel shook his head vehemently. "Of course not!"

"My parents would agree with you, as would most of the people here. They all think like that senile Abbot Antonius, who keeps telling my friend Magdalia to steer clear of books. I can't endure such talk. If a woman knows something, men become apprehensive because she refuses to be tyrannized any longer. If you're so scared of knowledgeable women, I can prescribe a simple remedy: Improve your minds. At least you wouldn't spend so much time idling in taverns and swilling till it comes out of your ears."

"Have you read Erasmus?" Michel asked.

"Yes. Have you?"

"Yes."

"Well? Is it reprehensible for a woman to read Erasmus?"

"No."

"You must get used to women behaving in the best way they can."

" 'Thus does the unusual become customary and the unacceptable acceptable . . .' "

" '. . . *fiet decorum quod videbatur indecorum.*' "

" '. . . and what seemed unbefitting will become befitting.' " Michel smiled. "I'm impressed."

"How arrogant of you."

"I pay you a compliment and you cast it in my teeth."

"Where's the compliment in being impressed because I've read Erasmus? You've read him too, after all, and I'm not in the least impressed. Everyone should read Erasmus. Sleep well."

She turned to go, but he laid a hand on her arm.

"How did you come to work for him?"

"I used to gather herbs in the forest for him as a child, and later on I read all his books. I was thirteen at the time." She laughed. "I made a list of all the printer's errors I found and gave it to him. For some reason, that impressed him. Good-night." She went out and shut the door behind her.

Looking out of the window, Michel saw her emerge from the house and make for the conservatory. "Shall I see you tomorrow morning?" he called after her.

She turned. "I'm always here."

Michel unpacked his bag and washed. He got into bed, took a book and leafed through it idly, unable to concentrate. At length he put it on the bedside table, got up, and went to the window. Looking across at the conservatory, he could just discern Marie through a tangle of flowers and foliage. She was seated at her table again, working by candlelight. At one stage she looked round, seemingly distracted by something. Michel smiled to himself, but she went back to work at once. Then, abruptly, she rose and placed a large screen behind her chair.

Michel lay down on the bed and blew out his candle. He was genuinely tired by now, but he couldn't sleep. He lay awake for a long time, and it was only toward dawn that he fell into a restless sleep. He dreamed again of Sophie tied to the stake. He tried to climb up and cut her loose, but the inquisitor's henchmen held him back. For the first time in this recurrent nightmare he was his present age, not a child any more. The brushwood flared up, ignited her clothing and scorched her flesh. Sophie burned like a human torch. Her fair hair fluttered in the hot updraft before catching fire. Michel managed to break loose at last. He ran up the steps, but just as he got there her head sagged forward on her breast. She was dead.

Scaliger was already breakfasting outside in the garden, together with his wife and Marie, when Michel emerged from the house with a glass jar in his hand.

"I trust you slept well?" said Madame Scaliger.

"Like a hibernating dormouse." Michel deposited the jar on the table. "I made it myself," he said. He sat down and glanced across at Marie, but she continued to eat without looking up.

Scaliger picked up the jar and opened it. "Ah, a fruit conserve of some kind." He took a little on a spoon and tasted it. "Quince jelly, excellent. You really made it yourself?" He handed the jar to his wife. "You must try some, Blanche."

"It earned me a little pocket money as a student," Michel explained. "I used to sell it in the market. The only problem is, one has to eat it right away. It won't keep."

Madame Scaliger, who had also sampled the jelly, passed the jar to Marie. "Don't worry, it won't have to keep for long, we'll eat it up in no time. It's truly delicious."

Scaliger rose. "Finish your breakfast in peace, then come to the library. We must talk." He looked at Marie. "You haven't tried the jelly."

"I don't care for sweet things," she said curtly.

Somewhat taken aback by her harsh tone, Scaliger shrugged and walked off in the direction of the conservatory. Marie rose at once and followed him.

Madame Scaliger saw that Michel was hurt by the

girl's brusque manner. "Marie meant no disrespect to your quince jelly," she said soothingly.

"Didn't she?"

"No." Madame Scaliger laughed. "It merely annoyed her that my husband left her sitting alone at table."

"Hardly alone, madame. You're still here – or do you also intend to get up and go?"

"I'll keep you company with pleasure, but it wasn't for my sake that you made so long a journey." She looked over at the conservatory. "His life runs like clockwork. He retires to his laboratory at a quarter past eight each day. In the afternoon he conducts experiments. And so it goes on, day after day, till late at night. I seldom see him except at breakfast."

"Other women see their husbands for hours on end, but what of it? I suspect that a few minutes in his company must compensate for all his absences."

She smiled wistfully. "When your own wife complains of neglect, try consoling *her* with the thought that a few minutes with a genius are worth more than an entire day with a dolt. You men are all the same!"

Michel bit off a big piece of bread. "I'm not married," he said, chewing vigorously. "That's to say, not as yet."

Marie was bent over the table when he entered the conservatory. Peering over her shoulder, he saw that she was painting a plant.

Marie stopped work and sat up very straight, as if fending him off. "He's expecting you," she said. Without looking round, she gestured at the door and went on painting. Her incivility surprised Michel, who wondered what he had done to offend her. He walked to the door in silence. Once it had closed behind him,

Marie stood up and angrily threw her brush down, spattering her work. She seized the sheet of paper and crumpled it into a ball.

Scaliger, seated at his desk with Michel facing him, gave the young man a long look. Finally he said, "Having now made a thorough study of your horoscope, I've a proposition for you. Remain here with me and I'll teach you all I know. Don't say anything now. Think it over and give me your answer tomorrow."

He rose, signifying the interview was at an end. Michel rose too.

"Meantime, Marie will show you around the town."

Michel looked surprised. "I hardly think she'd care to do so."

"Tell her it's my wish."

Soon afterwards, Michel and Marie were making their way across a meadow beside the Garonne. The roofs of Agen could be seen beyond the trees on the opposite bank. Marie walked so fast that Michel could scarcely keep up with her, and not a word had passed between them the whole way. He could sense how irked she was that Scaliger had obliged her to make this excursion with him. Struck by the absurdity of the situation, he caught hold of her arm.

"Let's go back."

"Very well." She turned and retraced her steps at the same brisk pace.

Michel hurried after her. "Why did you come at all, if you find my company so distasteful?"

"Because he asked me to."

"Do you do everything he asks?"

"Yes."

He laughed. "I can't believe that."

"It's true."

"But why?"

She came to a halt and looked at him. "Because he's clever. Because he's good and kind. Because he knows more than anyone else of my acquaintance. Why shouldn't I do as he wishes?"

"But you – "

"I don't want to talk about it." She hurried on.

He stood there, shaking his head. Then he called after her, "I know a fair amount too."

Marie didn't turn round, she simply walked on – she even broke into a run. She ran to the bridge and across it into the town. Michel sat down in the tall grass on the bank, picked up a stone and irritably tossed it into the river. The trout scattered.

That afternoon he went to look for Marie in the laboratory. She was carefully weighing out some powder and emptying it into a flask when he came up behind her. She ignored him and continued to concentrate on her work.

"You don't like me," he said.

"What makes you think that?" Again she avoided his eye.

"So you *do* like me?"

"I haven't given the matter any thought."

"Is it necessary to devote any thought to whether or not one likes a person?"

"Very well, I don't like you. Now will you leave me in peace? I've got work to do."

"I should be working too. I'm not accustomed to being idle."

"Why not read a book – or go to the ballet? There's a touring company from Paris in town."

"Would you come with me?"

"No."

"I know you have to work, but doesn't he ever allow you an hour or two to yourself?"

"For what purpose?"

"Well, going to the ballet, for instance."

"Why should I be interested in a stupid ballet?"

"I'm sure there are no tickets left in any case." He sat down astride a chair, rested his arms on the back, propped his chin on them, and regarded her with some amusement.

"Can't you leave me in peace?"

"I haven't said a word."

"You don't know what to do with yourself, is that it?"

Scaliger entered the laboratory. "Ah, I'm glad you're both here. You really must go to the ballet this evening, there's a company from Paris playing in town. I got some tickets from the mayor."

Marie shut her eyes and drew a deep breath. "You go, then. Your wife will be delighted, I'm sure."

"She's already going with a woman friend." He handed her two tickets. "Centre box, front row. Tickets like those aren't to be wasted. I'm sure you'll both enjoy it."

Michel couldn't help laughing. Marie glared at him.

"Did I say something out of place?" Scaliger inquired.

"On the contrary, monsieur," said Michel. "We were only just speaking of the ballet and how hard it must be to obtain tickets."

"So that's settled. Excellent!"

Michel got to his feet. "I'll come for you at seven, then," he said to Marie. "I shall look forward to it." And he strode gaily out of the laboratory.

"A likeable young man," said Scaliger as he bent over the experiment Marie had prepared for him.

A *pas de deux.* Entranced by its sheer audacity, the townsfolk were yelling and clapping so wildly that the music could scarcely be heard, for the crudity of the performance surpassed anything that had ever been seen in their theatre. The male dancer had just grabbed the ballerina by the hips, thrown her into the air, and flung her to the ground. She landed in the splits and rotated on her own axis, keeping her legs splayed in wanton invitation. Her partner fluttered around like an agitated butterfly, transformed himself into a menacing eagle, and suddenly pounced on her. She evaded him with a twist of her body and went whirling across the stage. He bounded after her, but again she evaded him by performing a series of lightning pirouettes. With a dramatic gesture, he indicated his bulging genitals. Mollified by this simple token of distress, she tripped daintily towards him like a sparrow, like a gazelle, and gently took hold of them. He made to fold her in his arms, overcome with relief and delight, but she coquettishly turned away once more. She never dispensed charity, her pose conveyed. He must earn his pleasure: she wanted to be taken by force. That sent him into a frenzy. He pawed the ground like a bull, grabbed her roughly by the hips, flung her into the air, and caught her by the feet. Poised at a dizzy height and lacking any means of support, she started to sway. Without warning, he let her fall. The theatre resounded to cries of alarm: she would surely break her neck. But before she could hit the ground he swiftly inserted one arm between her legs and caught her, steadying her with one hand on her haunches. Seated astride his arm, she lustfully rubbed her crotch against it, rocked to and fro, swivelled her hips convulsively. At that he lost control of himself and ripped off her outer garment of silk and lace. All she wore beneath it was a short, gauzy chemise. She wound her legs around his chest, locked them behind his back, and clung to him like a limpet. Very gradually, she sank backwards and downwards until she was lying supine on the stage. She entwined her fingers in his hair and clasped his head to her breast. He bit her. His lips were like coral, his teeth like precious stones. She arched her body and thrust him away, held him at arm's length above her. He spread his own arms wide in the manner of a hawk hovering on the wind. Slowly, she lowered him on to her body. Now they were lying one above the other, forehead to forehead, mouth to mouth, breast to breast, hip to hip, thigh to thigh, and so on down to their toes. Welded together, they lay there without moving until, at first almost imperceptibly, then more and more violently, they were rocked by an invisible billow that seemed to sweep them far out to sea, where waves were being whipped into foam by a raging tempest. She became a mare, a she-elephant, he a randy dog, a billy-goat, a wild ass. He rammed himself against her with all his might. And she? She, as he toiled away on top of her, looked out across the stalls with an expression of boredom and signalled to the spectators to egg him on a little. That brought them to their feet. They jumped up and bellowed to the man to act the tiger, the wild boar, the stallion. The brass farted and quacked and blared, the drummer belaboured his hissing cymbals, fiddles screeched as bows sawed away at their strings above the bridge. The conductor hurled his baton on to the stage and hammered wildly on an anvil. Utter pandemonium reigned.

Marie stared bemusedly at the theatregoers around her. Michel glanced at her. She looked so delightful when she was angry.

"May we go now?"

"This minute?"

"Aren't you bored?" She flushed, jumped up and left the box. Michel stayed long enough to see the ballerina wind her legs around her partner's neck, then hurried after her. He caught her up as she was running down the deserted staircase to the foyer. She came to a halt.

"I'm not going because I'm a prude, I want you to know that. I find such performances tasteless and vulgar. What's worse, their vulgarity is an attack on the world order – on happiness itself. I abominate it."

Trembling with rage, she ran on down the stairs and tripped over the hem of her gown. Michel just saved her from taking a nasty tumble. As soon as she had regained her balance she threw off his protective embrace. He looked at her and laughed.

"Why are you looking at me like that?" she snarled. "Is it so amusing when a person falls over?"

"I was just wondering why we fall when we trip."

"What?"

He produced the tickets from his pocket. "Look." He held them up, then let them slip through his fingers. "Why do they fall to the ground?"

"Because of their weight."

"Aha, and what exactly is weight, mademoiselle clever-boots? Why do all objects fall in a downwards direction?" He retrieved the tickets, tossed them into the air, and watched them flutter to the ground again.

"Why don't they fall upwards, why always down-wards? It's as if they're attracted by some mysterious force."

"Well, do you know the answer?"

"No, none of us has the least idea. I'm quite as ignorant of why a stone falls downwards as of why my rose-petal pills work. As for why you don't like me, I don't know that either."

"It was on your account that I had to waste a whole morning walking – that I had to watch an obscene ballet – that I was expected to converse on the subject of quince jelly. What else must I do on your account, can you tell me?"

"What would you rather do? I know: work. Forgive me, I'll see you home. Where do you live, anyway?

"Two rooms along the passage from yours."

"I see . . ."

Back at the house Michel unlocked the front door and stood aside for her, but she walked on.

"Where are you off to? Don't tell me you're going back to work?"

"Please have the kindness to leave me in peace at last. I want to finish off the work I've been hoping to do all day."

"I'm sorry, I don't know how to treat women. I behaved like an idiot. Forgive me."

Marie stared at him in surprise. She gave him a fleeting smile, nodded, and set off in the direction of the conservatory. He watched her go, half tempted to follow, but eventually went inside. Half-way up the stairs to his room he paused and thought for a moment, then turned and retraced his steps. He made his way through the drawing-room and down a long passage to the library, where Scaliger was still at work.

Scaliger looked up. "Is the ballet over already?"

"It is as far as we're concerned."

"Very tedious, a ballet of that kind. I don't blame you."

"I only came to tell you I've thought it over."

"And?"

"I shall remain here. If you still want me, that is."

Scaliger rose and embraced Michel. "I'm satisfied you're the person I've been waiting for all these years. You've come at last. I'm so happy." He released him and returned to his desk. "We'll start work tomorrow morning at a quarter past eight precisely. And now, good-night to you."

Moonlight was flooding into Michel's room. Lying awake in bed, he suddenly became aware of a murmur of voices outside in the garden. He got up and looked out of the window. Marie and Scaliger were down below, she talking angrily and he doing his best to pacify her, but without success. Michel couldn't gather what had upset her, but the two of them were clearly having an argument. Abruptly, she turned and walked toward the house.

"Marie, come back," Scaliger called after her. "Don't be foolish."

But Marie wouldn't listen. She disappeared into the house without a backward glance.

Scaliger shook his head, then made his way to the conservatory.

Michel opened the door of his room and emerged into the passage just as Marie came panting up the stairs. Her face was flushed with anger, her hair in disarray.

"What's the matter?"

"Leave me alone!"

She started to brush past him, but he caught her by the arm. "Were you quarrelling on my account? Why? Don't you like my being here? Are you jealous? Jealous of *me*? I don't understand you."

"You're spoiling everything! Everything!" She threw off his hand and walked on.

"I'll go if you want me to," he called after her. "I'll leave tomorrow morning."

She paused. "You don't understand in the least."

"Marie, listen to me! Please listen!"

"Sooner or later he would have entrusted all his secrets to *me*. He'd been waiting years for someone in whom to confide his knowledge. He was growing more and more impatient – even desperate at times – and I felt sure he would be bound to tell me in the end, rather than allow it all to be lost."

"Tell you what?" Michel went to her and grasped her hand. "Tell you what, Marie?"

"But now you're here he's happy, and I . . . I was always happy in his company. Now I'm not. You . . . You'll have to be very strong to endure it all – all he'll tell you in the days to come. You've every reason to be afraid."

"Afraid of what?"

"Of the truth. It's terrible."

She broke free again and ran along the passage to her door. Michel watched her go, wondering what to do. There was no point in talking to her now, she wouldn't listen, so he went back to his room.

*   *   *

He had drifted off to sleep at last, when, quite suddenly, he started up in terror. A shadowy figure had emerged from a dark void and was floating slowly past him into nothingness. Behind the figure trailed a long black veil that enveloped it from head to foot. It disappeared, leaving nothing but darkness in its wake. He sprang out of bed, ran to the door, wrenched it open, and sprinted along the passage. "Marie!" he shouted as he wrenched her door open too. "No! Don't do it, Marie! Please!" And then he saw her.

She was standing on a chair in her nightgown with a noose around her neck. She had tied the rope to the chandelier suspended from the ceiling. Just as Michel burst in, she kicked the chair away and dangled there. He ran to the chair, righted it, mounted it, clasped her around the body and tried to loosen the rope, but to no avail. He looked about him wildly, spotted a penknife on the table. Gently lowering her, he jumped down and ran to the table, seized the knife, climbed back on the chair, held her up again so that the noose wouldn't throttle her, and tried to cut the rope. No use, the rope was too slack. Supporting her with one arm, he tugged at it desperately. Still no use. He released her once more, jumped up, clung to the rim of the chandelier, breasted it, and let himself fall like a dead weight – once, twice, three times. At long last the mounting gave way. Marie, Michel and the chandelier landed on the floor in a heap. Hurriedly he removed the noose. Marie coughed and retched violently. He fetched a glass of water from the bedside table and held it to her lips. When she had drained the glass he tossed it aside and bent over her, kissing and caressing her with wild abandon.

"Marie, Marie, why did you do it? Marie, you

silly girl, I love you. Do you hear me, Marie? I love you."

She smiled faintly, rubbed her neck and coughed some more.

He knelt down beside her and carefully helped her into a sitting position. Supporting her with one hand, he used the other to conduct a careful examination of her neck and spine. He felt the whole length of her back, then gently worked her head to and fro. Nothing was broken. Relieved, he stroked her hair, held her in his arms, clasped her to him. "Why did you do it?" he whispered, embracing her tenderly. "Why?"

"I've lost him," she murmured. "And now I've lost you too. I'm all alone. I can't go back, not to the others. I can't any more. I know too much."

Michel kissed her on the lips. At that she put her arms around him and drew him to her, over her. She returned his kisses passionately, avidly, desperately.

"I love you too," she whispered.

Scaliger appeared in the doorway and looked in. Alerted by a distant crash, he had come to see what was amiss. What he saw was a ruined chandelier and, beside it, two young people making love on the tumbled clothes they had torn from their bodies. He watched them for a moment, and it was only when Marie cried out in ecstasy that he quietly closed the door. He leaned his forehead against the panel and stood there awhile in turmoil. His despair and unhappiness and longing were such that he didn't know how he would endure the pain. Slowly, he turned and climbed the stairs to his room, a bent-backed, sick, decrepit old man.

Immediately after breakfast the next morning, Scaliger went with Michel to the library. He lit a candle and handed it to him, lit another and placed it on the table. Then he drew the curtains. Taking a Bible from the table, he held it out.

"Swear. Swear that you will never speak with anyone but an initiate of what I shall shortly communicate to you."

Michel looked at him in surprise. Then he put his hand on the Bible. "I swear it."

"Should you do so, your life will be forfeit. The Inquisition will not kill you, one of us will do so." Scaliger replaced the Bible on the table. "You will settle here in Agen and earn your living as a physician. Then the authorities will not trouble you. You will move into the small house at the end of the garden, which belongs to me. You can enter the garden by the back gate, so you will always have access to me without anyone knowing how often you visit me, for your real work will be here. You must also marry and have children – lead an entirely normal life. Will you have the strength of purpose to do that?"

"I shall send for Raoul, my old apothecary. He can take a great deal of the everyday work off my shoulders."

"Can he be trusted?"

Michel nodded.

"Good."

Scaliger took one of the candlesticks, went over to a secret door, and opened it. He stepped aside to let Michel enter the dark, narrow passage beyond, then shut the door behind them. The passage, which was not a long one, ended in a small, circular chamber with a very high ceiling. Michel held the candle above his head for a better look. It was lined with shelves, and there were books everywhere – manuscript books, not printed editions. These volumes, most of them bound in leather, were very old, and many were yellow and dog-eared with age. The room was bare save for a table and two armchairs in the centre. Michel looked around him in wonder, not venturing to touch any of the books.

Scaliger waited for a moment. Then he said, "We have an enemy: the Church. Never forget that. Copernicus is right: the earth revolves around the sun. The Church suppresses the truth and those who seek it. Anyone who says as much in public is burned at the stake." He rose and indicated one of the volumes. "Copernicus, *De revolutionibus*. It deals with the rotation of heavenly bodies." He pointed to various other books. "Avicenna, Heraclitus, Plato, Aristotle, Plutarch. This is Al Ghasali's *Elixir of Happiness* in his own hand – the sole surviving copy. Albertus Magnus. Paracelsus. Cornelius Agrippa. Here is *De mysteriis Aegyptiorum*, and here Iamblichus' manuscript on the magic of Chaldea and Assyria. That book there is *De daemonibus* by Michael Psellus, and that one the writings of the Cabbala. I also have The Keys of Solomon and the Rites of Branchus, a priestess from Delphi."

He sat down again made a vague gesture that took in the entire room. "You would be burned at the stake for possessing any one of these works, and if they themselves were consumed by fire it would be a catastrophe. The world would be the poorer without them. They contain centuries' worth of secret knowledge. The men who wrote them were holy men, even if the Church believes them to be sorcerers fit for burning. Most of them had the ability to see into the future. You must learn how they did that. Nothing happens by chance; every occurrence accords with God's plan for the world." He opened a drawer, produced a small bowl filled with red powder, and held it out.

"What is it?"

"The key to your unconscious mind. More precisely, the door to the future."

"Nutmeg?"

Scaliger nodded. "Among other things. You must treat it with respect. Ingest too much, and you would die. It's a potent poison – your body must grow accustomed to it by degrees. Take a little more each day, and your visions will become clearer." He removed some sheets of paper from the drawer and handed them to Michel. They bore drawings in red chalk. Michel studied them. One showed a huge, menacing cloud shaped like a mushroom.

"I've seen that before," Michel whispered.

"What? Where? The drawing?"

"No, not the drawing itself, the mushroom cloud – in a dream. There was a vast explosion, greater and more terrible than any the world has ever known. When that mushroom rises into the air, all that will be left is death. Who drew it?"

"Our friend Leonardo." Scaliger showed him another drawing, this time of a peculiar boat.

"What's that?"

"Our friend Leonardo conceived it too: a vessel that travels under water – a submarine. People will devise the most fearsome inventions in years to come." Scaliger replaced the sketches in the drawer. "You will devote the coming months to systematic reading under my guidance. You will study until your brain has absorbed this library word for word, line for line, numeral for numeral. You will read only here in this room. You will remove no book from it and commit nothing to paper. You are not to make a single note. If the least suspicion falls on us, we're lost."

Michel was overcome with amazement. He scanned the books in turn and carefully removed a few from the shelves. They were true sanctuaries of human knowledge, he told himself. It was an indictment of the present age that such treasures had to be hidden away. He replaced the books and ran his hand lovingly over their spines.

"It's beyond belief," he said.

"We'll start tomorrow. I still have some work to complete today."

"Does Marie know what is in here?"

"No, and she must never find out." Scaliger smiled. "Not even when she's your wife."

Michel looked startled.

Scaliger laid a hand on his shoulder and looked into his eyes. "You must treat Marie with the greatest care. She's easily upset and very sensitive – vulnerable in the extreme. I love her like a daughter. It would distress me beyond measure if she were made unhappy."

"My one desire is to make her happy. I love her."

"And Marie? Does she love you?"

"I'm not sure. I hope so – in fact it's my dearest wish. She's so unfathomable. I'm often unable to tell where I stand with her."

"Shall I speak to her?"

"No, I should prefer to do that myself."

"Very well, but don't delay."

Michel nodded.

Scaliger extinguished all the candles except the one in his hand. They walked back along the passage and shut the door behind them. "Let me explain the secret mechanism," Scaliger said, "so that you can work here when I'm away." He showed Michel the hidden lever that released the door. "But please, no one else must enter that library – no one, you understand, only the two of us. Unless, of course, we receive a visit from one of our friends."

"Our friends?"

"The finest minds in Europe, and all united by one thing: curiosity – an urge to discover the truth about life, free from all religious and ideological dogmas. The old world is at an end. We are building a new one. Do you understand, Michel? It's not a matter of doing this particular thing or that; our goal is universal. Lose sight of that, and all our work will be in vain."

Marie was sitting over her drawing when Michel came up behind her. He rested his hands on her shoulders, bent down and kissed her. He looked at the plant. "Very nice," he said, but his thoughts were elsewhere. "Marie, we must talk."

"Yes?"

"We're already married in the sight of God. I should like us to be so in the sight of men."

She rose and put her arms around his neck. "Have you given it careful thought?"

"Indeed I have. Don't you want to marry me?"

"Did he confide his secret in you?"

Michel didn't reply.

"Do you think I don't know there's a secret chamber behind the library – one in which he closets himself at dead of night?"

"I'm not at liberty to speak of it."

"Do you think I'd marry a man who has secrets from his wife?"

"I'm not at liberty to speak of it," he repeated.

She laughed. "Then how do you conceive of our married life? You spending night after night in that library while I keep to the kitchen and make quince jelly – and discuss the weather with you when you deign to appear? You can't be in earnest."

"Please don't pester me, Marie. I mustn't speak of it. His wife knows nothing either."

"I'm not his wife."

"Won't you marry me, then?"

Marie kissed him tenderly. "I want it more than anything else in the world. But if we do marry, Michel, we shall not be able to lead a married life as other folk do. Think carefully." She hugged him. "I want you so much."

They married a week later, Scaliger and Madame Scaliger acting as witnesses. Marie's mother was uncertain whether or not to be happy with her daughter's choice. The young man was clever and well-educated and charming – yes, and famous – but he had no money. How would he support a family? Once the initial demand for his services as a physician had waned and people were accustomed to him, the young couple would be on short commons. Madame Auberligne had tried to talk her daughter out of such a marriage, but it was hopeless: Marie had set her heart on the fellow, and there was no dissuading her. She refused to discuss the matter any more than she would ever discuss anything that had once taken root in her head. Very well, Madame Auberligne told herself: let the girl have her way, but it would be no use her complaining later on, when everything turned out as she, her mother, had foreseen. Monsieur Auberligne, who took a more practical view of the matter, urged his wife not to be upset. On the contrary, she should be glad that their daughter had found herself a husband at all, for how many other men would want a wife who always knew better and intended to pursue a profession after the wedding? No one else in the district would have tolerated such a prospect. So he embraced Michel and expressed his pleasure at having acquired a son – one who might some time care to go hunting or play cards with him. He slapped the young man on the back, and that – as far as he was concerned – was that.

They moved into the cottage on the edge of Scaliger's garden. Michel set up his practice there, and Raoul, his old apothecary, came to assist him. They were very busy, for Michel's reputation had travelled to Agen in the wake of his spectacular cures during the plague epidemic. Everyone wanted to be treated by him, especially the women of the town, who were curious to see the new physician for themselves. Meanwhile, Marie continued to work for Scaliger in the conservatory across the way, though she also pursued studies of her own. Michel spent the mornings and afternoons at his practice. In the evenings he retired to Scaliger's secret library and worked there until the small hours. He slept little, not that he had ever been one to sleep much.

He was still in the library one morning, having studied all night long, when Scaliger came in.

"It's eight already. You must be going."

"Yes, in a minute."

"You mustn't keep your patients waiting."

"No."

Scaliger chuckled. "Then go."

Michel shut his book. "When can you spare me some time? I need to talk with you." He indicated the crowded shelves. "My head will burst if I don't soon speak with someone about all the things I'm learning here."

"It was the same with me. The brain finds them hard to assimilate, I know. I have to go to Paris for two weeks. We'll talk when I return."

Michel was walking home through the garden when Marie came in the opposite direction, making for the conservatory. These brief encounters in the garden were often the only times in the day when they saw each other. He kissed her.

"Your first patients are already there." She stroked his head. "You look tired."

"I'm all right. What are you doing today?"

"Working on my lichens."

"Scaliger is off to Paris for two weeks."

"I know. Rosalie will give you breakfast. Mind you eat something before you start work." She patted his cheek. "You really should lie down for an hour or two now and then."

Michel breakfasted on his feet in the kitchen. Rosalie, the maidservant, made him some scrambled eggs. He wolfed them and was drinking a cup of milk when Raoul came in.

"Are there many there already?" Michel asked.

"More and more every day. Most of them aren't sick at all. They come out of curiosity."

"No serious cases? Here, eat something."

"I already did, thank you. No, nothing serious as far

as I can tell." He smiled. "But the ladies don't want to hear that from *me*."

Madame Auberligne appeared in the doorway. "Where's Marie," she demanded.

"Good morning, mother-in-law."

"Good morning," she said impatiently. "My daughter — is she over there again?"

He nodded.

"I don't know why you stand for it. No self-respecting husband lets his wife go out to work."

"You make it sound as if I send her to the treadmill."

"It's worse than that: you send her to another man. People are whispering things."

"What sort of things?"

"That the old man is cuckolding you. That you may be failing in your marital duty — that you may even be incapable of performing it."

"Is that why so many ladies come to consult me, to find out for themselves? I can satisfy them of my capabilities if you'd like me to, mother-in-law." He laughed. "I must go now. There are plenty of womenfolk here already."

"You're quite impossible."

"Marie will be in the conservatory, if you want a word with her."

"I wanted a word with you as well."

"Good, so now you've had it. Was there something else?"

"I don't know why I trouble my head about you at all, the pair of you. Have it your own way, but don't come running to me if problems arise."

"What manner of problems?"

But Madame Auberligne merely said *"Au revoir"* and stalked out.

Michel shook his head. "What did she really want?"
Raoul shrugged.

"Problems?" Michel persisted. "What can the woman have meant by that?"

"What should she have meant?" said Raoul. "She was simply playing the *grande dame* and throwing her weight around."

"I hope you're right."

The waiting-room benches were fully occupied by the time Michel walked in. "Good morning, ladies," he said as he made for the inner door that led to his consulting room. "Which of you was here first?" One of the women promptly rose and followed him.

He proceeded to examine her. Standing beside the window, he took her head in his hands and peered into her open mouth. "You must keep an eye on those tonsils, they're a trifle inflamed. That apart, I can find nothing wrong with you."

"But I'm in pain, doctor. That's why I came."

"Where does it hurt?"

She pointed to her bosom. "Here."

"Your heart? Kindly get undressed."

"Undressed?"

"Yes, if you're in pain and I'm to examine you properly."

"Do you do this with all your women patients?"

"If they're in pain, yes."

The woman giggled and started to unlace her bodice.

"Kindly undress behind that screen, and expose the upper part of your body only."

Faintly disappointed, she went behind the screen. "Do many women have pains there?" she inquired.

"The cases have become more frequent of late, yes."

"And what are they suffering from? Is it something bad?"

"Very seldom." Michel sat down on the windowsill and looked out. How bored he was by all this stupid, lascivious, flirtatious nonsense. There was nothing wrong with her, nothing whatsoever. She was simply wasting his time, like most of the women who frequented his waiting-room. He rubbed his eyes. These consultations were even more tiring than his work at the hospital had been. He yawned. "At least," he added, "I believe I've been able to help them all until now."

"In what way?"

"By asking them to come and see me with their husbands."

The woman stared at him incredulously over the top of the screen. "What!"

"I explain to their menfolk that the female breast is a very sensitive organ. It must be massaged, gently and regularly, because if the blood flows too sluggishly it may stagnate and induce painful cramps in the heart."

"I see. And massage helps?"

"Yes, nearly always."

The woman emerged from behind the screen stripped to the waist. "But most men would be far too rough and clumsy to administer such treatment."

Michel handed her a small towel and gestured to her to cover her breasts. "I'll gladly show your husband how it should be done, if you wish."

Reluctantly, she took the towel and held it up in a rather haphazard fashion. "Don't you perform this massage yourself, doctor? I mean, so that one knows exactly how to do it?"

"Every night without fail, but only on my own wife. Please turn round."

She complied. Michel percussed her spine from neck to waist and examined her lymphatic channels. He did so conscientiously, not wishing to be accused of skimping his work, but it was all he could do to swallow his distaste. "Give thanks to God," he said eventually. "You're as fit as a fiddle. You can get dressed now."

She turned to face him with her breasts exposed and looked at him expectantly. "And the massage, Doctor?"

Michel ignored this. He went to a cupboard and took out a small sachet. "Here's a powder for your tonsils. That's all you need."

"But what of these pains in my chest? I can still feel them."

"Your blood is too congested," he told her, "hence the symptom you mention, a deep-seated ache. The treatment for that disorder is entirely different. No gentle massage – that would be highly inadvisable."

"So what's the proper treatment?"

"You must sluice yourself liberally with cold water from head to foot, night and morning. Any massaging of the breasts at this juncture would be injurious."

"But if the pains return, how shall I know if a gentle massage might not have been the best treatment after all, if my blood is flowing too sluggishly?"

"Then you must consult me again, and we'll find out."

*   *   *

He hurried across the garden to the conservatory and flung the door open.

"I can't endure these women. They're not ill, not a single one of them."

Marie laughed. "My mother warned me to keep a closer watch on what goes on in your consulting room."

"And the vulture told me to stop sending you out to work because everyone suspects you're having an affair with Scaliger."

"They should mind their own business." Marie's voice took on a sudden note of enthusiasm. "Michel, I think I'm on the track of something immensely important. You know feldspar, the mineral that occurs in all the mountains around here? Well, it contains a great deal of potash, which makes it prone to disintegration. Wherever the bare rock has crumbled away to dust under the effects of wind and weather, one finds lichens, those almost leatherlike organisms in red, yellow and other eye-catching colours."

She led him over to a specimen cabinet in which lay some lichen-encrusted stones. "We find them everywhere on the borderline where vegetation gives way to bare rock. That's why the most primitive varieties of lichen are almost indistinguishable from the rock itself." She picked up one of the specimens and handed it to him. "They have no cells or fibres or anything in common with the internal structure of other organisms." She took the stone from him and replaced it in the cabinet. Then she went to another cabinet and pointed to a second stone. "But add water and heat, as I have been doing for several months, and then, as in Nature when it rains a great deal and the sun shines brightly afterwards, they develop into something most remarkable." She indicated a particular spot and handed him a magnifying glass. "You see? They turn into liverwort and flowering mosses, and – hey presto! – we have a fully-developed species of plants. Do you realize what that means?"

"That there's an unbroken transition between inorganic and organic matter?"

Marie was really excited now. "Yes, between rock and plant and plant and animal, just as Scaliger has demonstrated in the case of corals and worms – just as we can observe in the case of carnivorous plants. And the same applies to every higher order. Primitive animals, like primitive plants, develop from inorganic material because of minor changes in their metabolism. In the beginning, Michel, was the stone, not the Word!" She took the stone from the cabinet and held it up. "That's what we're descended from – you and I and the neighbour's dog. What do you say now?"

"I say congratulations." He took her in his arms and kissed her. "Write it all down."

"And then? You know what would happen if I published it."

"Write it down. We'll send it to our friends."

"What friends?"

"I fear I'm not at liberty to tell you."

She flew into a sudden rage. "You can't tell me, but I'm expected to record my discovery for the benefit of these so-called friends, who are strangers to me, so that they can read my notes and discuss them. Discuss them without me, because I don't belong in their exalted company – because I'm a woman! Are you serious? Are you all mad?"

"Marie, calm yourself!"

"I've no intention of calming myself. On the contrary, I'm growing more exasperated by the minute – and with you most of all." She mimicked him. " 'I fear I'm not at liberty to tell you. . .' No, but I'm at liberty to tell you of my discoveries, aren't I, so that you self-important males can preen yourselves on them when you meet in secret. You make me sick! You're in no more danger than I, you're simply more conceited. How dare you talk such nonsense to me! I hate you. I hate you! I come to you at once and tell you everything, but how much do *you* tell *me*? Well? Do you tell me anything about your secret doings every night? I've been discreet hitherto, but that's over. I want to know, and I want to know now! I refuse to be treated any longer like a silly little flibbertigibbet. Find yourself another woman – one of those stupid cows who ogle you every day. Take her and go – and leave me in peace!"

"Marie, please!"

"What does 'Marie, please' mean? That I'm to hold my tongue, is that it? I'm expected to let you tup me – "

"Marie, that's enough!"

" – but talking, no, you reserve that for the illustrious Monsieur Scaliger, man to man. Tup him, then, but leave me in peace!" Trembling with fury, she turned and ran off.

Michel ran after her. "Marie! Marie, wait!"

She ran across the broad expanse of lawn and down to the lake, where she seated herself on a bench beneath a willow tree near the water's edge. Michel could see, as he drew nearer, that she was crying.

He sat down beside her and took her hand. "I don't want you to endanger yourself."

"No, but *you* can do so. You truly don't think of anyone but yourself."

"Marie . . ."

"I married you and you married me, am I right?"

"Of course, but what are you driving at?"

"In other words, we were two individuals who freely decided to marry."

"Yes, but – "

"No buts. Yes or no?"

"Yes."

"Very well. Then each of us has equal rights."

"What are you implying, Marie?"

"What I'm implying is that we bear joint responsibility for this marriage, and that we have the same rights and obligations. Either I present the results of my investigations to your friends in person, or they don't learn them at all. If one of us runs a risk – "

"The other should too?"

"Exactly! The other should too." She hugged and kissed him, laughing and sobbing simultaneously. "Michel, I couldn't live another day if anything happened to you."

"I'll discuss it with Scaliger."

That provoked a lightning change of mood. She thrust him angrily away. "Scaliger, Scaliger, always Scaliger! Haven't you any will of your own? Whom did I marry, you or him? I *could* have had him, believe me, if I'd wanted to."

"Is that so?"

"You don't believe me? I could still have him today."

"Look, Marie, this is becoming absurd."

She nodded. "So it's absurd. You'll see."

"I must be getting back, the waiting-room is full.

Let's talk about this tonight, quietly." He rose to go, but she caught hold of his hand and drew him down on the bench again.

"Michel, I want you to show me the secret library."

"What!" Michel stared at her aghast. "I couldn't. I had to give him my word. I swore it on the Bible."

She got up and ran her hand lightly over his hair. "Then I'll ask him myself."

"He'll never show you that library."

"What makes you so sure?"

She hurried back across the lawn to the house.

That night, when everyone else in the house was asleep, Michel showed her the secret library after all. He operated the mechanism that opened the hidden door and handed her a candle. They stepped swiftly into the narrow passage, and he shut the door behind them.

Marie surveyed the secret chamber with awe. She toured the shelves, sometimes pausing to take down a book and leaf through it. "Michel," she whispered, "this is wonderful. The answers to all the world's secrets are here."

He nodded.

She stared at him in sudden alarm. "Who are you, Michel? Who are you that he should show you all these marvellous things and take you into his confidence? Why you? Why you of all people?"

"I don't know. He cast my horoscope."

She held out her arm. "Look, I'm all gooseflesh. This place frightens me, Michel. We're venturing too far, the two of us — I with my lichens and you with these books. Let's draw back while we still can." All at once she embraced him wildly. "I don't want to lose you, Michel, do you hear? Let the world go its own way. I love you and I don't want to lose you. Just be a physician and forget all this. Let's live like ordinary folk – let's move to another town before it's too late."

He put his arms around her neck and gazed at her earnestly. "It's already too late, Marie. I know too much – too much of the terrible truth about this world of ours."

She heaved a deep sigh. "I've sensed it lately when you hold me in your arms. You're never really with me – your thoughts are elsewhere. Please let me out, I want to leave this place. Let's go, please."

They made love that night. It was dawn by the time they released one another, bathed in sweat and exhausted. Michel rolled over on his back with his arm around her. She pillowed her head on his chest. The sun's first rays were streaming into their bedroom.

"You must get up," she said, nestling even closer.

"I know."

She laughed. "Get up, then. I'm sure the ladies of the town are already thronging your waiting-room."

"Yes, at once. I wasn't too rough with you?"

She kissed him. "What makes you say that?"

"I was thinking of the child."

"What could be better for the child than to learn about love while it's still in my belly? It should cry out with delight when the blood races through my veins." She fondled him hungrily and laughed. "You really must get up."

He laughed too. "Then stop that."

"I wouldn't dream of it."

Having kissed her and gently released himself, he got out of bed and started to dress.

Marie sat up and wedged a pillow behind her back. She gently stroked her round, protuberant belly. "It's stirring already." She took his hand and laid it on the bump. "Can you feel it too?"

"Indeed I can." He put his ear to her belly and caressed her tenderly. "That child is really being spoiled with love."

"Yes," she whispered, "and we both can't have enough of it."

The Scaligers had invited Michel and Marie to eat with them one Sunday. It was a warm, sunny day in late summer, but the golden leaves were a reminder that winter was on the way. Far gone with child by this time, Marie was rapidly approaching her time. She made a thoroughly contented impression. Michel had stationed himself behind her and was rubbing her back.

After the meal Scaliger inquired if the young couple would care to see the new statue of the Virgin which was to be displayed in the church square that day before being installed in one of the side chapels.

Marie, who said it was quite some time since she had been into town, pronounced this a good idea. Michel looked a shade worried and wondered aloud if the outing would be too much for her.

"We can always take the carriage if you prefer not to walk," Scaliger suggested.

Marie laughed. "I'm not ill, gentlemen, I'm only going to have a child."

" 'Only' is a fine thing to say!" Michel protested.

" 'Only' is right," said Marie. "Do let's go right away, or I may give birth in the market-place."

They took a leisurely stroll through the streets.

Michel and Scaliger walked on ahead while Marie and Madame Scaliger followed slowly on behind.

"The mayor had a word with me yesterday," said Scaliger. "I put your name forward as a candidate in the next municipal elections. He agreed."

"You think that's wise?"

"Very much so. You'll have to waste a lot of time with those imbeciles, admittedly, but your position will be safer. They'll think twice before attacking a town councillor."

"Why should anyone attack me?"

"There's something in the wind. When stupidity mates with bigotry, the fruit of their union is violence. Be sensible and stand for election."

"If you think it's the right thing to do."

They had reached the church square. A few onlookers were watching the new statue being hoisted on to a plinth for the townsfolk to admire. Michel and Scaliger exchanged a horrified glance.

"It's appalling," Michel whispered. "A monstrosity." He drew nearer while Scaliger waited at the entrance to the square for the ladies to catch up.

Michel was now standing only a few feet from the statue. "What in heaven's name is that frightful creature above the Madonna's head?" he demanded of the onlookers.

"A cherub," said a man who had been nervously supervising the erection of the statue to ensure that no accident befell it.

"Really? To me it looks more like a demon put there to frighten little children."

"Is that what you think?"

"Yes, don't you? It's truly appalling. I'm shocked."

"I cannot endorse your opinion."

"Fancy spending our taxes on it! It's a scandal. What are they going to do with the thing? They surely don't propose to set it up inside the church?"

Scaliger was approaching with the two women. Seeing that Michel was embroiled in an argument, he hurried up to him. "Allow me to introduce you, Michel." He indicated the man Michel had crossed swords with. "This is Monsieur Grenelle, the sculptor responsible for this wonderful statue. Monsieur Grenelle, meet Monsieur de Nostradame, the finest physician in Agen."

"I hope he knows more about medicine than he does about art," Grenelle snorted furiously. "About that, he knows nothing whatever!" He turned abruptly on his heel and strode off to join a group of admirers, who were eagerly extolling his handiwork. But their encomiums failed to appease him. He kept looking back at Michel, who had taken Marie's arm and was leaving the square with the Scaligers.

Scaliger wagged his finger at Michel. "You should be more careful whom you offend."

"Bah! Who offended whom? *I* was offended. My eyes were offended by that wretched piece of work."

"Monsieur Grenelle, to whom I just had the honour to introduce you, is adviser to the high court of the Holy Inquisition on all matters pertaining to art. Weren't you aware of that?"

"Oh, damnation!"

Scaliger chuckled. "Quite."

"What now?"

"Now we must be very adroit. If I know the man, he'll be thirsting for revenge."

"But why didn't you warn me?"

"Because I had no idea you didn't know him. Know thine enemy, Michel. It's an invariable rule."

Marie's pains began as they were walking across the market-place. Scaliger hailed a carriage, which quickly conveyed her home.

Marie, clad only in a flimsy nightgown, clung tightly to the arms of her chair. Her feet were immersed in a bowl of warm water. She winced as another pain came.

Michel patted her. "Keep calm and breathe deeply – draw the air deep down inside you. Yes, that's it. In deeply and out slowly, the way we practised it. Yes, very good."

Marie smiled despite the intensity of the pain. "Which of us is having this child, Michel? You mustn't get so agitated." She put out her arms, took his head in her hands and kissed him. "We'll do it, never fear."

He chuckled. "What a wonderful woman you are!"

The room was full of women, all of whom wanted to be present at the birth in the customary way. Rosalie came in with a tray of refreshing drinks and handed them round. One woman shut the window and draped some thick blankets over it to keep out the draughts, another stacked wood on the hearth and prepared to light a fire. Madame Scaliger was standing behind Marie, stroking her hair. The midwife entered with a bowl of boiling water and deposited it on the floor beside the chair. There were white cloths everywhere. A cradle stood waiting in the corner. The table was draped in white sheets, and neatly arrayed on it, against the possibility of complications, was a set of clean, sparkling instruments: obstetrical forceps of various sizes, scalpels, knives, pincers, needles and thread.

Madame Scaliger massaged Marie's neck to prevent

her from tensing up. "It'll soon be over," she said. "It always takes longer the first time, everything's so narrow. The second time, believe me – whoosh, and it's out. It only hurts as much as this the first time."

Marie smiled and nodded, then grimaced with pain as the next contraction made itself felt.

Michel looked round. He had been unaware of what was going on elsewhere in the room. "Thank you all for coming, ladies," he said. "It's exceedingly kind of you, but I should prefer us to be alone for the birth. We'll call you as soon as the child arrives. Thank you again, and please, no fire." He went to the window, removed the blankets, and flung it wide. "Air is what we need, and light. I want the child to rejoice in this glorious sunshine."

The women trooped out in a body. Thoroughly disapproving of Michel's unconventional approach to childbirth, they shook their heads darkly as they went. Madame Scaliger made to follow them, but Marie caught her by the hand. The older woman smiled. She resumed her post and continued to massage Marie's neck. Another contraction. Marie's hands tightened on the arms of the chair. Then, when the pain had subsided, she beckoned Michel over and whispered a few words in his ear.

"Arabic?" He stared at her in surprise. "How do you come to know the language?"

She smiled. "I've been studying it on those long, lonely nights when you desert me in favour of your work."

"But why? For what purpose?"

"Will you do me a favour?"

"Ah, I guessed as much! What now?"

She spoke even more softly, so that Madame Scaliger

could not overhear. "That time I was with you in the library, remember? I saw – "

"Say no more, please!"

"Scaliger has a manuscript of the *Ghàyat al-hakim* by Abu'l-Qásim Maslama ben Ahmed el-Madjrti. I want it."

He shook his head firmly. "No."

Another contraction. Marie breathed in deeply through her nose and slowly out through her mouth. Before the pain had subsided, she whispered, "According to ibn-Khaldun, it's the most important and definitive work on the magic of Arabia. I simply must have a sight of it."

"But that's impossible. Scaliger is forever in and out of that library – you can't go there."

"But you can. Fetch the book and bring it to me."

"I can't."

"My treatise on lichens impressed you greatly. Him too, he told me so himself. Aren't I permitted to continue my research? Must I leave it to you men?"

"Please don't start that again."

"Abu'l-Qásim states that all matter is pervaded by the divine spirit, but in varying degrees. The emanation of the deity communicates itself to the world by way of intermediate creatures. The more highly developed those creatures are, the more they approximate to the nature of gods and demons, whereas the more intimate their connection with primitive matter, the more they assume the form of divine forces that slumber within animals, plants and stones, waiting to be awakened."

Marie waited for the pain of the next contraction to fade. She was very excited, but not at the imminent birth of her child. All her thoughts were of the book she craved. She had to have it, why couldn't he understand?

"Don't you see what I mean? That book would confirm what I wrote about the lichens. The number of series or chains, as Proclus terms them – the 'sympathy' existing between things that belong together and are interrelated but do not at first appear to belong together at all – are harmoniously attuned to each other in their effects. I know I'm making progress in this field. It would also have undreamed-of consequences for medicine. Since the complex substance always contains the simpler one, it must be possible to determine exactly which remedy will assist and cure by reinforcing that substance. I need that book badly."

He sighed. "You're impossible."

Marie laughed. "You knew that when you married me." She gave a cry as an another pain assailed her with unexpected intensity.

"The pains are coming every half-minute," the midwife said soothingly. "It'll soon be over, madame. Very soon."

Michel knelt beside her, reached beneath her nightgown and spread her thighs a little. He smiled up at her.

Another contraction came.

"Yes, and now you must push. That's right, push with all your might. Good, well done. Yes, that's it, and again. It's almost there, Marie. A little more, just a little more. Yes!"

The baby uttered a loud cry. Michel held it up and showed it to her: a boy. The little thing was smeared with blood, but blood of a colour remote from sickness and death. It was the bright, clear, wonderful, luminous colour of life. Madame Scaliger mopped the beads of sweat from Marie's brow. Marie beamed.

"It's a boy, Marie. We have a son!"

Marie smiled. "We'll call him Julius," she whispered. Feebly, she raised her arm and stroked the child, which Michel was still holding. He severed the umbilical cord and knotted it, then carefully laid the child on Marie's breast. She hugged it gently to her. The midwife disposed of the afterbirth.

"Aren't you going to wash him first?" inquired Madame Scaliger.

"The young man has long been accustomed to the throb of his mother's heartbeat. Let him hear and feel it again. The natal process is a great strain on any infant. He needs time to recover." Michel beckoned to Rosalie, who handed him a fluffy white blanket. He draped it over the baby, then seated himself in an armchair beside Marie and held her hand. She was truly exhausted now. As for the child on her breast, it had found the nipple and was already sucking.

Beside the table in the centre of the secret library stood a tripod, and on it reposed a basin of water whose surface reflected the flame of the single candle beyond it. Michel, seated in front of the basin with Scaliger standing at his elbow, slowly poured a few drops of essence into the water, which became slightly discoloured. Scaliger went to the table and fetched a bowl of red powder. He removed a little with a miniature scoop and handed it to Michel.

"Let it slowly dissolve on your tongue."

Michel scattered the powder on his tongue and leant back with his eyes shut.

Scaliger replaced the bowl on the table and sat down.

"I shall stay with you. I want to observe your reactions. Don't be afraid, I won't leave you."

Michel opened his eyes. He bent over the bowl and gazed at the water, which was full of iridescent streaks. Then his eyes turned up until only the whites were showing, and he fell into a deep trance. His hands rested quietly on the arms of the chair, his breathing was deep and regular. Not a sound. Absolute silence reigned.

All at once Michel gave a loud, harsh cry. His eyes were wide and staring now, his features twisted with fear and anguish. Saliva trickled from his mouth. He jumped up, swayed and fell, upsetting the tripod and the basin. The water drained away. He crept into a corner and huddled there, screaming again and again as if tormented by a thousand demons. Scaliger hurried to his side, put his arms around him, gently massaged his temples and talked to him in a low, soothing voice. They sat side by side on the floor for half an hour, by which time Michel was somewhat calmer. Then Scaliger helped him up and shepherded him out of the library.

They walked slowly through the garden, Michel with one arm around Scaliger's shoulders because he was still weak and unsteady on his feet. He was so exhausted he wanted to sit down – or, better still, lie down and sleep. He had never felt so sorely in need of sleep, but Scaliger wouldn't let him rest. He made him walk and go on walking until the effects of the drug had worn off. Little by little, Michel's eyes lost their dazed look.

"That dose was too strong for you. I gave you very little, but I underestimated your sensitivity."

"Why does my imagination generate such terrible

visions?" Michel muttered. "I must give the matter some thought."

Scaliger shook his head. "Those visions were no figments of your imagination, my poor friend. You saw the future in all its frightfulness. We must be very careful. I've never before seen anyone react so violently."

"If that's the future, all our efforts and endeavours are in vain. There's no hope for the world."

"Yes, it's a hard road to travel."

"Sometimes, Julius, I think I'm going mad."

"You know more than most people know, and you've seen more than most people have seen."

"Such terrible, atrocious things. So much human misery and cruelty. So much pain. Sometimes I think it would be better if I were ignorant of it all."

"I did warn you."

"But how do you live with all that terrible knowledge?"

"By persevering with my research. I'm sure that, if we ever fathom the mysteries of creation, all will be well. God will manifest himself to us in his infinite mercy and goodness, in all his splendour and glory. I tell you, Michel, a golden age will dawn when we finally comprehend his plans and intentions. The ancients knew far more than we do. It's only from studying their secret texts that I derive the strength to endure the stupidity and beastliness around me."

Michel was still feeling decidedly weak. "I'd like to go back."

"To the library?"

"Where else?"

"Perhaps you'd do better to rest awhile."

"If a man falls off a horse he must remount it at once

and ride on, or he'll never summon up the courage to ride again."

They walked back to the house, where Michel worked until the small hours.

He returned home to find Marie at the kitchen stove. Clad only in her nightgown, she was standing barefoot on the flagstones.

"Still up? What are you doing, making quince jelly?"

"Not exactly."

He laughed. "So what's that?"

"It's quince jelly, yes, but I've been conducting a little experiment. I think I've found a way of making it keep." She took a spoonful of jelly from the pot and handed it to him. "Try it, and tell me if it tastes any worse than yours."

He sampled it. "Delicious."

"For my own part, I think it's even more delicious than yours," she said with a laugh. "I'll give you the recipe if you like." She broke off to cough, patting herself on the chest. "You look tired. You shouldn't work so hard."

"I know, it's becoming too much for me. I'm haunted day and night by the most appalling visions. Flames everywhere, huge tidal waves, colossal earthquakes, wholesale destruction."

"Have you talked to Scaliger about it?"

He nodded.

"Well, what does he say?"

"It worries him, too, that I react to everything so violently. I want no more of it."

"I warned you, but now it's too late. You'll never be rid of those visions." She coughed again, harder this time.

"Your cough grows no better."

"It's nothing. Except that the children have one too. It's such a harsh, racking cough, it worries me."

"I'll give you all something for it." Michel went to the cupboard took some pills from a bowl. "Take them, and dissolve some in lukewarm water for the children."

"Your miracle pills?"

"My miracle pills, yes. Open your mouth." He inserted a pill under her tongue. "Don't chew it."

"But I don't have the plague."

"Anything that combats the plague ought to be able to cure a little cough." He produced a manuscript volume from his bag and handed it to her.

She looked at it, unable to believe her eyes. Then she clasped it joyfully to her breast. "The *Ghàyat al-hakim*!" She hugged him. "At last! Thank you. Did you ask Scaliger's permission?"

"No. He would never have given it – and I'm a fool for having brought you the book. If he finds out he'll never let me enter that library again. But you wouldn't give up, and I'd sooner break my promise to him than suffer your looks of entreaty any longer."

"This is wonderful! So many of my questions will be answered at a stroke." She had an even more violent fit of coughing. "This cough is really becoming a nuisance. What is it, doctor? Can't you cure a simple cough?"

"Not if my patients stand in the kitchen barefoot and half-naked, making quince jelly in the middle of the night."

"Then come to bed quickly." Marie walked to the door with the manuscript under her arm, then turned and held her hand out. Michel went to her and took it. Before retiring to bed they looked in on the children.

The boy was nearly three now, the girl just six months old. Both were asleep. Michel laid his hand on each forehead in turn. They felt a trifle feverish.

"I made them some poultices," Marie whispered.

"We'd better renew them."

Marie renewed the poultices while Michel rubbed the children's chests with camomile. The boy woke up for a moment and coughed, but not for long. He saw his father, smiled, and went straight back to sleep. Michel stroked his cheek. Then he kissed both children and went off to the bedroom with Marie.

He fell asleep at once. Marie, gently running her fingers through his hair, began to read the manuscript. She wheezed, thumped herself on the chest, shook her head in annoyance.

Just then there came a sudden loud knocking on the back door. Michel awoke and sat up with a start.

"What was that?"

"There's someone at the door."

"At this hour?" He got up, put on a dressing-gown, and opened the door to the garden. Scaliger was standing outside in the rain.

"You must leave for Arles at once. The plague has broken out again, or so a messenger reports. Go there and find out if it's true. If you act quickly enough, the worst may be avoided."

"I'll take Raoul with me."

"Assess the situation first. Then give Raoul his instructions and come straight back. Raoul knows what to do. Your work here takes precedence."

Michel and Raoul reached Arles in the late afternoon of the following day and went straight to the hospital. It was a damp, dirty, windowless building lit only by

an oil lamp thick with soot. Raoul went off to get a
pine-resin torch. The sick were lying everywhere on
plank beds or on the bare floor. Many were already
dead. There was no one to tend them: no physician,
no nurse, no priest. They had simply been abandoned.
Michel surveyed the scene with boundless fury.

"They're incorrigible, those fools. Every physician in
the land must know how we fought the plague, but they
simply don't care."

He made his way across the room. All at once,
in a corner dimly illuminated by the smoking lamp,
he caught sight of three figures lying motionless: a
woman and two little children. Michel turned pale
and trembled, gripped Raoul by the arm and mutely
pointed to the three. He snatched the torch from Raoul
and held it up. All three were dead: Marie, his son and
his daughter. With a terrible cry, he dashed over to
them. Then, as the torchlight illuminated their inert
forms more clearly, he saw that it wasn't Marie after
all, nor his son, nor his daughter. His eyes had deceived
him, God be praised. He breathed a sigh of relief. There
was no resemblance at all. How could he have been so
mistaken? He rubbed his eyes, stepped back and looked
again. He shook his head: there was no resemblance
even from that distance. And then, quite suddenly,
relief gave way to panic.

"Raoul, you know what to do. It's the plague. They
must all be removed from here. Burn their clothes,
make them wash, give them some pills. Burn the dead,
then procure some gunpowder and blow this pigsty to
kingdom come. I must return to Agen – I must leave
at once."

Raoul stared at him.

"It's Marie and the children. I must go back."

"But why? Has something happened to them?"

"I hope not – I hope I'm wrong, this time at least."

He rode through the night, pausing only to water his horse. At dawn, when the beast could go no further, he roused a postmaster from his bed and exchanged it for another. On he rode, wielding the whip unmercifully.

It was raining when he finally reached Agen that evening. The streets were deserted. His mount was trembling and bathed in sweat, its muzzle streaked with foam. He made for his house, but Jean, Scaliger's manservant, stopped him at the entrance to the street.

"You can't go home, monsieur. The inquisitor is there."

Michel dismounted. "Where are my wife and children?"

"They've been taken to the hospital."

"What! Why, for God's sake?"

"I don't know. Monsieur Scaliger is on his way there at this moment."

Michel vaulted on to his horse again, but Jean wrested the reins from his grasp. "You can't go there. The inquisitor has posted sentries everywhere."

"But why?"

"I can't say."

Michel retrieved the reins, whipped up his horse and galloped on.

"Have a care, monsieur," Jean called after him. "They'll kill you!"

Michel pulled his hat down low over his eyes and rode past his house like the wind. Two of the Inquisition's sentries were stationed outside the door.

More sentries had been posted at the entrance to the hospital. Scaliger was just crossing the square.

Michel jumped off his horse. "What happened?"

"I don't know yet. The inquisitor and his men burst into your house, meaning to arrest you. Marie couldn't catch her breath, she became so agitated, and your children were in a similar state. The poor girl could scarcely speak for coughing. Rosalie told me – Marie just had time to send her to me before they took her away."

Michel started towards the hospital, but Scaliger restrained him.

"You can't go in there."

"But I must help her."

"How will it help her if they arrest you on the spot?"

"What should I do, then?"

"Keep calm. I'll go to her – I'll examine her and the children and then consult with you. You can tell me what must be done for them. Go to my house. I'll be as quick as I can."

Scaliger hurried over to the hospital and spoke briefly to the sentries, who let him pass.

Michel rode around the corner, tethered his horse to a tree, climbed over the wall and jumped down into the hospital grounds. Bending low and hugging the shelter of some bushes, he made his way to the building. One of the rooms was illuminated by candlelight. Cautiously, he stole over to the window, which was open, and peered in. Marie and the children were lying on the floor, for all the world like the dead woman and her children at Arles. Michel caught sight of his physician's bag on the floor near the door. The door, too, was open, and he could see a sentry on guard in the passage beyond. Marie was coughing terribly. She struggled across the floor to the window to get some fresh air.

"Marie!" he whispered.

She looked up, startled, then put out her hand. He grasped it.

Marie was breathing stertorously, every breath a torment. "They found the *Ghàyat al-hakim*," she whispered. A violent spasm of coughing racked her body. "Run! They'll kill you if they catch you here."

Just then the sentry came in. Michel quickly released her hand and ducked down below the sill. The man surveyed the room suspiciously.

"Did you say something, madame?"

Another fit of coughing. "I . . . I was praying to the Holy Virgin . . . to deliver me from my torment."

Moments after the sentry had returned to his post in the passage, Scaliger appeared. Michel saw him speak soothingly to Marie, then examine her and the children. At last he caught sight of Michel, who gestured to his nose and throat and pointed to Marie. Scaliger nodded and proceeded to examine Marie's throat.

Michel ran back to the wall. He untethered his horse, rode back to the square, and waited in the shadow of the arches surrounding it. A minute later Scaliger emerged from the hospital and came over to him.

"Their throats and noses are thickly coated and congested. Mucous membranes swollen, pulse shallow and fast, blood pressure extremely low. They have difficulty in swallowing, as if their soft palate were paralysed. Attacks of breathlessness, too. At first I thought it was a severe case of tonsillitis, but it can't be that. What should I give them? Marie had the presence of mind to bring your bag with her."

Michel thought for a moment, nervously chewing his knuckles. "What can it be, for God's sake? I'm unfamiliar with the illness. Breathlessness, swollen mucous membranes, racing pulse, danger of asphyxia. They mustn't be allowed to suffocate, that's the main thing. Give them ... Yes, lungwort might help: three spoonfuls of the powdered herb dissolved in a litre of wine – or the same of sage leaves. And stones – apply some topazes to their throats. Rock crystal, too. But how are we to get hold of them? All the stones are at my home."

"It would take too long in any case."

"Then there's only one alternative – if you can undertake it."

"What?"

"A laryngotomy. You must make the incision here." Michel indicated the spot on his own throat. "It must be done with a sharp knife. Quickly, or they'll asphyxiate. But the blade must be clean."

"Very well. Now go to my house. You must leave before the night is out."

"I can't – I can't desert my wife and children."

"You'll be no use to them dead. Go!"

Scaliger hurried back to the hospital. Michel mounted his horse and set off, but not in the direction of Scaliger's house. He rode back to tree beside the hospital wall. Without even troubling to tether his horse, he jumped over the wall and ran straight across the grounds to the window.

By some supreme effort of will, Marie had struggled to her feet and was clinging to the window-frame for support, scarcely able to draw one rattling breath after another. Her face was already turning blue. When she saw Michel she despairingly stretched out her hand. He grasped it.

"Save yourself, please," she whispered. "I love you, Michel ..."

Just then Scaliger appeared in the doorway. The sentry barred his path. He remonstrated with the man, but in vain, then tried to thrust him aside, only to be knocked to the ground. He scrambled to his feet, but the sentry menaced him with his pike and motioned to him to leave the building.

Falteringly, Marie stroked Michel's head one last time. "Michel. . ."

"I love you, Marie," he murmured, clinging to her. "I love you. . ."

Then her body went limp, and she slumped forward over the sill.

The sentry came in. Michel ducked down, hugging the wall, and subsided into a crouch. The tears were streaming down his cheeks.

Silence reigned in the library. Flanked by the Scaligers, of whom Madame Scaliger was sympathetically holding his hand, Michel sat staring into space like a man in a trance. Then the spell was broken by Jean, the manservant.

"The inquisitor is outside, monsieur."

Scaliger exchanged a look with his wife and hurried from the room.

Sure enough, the inquisitor was standing outside in the street accompanied by Monsieur Grenelle, the sculptor, and three soldiers bearing torches. Scaliger opened the door.

"Monsieur," the inquisitor said with a little bow, "we must speak with you."

"At this hour?"

"The matter will not wait. The Holy Inquisition – "

"I'm very tired," Scaliger broke in. "A dear friend of mine has just died, together with her two children.

You must excuse me. I'll gladly answer your questions tomorrow, but not now. Good-night."

"Where is Monsieur de Nostradame?"

"In Arles. He went there to fight the plague. What do you want with him?"

"His wife was reading a certain book when we searched his house. We wish to know how he came by it."

"What book?"

The inquisitor smiled. "The *Ghàyat al-hakim*."

"I'm sorry, I've no idea how he came by it. Good-night to you."

Scaliger shut the door.

The inquisitor was temporarily speechless. Not so Monsieur Grenelle.

"Let's break the door down!" he cried angrily. "Fancy shutting the door in your face, Eminence! The effrontery of the man!"

The inquisitor thought for a moment. "He won't escape us — we can arrest him tomorrow. As for Nostradame, he's not there in any case. We have time enough."

"The arrogant fellow," fumed Grenelle. "I wouldn't trust him an inch."

The inquisitor shrugged. "We'll post a sentry outside his door."

Michel was still sitting there like a statue when Scaliger returned to the library.

"You must leave at once."

Still no reaction.

"I'm not thinking only of you, Michel. Forgive me, you know I share your grief, but time waits for no man. The inquisitor was here with your friend Monsieur

Grenelle. They'll question me tomorrow and search the house. The secret library must be removed. You leave at once." In desperation, Scaliger slapped Michel's face. Michel came to life with a start. "You must go this minute. The library will follow. You're to wait at an inn outside Clermont, the 'Chapeau Gris'. Where can I send the library?"

"To my brother. He's the mayor of Salon."

"Is he to be trusted?"

"He's my own flesh and blood."

"Very well." Scaliger paused for a moment. "How did Marie come by the *Ghàyat al-hakim*?"

"I gave it to her."

"I expressly forbade you to do any such thing."

"She needed it for her work. If you'd given her access to the library, none of this would have happened."

"I won't quarrel with you, Michel, not now. Come." Michel rose to his feet. Scaliger embraced him.

"I hope we meet again in this life. You'll find the list of friends in *Speculum astronomiae* by Albertus Magnus. If you need help, consult your colleague Doctor Rabelais."

"Is *he* a friend?"

"One of the best."

Michel bade Madame Scaliger an affectionate farewell.

Jean opened the small gate in the wall at the far end of the garden. He stole out into the street and looked around, then beckoned to Michel, who mounted his horse and galloped off.

He rode to the hospital, climbed over the wall, and crept to the window for a last sight of Marie and the children. Just as he got there, Madame Auberligne and her husband entered the room. They stood looking down at the three pathetic corpses.

"He saves half the world from the plague," sobbed Madame Auberligne, "but he leaves his own wife and children to die. Who knows, he may even have murdered them himself. Whatever the truth, he must pay back Marie's dowry."

They stood there in silence for a moment or two, then turned and left the room.

Michel, peering over the windowsill, took a last look at Marie and his children. As he watched, the sentry came in with two assistants. One of them took Marie by the ankles and hauled her out into the passage. The other two threw the children over their shoulders like sides of meat and followed. Michel turned away and stood with his back to the wall beside the window. The tears were streaming down his cheeks.

PART THREE

The Monk

Scaliger and his wife, assisted by Jean and Rosalie, were stowing the books from the secret library in packing cases. They left a quarter of each box empty, inserted a false bottom, and filled the remaining space with bottles. Having covered the bottles with a layer of straw, they nailed the lids down tight. Finally, the boxes were carried out into the garden by another two servants.

Scaliger paced nervously up and down while this operation was being completed. "As quickly as you can," he said. "Grenelle and the inquisitor will be back tomorrow. We'll all be done for if they find those books here." He laid his hands on Jean's shoulders and looked into his eyes. "Jean, I want you to go with them and remain with them. When you get to Salon, I depend on you to make sure they're stored in a safe place."

Standing outside the "Chapeau Gris" were a carriage and two wagons laden with packing cases. Jean emerged from the inn and looked to see if the coast was clear, then turned and beckoned to Michel. With his hat pulled down low and his collar turned up, Michel walked quickly to the carriage and got in. Jean climbed up on the box of the first of the wagons, and the little convoy set off.

Some hours later they were driving along the banks of a river flanked by lush green water meadows. The distant mountains in the background were shrouded in a bluish haze. Michel had half lowered the window and was looking out, his cheeks fanned by a warm evening breeze. The sun's last rays were casting a reddish glow over the meadows alongside. No scene could have seemed more peaceful.

Until, all at once, it dawned on him that the meadows were not tinged with sunlight after all: they were steeped in blood. Just then he heard a whistling sound overhead, so unendurably loud that he feared his eardrums would burst. A geyser of turf and soil erupted, followed a split-second later by an immense explosion. More explosions followed as strange, air-borne machines swooped low and dropped their lethal cargoes. He was in the midst of a battlefield. Another kind of machine, a monster encased in metal plates, crawled up the banks of the river and lumbered past his carriage, only to be hit by some explosive missile and burst into flames. Soldiers wearing dappled uniforms and helmets of unfamiliar design were crouching in trenches, firing guns that spewed bullets in an endless stream, far too fast to count. One badly wounded man, bleeding profusely, staggered towards the carriage with his arms out. Just as his bloody hand touched the window, a hail of bullets struck him in the back. His imploring eyes went blank and uncomprehending. He stumbled and fell, and as he fell his hand slid down the glass, leaving a smear of blood behind. Fireballs were bursting all along the river valley, shattered bodies lay everywhere . . .

Michel cried out and clapped his hands over his ears. The carriage came to a halt and Jean ran up.

"What is it? Are you ill, monsieur?"

"What? No, no, Jean, it's nothing — just a passing fancy. All's well, thank you."

Michel rubbed his eyes and looked out of the window. The verdant meadows, the river bank, the distant mountains — all was as it had been, but with one exception: a smear of blood on the glass. He leaned out and touched it. The blood was still fresh. It adhered to his fingers.

"What is it, monsieur? Are you hurt?"

Michel stared at the blood on his hand. He touched Jean to make sure that he was really there. Then he opened the door and got out. "No, no, it's nothing, truly. Listen, Jean, you know where my brother lives?"

"Yes, monsieur. He's the mayor of Salon."

"Go there. Tell him that I shall follow — tell him to store the cases in a safe place. I need a little peace and quiet. Please leave me and drive on."

Michel hurried down the river bank. He tripped over, picked himself up, and ran to the water's edge: he couldn't wait to wash the blood off his hand. Jean stared after him. Then he shrugged, resumed his seat on the box, and signalled to the other two drivers to whip up their horses. The convoy proceeded on its way.

Michel had been in the mountains for two days now. Lumbering up the narrow track ahead of him was

an ox-cart. A peasant was leading the beast by a
halter wound around his wrist. The man had allowed
Michel to ride on the cart until the track became
too precipitous. Now they were both obliged to go
on foot.

He looked up at the jagged peaks ahead, and as
he looked a strange thing happened: they began to
sway and disintegrate. Huge boulders broke away and
rolled down the mountainside with an earsplitting roar,
flattening every tree and bush in their path. One of
them smashed into the cart and sent the peasant and his
ox hurtling over the edge of the precipice that flanked
the track.

Michel stood transfixed, trembling in every limb.
He stood there for what seemed like an eternity.
Time went by, but nothing stirred. Not another sound
could be heard. At last he walked on – on and on
for hours, like a man in a trance. He crossed the
pass and descended into the valley on the other side.
Ahead lay a plain, and in the distance he made out a
monastery. Some monks were working in the fields. He
ran towards them, calling and waving. Then everything
went black. He fell headlong and lay there without
moving.

All he saw at first was a blurred ring of lights.
Gradually, as his vision cleared, it dawned on him
that they were numerous candles stuck in a kind of
tin crown. More than that, the wearer of the crown
was a monk whose face was looming over his own.
The monk nodded and smiled.

Michel was lying on a plank bed in a cell. He sat
up, shut his eyes, and tried to collect his thoughts. The
monk shook him. He opened his eyes again. Cackling

shrilly, the man took a bowl of soup from a stool and perched on the edge of the bed.

Michel looked round, bewildered. "Where am I?" he said.

"In hell."

He tried to get up, but the monk, who was immensely strong, thrust him back and held him down by main force.

"Eat."

He raised a spoonful of soup to Michel's lips. "Don't you pray before eating? Never mind, I've already done some praying for you. Eat, just eat." He proceeded to feed Michel like a baby, but before Michel could swallow one spoonful another was already forcing its way between his lips. The soup ran down his chin.

"They're all thieves in here," the monk whispered. He laughed briefly. "They stole my reason and your money. I've forgotten everything. They say it's better that way. They give me food. They beat me, too. A woman died. I have to take the consequences. That was yesterday, or was it tomorrow? That's when Our Lord will rise again, so they say." He broke into song. "I believe in God the Father. . ."

Michel heard a high-pitched bell begin to toll. The monk stopped singing at once. He replaced the bowl on the stool and rose.

"Come."

Michel tried to stand up, but he was still too weak. The monk took him by the scruff of the neck and hauled him to his feet, then dragged him out of the cell and along a passage. On reaching a bend he put a finger to his lips and peered cautiously round the corner. Clasping Michel around the hips and slinging him over one shoulder, he made his way along the passage and down a narrow flight of steps. Michel could now hear monotonous chanting punctuated by cries of ecstasy. The monk dumped him in front of a small, barred aperture in the wall only a few inches from the stone floor. He found himself looking down into a big hall filled with other monks stripped to the waist. They were flagellating themselves, some with birch rods, others with heavy chains. Their backs were streaming with blood, but they were alternately chanting and crying out in rapture.

The monk pointed down through the hole in the wall. "They say I'm stupid, but I'm not. I'm not stupid at all. I shall pray for you." He stroked Michel's face. "You're a good man, you are."

He picked Michel up again, slung him over his shoulder, and walked on. Two cowled figures came in the opposite direction. The monk dropped Michel, grabbed them, and hurled them bodily against the wall. They slid down it and lay there without moving. Taking Michel by the hand, the monk led him down some steps to a small cell. There was a crucifix hanging on the wall. The monk took it down, to reveal a small niche with a woollen thread dangling from it. Removing his crown of candles, the monk lit the thread, deposited the crown on the floor, slung Michel over his shoulder yet again, and carried him down some more steps to a small, iron-barred door. The bars had evidently been sawn through, because the monk kicked the door down with ease and dragged Michel through.

There was nothing beyond the door but undergrowth. The monk took Michel's hand and towed him through the bushes. And then they were out in the open at last, in a field below the monastery. The night sky was clear, the moon full. The monk broke into a run, still towing Michel behind him, and did not stop until they reached the shelter of an oak tree. As Michel crouched there trying to catch his breath, there was a sudden, monumental explosion. The entire monastery went up in a sheet of flame. Fragments of stone came whirring through the air.

The monk emitted another of his strident laughs, listened for a moment, tried to reproduce the sound exactly, and shook his head. "I can hear myself laughing," he said. "Hey!" He dug Michel in the ribs. "Tell me, why do I laugh all the time? I can never remember what I'm laughing at."

Michel stared at the blazing ruins. "Are those flames real?"

The monk nodded.

"The monastery that just blew up – was it real, or did I only dream it?"

"It was real right enough."

"You did that, didn't you?"

"I did."

"But why?"

No answer.

"You killed them all. Why? Tell me why!"

The monk's silence persisted for a few moments longer. Then he whispered, "They used to take children from the villages around here and butcher them. They would dry the hearts and livers and kidneys and grind them to a powder, which they dissolved in wine and drank. That I never did, not I! I may be mad, but I made a powder of my own and set fire to a long woollen thread, and bang!" He extended his arm and made a sweeping gesture than embraced the monastery and its surroundings. "They'll slaughter no more children here, do you understand? Do you?" He straightened up. "Come!"

They walked throughout the night. The next morning they came to a meadow where some wild quince trees were growing.

"I'm hungry," the monk announced.

Michel picked a few of the fruit and they sat down to eat them. "You don't pray either, before you eat," he said.

"I pray all the time – I pray every step I take. I start when I rise in the morning and I stop when I lie down to sleep at night. I've prayed for you too. Eat. . ." The monk scratched his head. "But if I forget to pray for you, you must pray instead – for safety's sake. What shall we do now, lie down and die? I've no wish to die, have you? What else can I do, though? My guilt is so great for any man to pray it away."

Michel got up and took off his coat. Having picked some more quinces, he wrapped the coat around them and secured it by tying the sleeves together. The monk shouldered the bundle and walked on with him until they came to a farmhouse. Michel knocked, but the place was deserted.

"War," said the monk. "All dead – butchered. Why?"

Michel tried the door, which proved to be unlocked. They went inside and lit the stove. Michel cut up the quinces and put them on to boil while the monk stirred them with a big wooden ladle.

"The monks in that monastery," said Michel, " – why did they kill little children and drink their powdered organs in wine?"

"What monks? What monastery? Children were killed, you say? By whom?"

"You don't remember?"

"I forget everything. Remembering things makes me feel sick and ill – it hurts my head. It's only when I pray and think of nothing that I can feel God inside me."

"Did you kill children too? Is that why you've no wish to remember?"

The monk shook his head.

"Did you drink their heart's blood?"

The monk shook his head again and went on stirring.

"I think you cut out the children's hearts and livers and kidneys. I think you ground them to a powder and mixed it with wine and drank it like all the rest."

The monk spun round. "No!" he shouted.

"Then why do you want to forget everything?"

"Because I must."

"Why?"

"You're tormenting me."

"No, you're tormenting yourself. It takes you all your strength to forget everything."

"I've no wish to talk about it."

"You do remember?"

The monk nodded.

"But you're reluctant to talk about it?"

The monk nodded again. Then, in a low voice, he said, "They killed my child – the girl child I'd fathered on the carpenter's sister. I saw its heart in a cooking pot." He gripped Michel by the shoulders. A terrible expression settled on his face as the memory came flooding back. "They made me flay the child and cut up her flesh into little pieces – they beat me until I'd finished. Later I found her remains on the compost heap. With others. The rats had devoured their lungs and intestines. Their eyes, too."

Michel put his arms around him. "And I wanted to enter a monastery because I thought I would find peace there. Peace and a respite from all the horrific visions that haunt me." He laughed aloud.

"Why do you laugh?"

"I don't know."

Market day in a small town. Michel and the monk had set up a stall and were selling their quince jelly. Hectic activity reigned on all sides. Many other stallholders were crying their wares, women offering fruit and vegetables for sale, children scampering everywhere. Michel and the monk were doing a brisk trade. The monk handed the jars across the counter while Michel took the money and dropped the coins into a wooden box on the ground beside him. A small boy came and stood in front of the stall.

"Does it taste good?" he inquired.

Michel laughed. "Would you like to try some?"

The boy nodded. Michel took a big spoonful of jelly from an open jar and let him sample it. The boy smacked his lips with delight, so Michel smilingly presented him with a jar.

And then he heard a deep, swelling roar. A flying-machine, this one seemingly supported in the air by some narrow wings rotating above it like sycamore pods, came skimming over the rooftops towards him. The roar became an ear-splitting crescendo. Michel cried out and threw himself to the ground. Something fell from the flying-machine and exploded with tremendous force. Shots rang out, so close together that they sounded like a gigantic sheet of canvas being ripped from end to end. The little boy was hit, the jar of quince jelly went rolling across the cobblestones. Several of the neighbouring stalls went up in flames. A building on the other side of the square collapsed. Then a column of self-propelled vehicles swept into the market-place, some small, some much larger and filled with helmeted soldiers. People scattered in panic, unable to escape because every exit had been cordoned off. The soldiers jumped down and fired into the close-packed townsfolk, killing many of them. Some laid hold of women and girls, dragged them behind the stalls, tore off their clothes, and raped them on the spot. Michel saw one soldier drive his bayonet into the woman he had just violated and slit her belly open. He hurled himself at the rapist and tried to throttle him, but other soldiers pulled him off, kicking and punching him unmercifully. A disembodied voice of immense power rang out: it ordered the men to assemble on the left of the square, their womenfolk and children on the right. The flying-machine, which had been hovering overhead, landed amid a swirling cloud of dust. One little girl clung to her father, unwilling to be parted from him. He was still pleading with her to go when some soldiers shot her down in cold blood.

"I don't want to see any more!" Michel shouted. "No more of these visions, for pity's sake, or I'll tear my eyes out!" He was lying on the cobblestones, trembling all over. The monk took him in his arms.

"You mustn't tear your eyes out. God wishes you to see more and further than any other man alive."

Michel shook his head.

"Yes," the monk insisted, "you must obey his call, do you hear? Not to do so would be a sin."

"I don't want to."

"You have no choice. But beware: if people notice that God has chosen you, they'll persecute and kill you. They'll leave you in peace only if they think you're mad." The monk gave a shrill laugh and looked round warily.

"So you're not mad at all?"

The monk stared at him blankly. "What do you mean? Who's mad? That's what they say I am, because I ask God not to make me normal like them. I pray for you, too. You must also pray." He picked up a jar of quince jelly and handed it to a woman. "Why not take two?" he suggested amiably. "There aren't many left. Your husband won't leave you any once he's tasted it." He gave her a spoonful to try.

The woman sampled it and nodded. "I'll take them all."

"Truly?"

"Yes, all of them."

The monk laughed and gave Michel a delighted hug.

They picked some more quinces the next morning and spent the day making jelly with them. This time the monk prepared the fruit while Michel stirred it. "Excellent," Michel told him. "Now you know how it's done."

"You really mean to move on?"

Michel nodded. "Don't sell it any more cheaply. The price is a fair one — it'll bring you enough to live on."

"Roam wherever you please," said the monk, "you won't escape your destiny. I shall be sad to lose you. Where will you go?"

Michel shrugged. "I don't know. Italy, perhaps, and down to Sicily. Then north again into Switzerland and up as far as the Low Countries. It's all the same to me. I shall go wherever the plague is raging."

"What of the books your brother is keeping for you?"

Michel looked startled. "How do you know about them?"

"You mentioned them in your dreams. From now on, take care never to sleep beside a stranger."

"I never wish to see those books again – never again, for as long as I live. I mean to be a physician, nothing more."

PART FOUR

The Contessa

The Contessa owned one of the most splendid properties in the wine-rich countryside near Florence. She and Michel were sitting together on the terrace, which afforded a magnificent view of the vineyards that stretched away below them. Ensconced in her wheelchair with a glass cupped between her tremulous hands, the old lady was sipping her favourite sweet liqueur. She was thin to the point of emaciation and pale as death, but her hollow cheeks were rouged and her thin lips painted scarlet. Her voice was hoarse and throaty, the breath wheezed and rattled in her chest, and she was short-sighted, but nothing could dampen her spirits. Michel was playing chess with her. She moved a pawn and looked at him triumphantly.

"Well, what do you say now, sir? Do you resign? Don't compel me to humiliate you."

Michel moved a pawn of his own.

"What's that? What have you done?" The Contessa laughed with a sound like a saw-blade hitting a nail. "Ah, that's not fair. You're after my queen, aren't you?

The men are always after the women. Quite right too, or the world would come to an end. Imagine what would happen if men suddenly ceased to lust after women. It's unthinkable!" She sighed. "You've no idea how greatly I relish your company. When I think of all the quacks who have treated me hitherto! They confined me to my bed, bled me again and again, kept the curtains drawn. No wonder I look like a ghost. You're the first physician to allow me fresh air and sunshine. I've felt as frisky as a new-born lamb since you've been here. Give me your hand. When I hold it I feel so much strength flowing into me I could tear up trees by the roots and reduce them to kindling." She paused. "But I'm told you intend to depart. It's not true, surely?"

"I fear so."

"Nonsense, you must stay here. You'll want for nothing, believe me."

"I must move on."

"Why so restless? Find yourself a wife and father some children. You're the proper age."

"My wife died. So did my two children. I failed to save them."

"What! When was that?"

"Nearly ten years ago. I've been on the move ever since. Basle, Berne, Milan, Venice, Parma, Padua, Rome, Palermo, Amsterdam. Yes, it's nearly ten years now."

"And you're still grieving? You must have loved your wife very dearly."

"I did indeed."

"Where do you mean to go?"

"To the Low Countries, perhaps. A physician's services are always in demand."

"If your wife and children died despite all your skill, it was God's will, not the consequence of any failure on your part. You're a fine physician – you've no need to reproach yourself. Besides, it's cold and damp and foggy in the north. At least remain here until the spring comes."

"My bags are already packed."

"You want me to die?"

"With a constitution like yours? You could easily live to be ninety."

She laughed. "I already have."

"What?"

"I turned ninety-one last May, and I still have my wits about me." She gazed at him earnestly. "What is it that torments you, young man? Surely not your painful memories alone? Those a person can never escape – those he must carry in his baggage wherever he goes. We can't run away from things, they always overtake us in the end." She laughed. "Especially the ghosts of the past."

"Except that when I travel – when I'm in a different place each day, working to the point of exhaustion – it dulls my senses. Then I don't have to think and can get a little rest. Then I forget things for a while – and I so much want to forget them."

"Have your experiences really been so terrible?"

"When a man has travelled as widely as I have, there's nothing he hasn't witnessed. One sees people in their true colours only in time of crisis – their rapacity, their cupidity, their brutality and selfishness. I've seen mothers abandon their sick children for fear of infecting themselves, husbands murder their wives and bury them because they believed they could save their own lives by so doing. At Avignon I saw a

band of marauders burst into a mansion in which
an entire family lay dying. They ransacked the place
– stole money, jewellery and paintings, stripped the
clothes from the moribund, hacked fingers off in their
eagerness to acquire the rings that adorned them. It
never occurred to them, the fools, that they would
infect themselves. They all died, of course. I've seen
so much frightfulness, so much misery and despair.
When people abandon hope, when they give up and
submit, they're stupider than any cattle. At Toulouse
they simply danced, day and night, until they dropped.
The others didn't spare them a thought. Blind drunk,
they continued to dance amid corpses already being
devoured by rats. At Marseilles, sick men attacked
healthy women in the streets, tore off their clothes
and raped them. If they had to die, they wanted to
drain life to the lees and take the rest of the world
with them. Nobody tried to prevent such atrocious
doings. On the contrary, the city's inhabitants very
soon succumbed to a frenzy of lust. They lost their
heads to such an extent that the healthy copulated
with the sick. The poor stormed the houses of the rich
and avenged themselves for their poverty by violating
the womenfolk. If the unfortunate women's husbands
tried to defend them, they were killed. Other people,
who flagellated themselves in the hope that their
penance would protect them, bled to death of their
self-inflicted wounds. Common sense and faith in the
future had largely fled. Many threw themselves down
wells, many others hurled themselves from windows.
Everything was suddenly permitted: there was no law,
no curb on the baser human instincts. What I witnessed
was absolute licence, unbounded freedom for all to do
as they pleased, and it was then that I discovered what

pleases human beings most of all: killing and inflicting pain. When they're truly free and utterly unconstrained by any superior power, they're lower than the beasts. It suited them perfectly when our king decreed that members of the Waldensian sect be hunted down and killed. That enabled them to murder at the behest of higher authority and under its aegis. They tortured and butchered heretics or burned them at the stake. And if they found none, no matter, they invented a few."

The Contessa had been listening intently. There was a momentary silence. Then she said, "Yet you still tend the sick?"

"I must. I cannot do otherwise."

"If you care to stay to dinner, it may interest you to meet a fellow countryman of yours – a youngster of seventeen. A firebrand, so I hear, and very gifted. He's on his way home after spending some time in Rome. You may even know him: Monsieur Étienne de la Boétie."

"You're absolutely right, monsieur," Étienne said when he was sitting by the fire with Michel and the Contessa after dinner. "Giving the common herd free rein spells their complete ruination. But why should that be so? Because centuries of discipline – centuries of our wonderful religion – have brought them to such a pass that all they can do when permitted to act as they please is to kill and destroy. In reality, however, they're waiting for deliverance: for someone to come along and forcibly restrain them from continuing to act in such a manner. Someone who will punish them for their misdemeanours and put them in their place. Someone who will pardon them, too – some strict but kindly being who will praise and reward them for their obedience. They readily submit to serfdom, again and again, because that alone will grant them security. They believe themselves to be guiltless whatever they do, having surrendered all responsibility, and their fits of rebellion are only rare and brief. Such is the age in which we're living now – an age when all that was for so long pent up and suppressed is temporarily bursting forth because our rulers are weak and have failed to draw a line."

"So you favour strong rulers?"

"Far from it! They change nothing. Sir Thomas More, Campanella, Plato – I've read all that has ever been written about the ideal state, and what does it amount to? A collection of dreadful fantasies! I ask you: Utopia, the Land of Nowhere!" Étienne gave a scornful laugh. "They're futile dreams on the part of men whose conception of the state is limited to a place in which people are subdued, supervised, and punished – men who presume to dictate our every move: what we should eat; whom we should make love to and how often and when; what we should read; what music is permissible. How, I ask you, can a person develop within a society in which everything is controlled?"

"So what do you suggest?"

"The serfdom which the Utopians prescribe for our salvation is the very root of all evil, for the only solution they recommend is tyranny. But what is tyranny? What are tyrants and whence do they derive their power over us? What are they, these men entitled to forbid, command, supervise, punish, bestow honours? Why, human beings like ourselves! How dare they presume to set themselves over us, to tell us what is right and wrong, to wield the power of life and death? They have but two eyes and two hands like the meanest of mortals, so whence comes their power over others? Why, only from the many who give them that power! No ruler has ears enough to eavesdrop on every home and discover if his orders are being obeyed. The ears reside in the homes themselves, like the eyes that observe everything and the mouths that report it. And the hands? Whose are the hands that flog the many, or the feet that trample them in the dust? They belong to the many themselves. The ruler has but two pairs of limbs. He wields no power over his fellow men that was not conferred on him by them. They assist in their own enslavement. They despoil and betray themselves. No beast would tolerate the treatment they so readily accept."

Étienne's cheeks had turned crimson with fervour. He picked up his glass of wine and drained it at a gulp.

"How comes it, then, that the many have always tolerated such treatment since time immemorial?"

"They're afraid," said Étienne, " – afraid of being true human beings."

Michel looked at him searchingly. "And is their fear so unjustified?"

"Certainly not. It's altogether understandable, after so many centuries of subjugation. Whence are they suddenly to acquire the strength to assume responsibility for their lives and determine their own fate? But that, believe me, is the only road to follow. An arduous one, I grant you, but all the others lead to perdition. We have no choice. We're free and equal by nature, and everything follows logically from that. We must first slough off tyranny, which is simple enough. We need not even employ force against the tyrant, we need only retract our acceptance of enslavement. We need not take anything from him, we must simply withhold it, then the tyrant will wither and die of his own accord. Once we cease to assuage his appetite for power, victory will be ours."

"That, of course, is far more easily said than done."

"The most important thing is to recognize the laws of Nature and the laws of our own nature. Then we shall learn what the ancients knew: that we ourselves are a part of Nature, and that we develop in tune with it when we behave naturally. Only then will everything attain the equilibrium that precludes degeneracy. In the divine scheme of things, Nature aims at perfection, not destruction. It has conserved and perpetuated itself from the outset and will continue to do so *ad infinitum*. Everyone rejects the possibility of perpetual motion. What utter nonsense! We have its outward manifestation before our eyes every day: Nature, which reproduces itself again and again. I tell you this: if we're presumptuous enough to exalt ourselves above Nature because we consider ourselves the crowning glory of creation, Nature will avenge itself and destroy us. We're no more than ordinary natural elements despite our intelligence – our capacity for self-observation, which distinguishes us from cattle, should prompt us to recognize that fact. We haven't the strength to challenge Nature and gain the upper hand, strong as we are, yet that is what we daily attempt to do by subjugating, exploiting and despoiling each other. The history of nations demonstrates that they were never in direr straits than when someone made himself their master and abused them. We must harken to our innermost selves and recognize our own nature for what it is. Then we shall be just and good."

Michel nodded. "I'm no politician and take no

interest in politics. I have no time for such things, shameful as it may sound, but I'm impressed by what you say about Nature. We are indeed a part of it and must recognize the possibilities it offers. I foresee many obstacles on the road you recommend, but you're right: there is no other, neither economically, nor politically, nor morally." The Contessa had dozed off in her armchair. Michel yawned. "We should get some sleep too. It's growing late."

A footman entered bearing a letter on a salver and presented it to Michel. Somewhat surprised, he took the letter and opened it.

The Contessa woke up and rubbed her eyes. "What have I been missing?" she demanded.

Étienne laughed. "What can we tell you that you don't already know? Anyone as old as you, Contessa, must know all there is to know about life."

"I've learned how to live," she replied with a smile, "but as to understanding life itself, that I beg leave to doubt."

"Perhaps it's the same thing."

"Perhaps. I wouldn't know." The Contessa shot an inquisitive glance at Michel's letter.

"It's from my brother Paul," he said. "The plague has broken out in Salon. He asks me to come at once. Paul is mayor of the town."

"Poor France," said the Contessa. "So much misery, so many wars, and all for religion's sake."

"I don't believe religion lies at the root of it," Michel said. "Religion is merely the threadbare cloak in which those who seek power choose to wrap themselves. Wars have to do with politics and power, land and money, reputation and vanity, not with God." He looked at Étienne. "I agree with all you say, but it will be a very long time before people realize that they have no other choice – unless, of course, they prefer to exterminate the human race."

"There could be worse solutions," observed the Contessa.

"Really, Contessa!" laughed Michel. "We've been cudgelling our brains for some means of preventing just that."

The Contessa sighed. "Nothing will ever change, nothing at all. Not ever." She took a little bell from the table and rang it. "But don't be deterred by an old woman's fatalism. I relish the vehemence with which you youngsters debate such questions, it does me good. Most of the people I meet were born old – indeed, far older than I shall ever be. They venture nothing and run no risks, they merely conform, keep their heads down, and put up with things. They're fit for nothing but the garbage heap. I find it refreshing to hear you speak of a rosy future and whip yourselves into a frenzy. It sharpens my wits and makes me receptive. At least it passes the time, which is indifferent to all our concerns, in an intelligent manner. I'm reminded of the old days. Machiavelli often came visiting. He had a house at San Casciano, only half an hour's carriage-ride from here. He was bored beyond belief in exile – used to catch fieldfares on lime-twigs, spent whole nights drinking in taverns and played cards with the local farmers, desperately hoping to be recalled to office. That was when he wrote his book, *The Prince*, and that was how he survived, soliloquizing with the great minds of the ancient world. He often came here. He adored my lemon sorbet, not to mention my quails in cinnamon. Sometimes he would read us a chapter from his book, and it greatly amused him when his theories exasperated my husband. My husband, I should add, was a trifle naïve."

"Because Signor Machiavelli's theories annoyed him?" said Michel. "That, in my view, was the mark of a clever man."

"Clever? My husband?" The Contessa laughed. "If only he were still alive – he'd have loved you for that. You could have named your own reward. My Lorenzo was kind-hearted, to be sure, but a regular ninny. I was very fond of him. He forgave me everything – every act of folly, every love affair, however passionate. He knew, of course, that I was always true to him in spirit despite my wild goings-on." She sighed. "But how did I come to speak of that? Ah yes, Étienne, because you inveighed so fiercely against More and Campanella and Plato. Machiavelli, too, waxed very irate whenever conversation turned to them."

"I wax irate with those gentlemen for reasons other than Machiavelli's," Étienne said coldly. "Machiavelli was a thorough reprobate."

"Oh come now, what makes you call him that? He was witty, cultivated, and full of charm. He could be a most entertaining conversationalist."

"Possibly, but that's neither here nor there."

"We would sometimes perform one of his plays in the garden in summer – so amusing. You'd have liked him, I'm sure."

"I think not," Étienne said doggedly. "His book is vile from first to last."

The Contessa stared at him in bewilderment. "But why? Because he was second to none in his under-standing of human nature, which is vile indeed, and had the courage to give an account of it? Because he didn't cravenly gloss over it? He was brave enough to

look the Gorgon in the face. Is that such a crime? I
cannot agree with you."

A young footman entered.

"What is it?" the old lady demanded rather testily.

"You rang, Contessa."

"I? Why should I have rung for you? I've no intention
of going to bed, not at this hour. I can sleep when my
gentlemen guests have gone. I'm as fresh as a daisy.
Leave me." A sudden thought struck her. "No, bring
us a bottle of wine, a few slices of ham, some cheese
and olives, and then be off to bed with you, I won't
be needing you again tonight." She smiled at Étienne
and Michel. "I'm sure one of these gentlemen will carry
this old bag of bones to her bed, eh?" She turned back
to the footman. "Well, what are you waiting for?"

The man inclined his head and withdrew.

"Where were we?" said the Contessa. "Ah yes,
courage. Anyone who comprehends human nature as
Machiavelli did, yet continues to lead a reasonably
happy and contented life, remains sanguine, and does
not lapse into melancholy, must be a stout fellow. That
takes more courage and audacity than staving in an
enemy's skull in battle."

"It would have been better if someone had stove in
his skull before he wrote that book," said Étienne.

The Contessa smiled. "I see. So violence is not
entirely alien even to your conception of the world.
I'm reassured."

Étienne laughed despite himself.

"The pair of you would have got on well together,"
said the old woman, "even if you had spent the whole
time arguing."

"I'm far from sure," Étienne replied. "I always take
sides against Machiavelli with the Utopians, whom I

abhor in other respects. They, at least, perceived short-comings and were troubled by them – by epidemics and wars and rebellions, by the poverty and beggary that break the human spirit. It distressed them that land should go to rack and ruin, that cities should decay, that people should become depraved and do nothing but hate, enslave and kill each other. They aspired to a better world. They conceived of a brighter future – indeed, they yearned for it. Not so Machiavelli. He was merely the Devil's henchman, lackey to the great criminals whom he obsequiously advised on how to subdue, enslave and exploit the common herd, the mass of poor unfortunates, by means of lies and betrayal, flattery and violence. That book of his instructs those who despise everything, who are perversely, morbidly covetous and self-seeking, in how to satisfy their terrible urges to the full. He perpetuates an evil state of affairs in which there is no concern, no love or affection, and – worst of all – no future except one in which soldiers must be armed with ever better weapons and trained to become perfect killing-machines. That's how his frightful book ends, and that's what I find so repugnant. I'm only surprised that *he* should have been surprised that his pupils no longer wanted him at their table. It was he that advised them to mistrust men of his own stamp – but then, what man has ever shone the light of his knowledge on himself?" Étienne shrugged and smiled. "But I've no wish to dispute with you. It's so pleasant here, we shouldn't put ourselves in an ill humour."

"Not at all," the Contessa retorted. "The fiercer the argument, the better my humour, especially when I'm with young people. They're so touchingly innocent, and I'm always so profoundly moved by their vehemence and naïve self-assurance. But beware, young man:

there's a point at which naïvety ceases to be a virtue
and becomes mere foolishness. However marvellous
one's ideas, their fulfilment entails practical measures.
You too will learn that in due course."

"And I'll find those measures in Machiavelli, is that
it? No, if the means to an end are reprehensible, they
pervert the end itself."

"Better that the end should be perverted than you
and your fine ideas. Had Savonarola possessed an
army, his cause might have triumphed."

Étienne turned to Michel. "What do you say?"

"I fear that our hostess is right," Michel replied. "It's
easy enough to be moral when we're merely conversing
or cogitating. But what happens when we try to put an
idea into practice? We have to act. We also have to
fight for the idea in question, and you'd better accept
the fact. I already know what your excuse would be
in such circumstances: 'No more violence after this.'
That's what they all say. It becomes their justification
for murder. One last blow – one last, resolute blow
delivered with all one's might – and that indispensable,
ultimate use of force becomes not only just but justified,
for violence cannot be eradicated by gentleness. Only
violence itself can do that."

"Then the killing will go on for ever."

"Perhaps, perhaps not. There's certainly no end in
sight that I can discern. In any case, I don't think one
can rid oneself of a tyranny by simply withdrawing
one's allegiance. The tyrant himself must be killed."

"You, a physician, say that, when your task is to save
people's lives? An interesting contradiction in terms.
What if you were standing at the sickbed of a tyrant
and knew full well how to cure him – if you knew that
he would die without benefit of your ministrations?"

"As so often, that would be a question of mathematics. Would it be right for me to save one man if I knew that, once recovered, he would treat his many subjects with boundless cruelty?"

"Or possibly with unwonted benevolence," the Contessa interjected, " – that is, if his illness had purged him of evil impulses. Who can be certain of making the right decision every time? Can you?"

"When the king of Persia offered Hippocrates valuable gifts and a senior position at court if only he would treat him, Hippocrates replied that his conscience would not permit him to cure a barbarian who was solely intent on killing Greeks. He could not, he said, place his skill at the service of someone preparing to subjugate his native land. You can read that in his treatise *On Air, Water, and Earth*. For my own part, I think he made a wise and courageous decision. I once cured an inquisitor. He thanked God for his recovery and then, to please his Maker, sent a great many more people to the stake. Had he died they would still be alive. I chose the wrong course of action, that's as clear as daylight."

"A mathematical equation, is that all there is to it?"

Michel shook his head. "No," he said. "I have a vision of Paradise, the Garden of Eden, the Isles of the Blest, Elysium, Cythera, Arcadia. Every account of the creation of the world, in no matter what religion, tells of a wonderful garden where people live and love in peace and plenty. Where betrayal and deceit are unknown, where all are happy because no one person lives at the expense of others. I cling to that vision. I doubt if I shall never see that wonderful garden, but it did exist at one time, and I'm convinced that it will exist again in the far distant future. That notion consoles me and encourages me to hope that all our trials and tribulations are not in vain."

The footman brought the wine, ham, and cheese, and the three of them sat talking far into the night. At long last, Michel carried the Contessa to her bedchamber. She put her scrawny arms around his neck and nestled against him. "You smell good," she murmured, stroking his cheek. "Do I disgust you? There's still such a fire burning inside me, isn't it awful? That youthful footman you saw just now – he used to be my gardener." She giggled. "Now he waters my ancient flesh, but hush, not a word! If my relatives discover the truth they'll shut me up in a madhouse. I still enjoy my days on earth. The youngster is counting on a fat inheritance, of course, but I don't care, he can have it all. Do you think that's disgraceful of me?"

"No," said Michel, laughing. "I think it's wonderful."

PART FIVE

Anna

Darkness had fallen and the streets were deserted by the time Michel reached Salon. He asked a night watchman the way to the mayor's house, and the man accompanied him to the door. His knock was answered by Jean, Scaliger's manservant.

"You're still here after all these years?" Michel said, embracing him warmly.

"I and the books, monsieur."

"Ah yes, the books."

"My master desired me to stay here for as long as you were abroad, monsieur, for fear someone should find them under the wine bottles."

"They're still in their boxes?"

"Safely locked up in the cellar."

"Wasn't it sad for you to remain here without your master?"

"Your brother is a fine man, monsieur."

"Where is he? Are they all asleep?"

"They retire early here."

*　　*　　*

Paul had got out of bed and was sitting beside the fire with Michel, drinking wine. Ham, cheese and bread had been set out on the table, and Michel was eating with gusto.

"I'm glad you came so promptly," Paul said.

Michel nodded and took a sip of wine. "It seems an age since we last saw each other," he said. "Fourteen years is a long time, Paul."

"You must be tired. I'll take you to the hospital early tomorrow morning. Tell me what you need and you shall have it. The dead already number close on five hundred, and there are more of them every day."

"What of the civil war? Did that claim many lives as well?"

"That gang of Calvinists and Lutherans was creating havoc. They had to be exterminated without mercy. The whole breed needs to be destroyed root and branch."

Michel looked startled. "Why, Paul, you're a fanatic!"

"I'm no fanatic, brother Michel, I'm a loyal Catholic. I'm simply defending my faith."

"You're a Jew, Paul. You of all people should know what it means to be persecuted and butchered for religious reasons."

Paul grabbed him by the collar. "Never say that again!" he said angrily. "Never!"

Michel released himself. "Why, because you'd cease to be the mayor if someone overheard? Is that why you're so intolerant?"

Just then Paul's wife came in, having hurriedly pulled a coat on over her nightgown. Hélène was a pretty woman with sensual features, but the sour set of her mouth and the little vertical furrow above the bridge of her nose lent her a rather world-weary and disillusioned appearance. She embraced Michel with a beaming smile.

"Welcome to Salon, brother-in-law."

"I fear I've disturbed your night's rest, the pair of you."

Hélène continued to hold his hands in hers. "I'm delighted you're here. Let me look at you. You must tell me all about your travels. For my own part, I've never set foot outside Salon."

"Oh come," said Paul, "that's not true."

"No, I visited Montpellier once. And Aix. That's all I know of the world apart from what I've read in books. I adore reading." She laughed rather shyly. "I sometimes write little tales, too, but Paul doesn't approve."

"That's not true either," Paul protested.

"Oh yes, it is. You don't like your wife reading or writing." She released Michel's hands but laid her own on his arm. "He finds it a trifle bizarre. Men work and wage war, women belong at the kitchen stove – that's his scheme of things."

"Now you're exaggerating. I've given you some books myself before now."

"Yes, once ten years ago, and bitterly you've regretted it ever since." She put her arm through Michel's. "But there are one or two other women here like me. We meet in secret and read aloud to each other, and tell each other what we've been reading. That's because we can't discuss such things with our husbands."

Paul rose. "Spare Michel any more of your chatter, Hélène, he's tired. Show him to his room."

"You can give me a bed for the night?" said Michel.

"What do you think? Of course. You must lodge here with us for as long as you please."

*   *   *

Hélène escorted Michel to his room and lit some candles. Jean carried his bags in and withdrew. Michel opened the curtains, then the window.

"Is there anything else you need?" Hélène asked.

"No, thank you. It's very kind of you both."

"You needn't tell me about your travels unless you wish. I won't pester you."

"It would give me pleasure."

"Our marriage is a happy one, really. I wouldn't want you to think — I mean, just because of that little argument just now. . ." Hélène laughed. "We're always arguing." She took her candle and looked at Michel. "There's really nothing more you need? Good-night, then." In the doorway she turned with one hand idly stroking the wooden panels. "I'd pictured you quite differently, after all Paul has told me about you."

"Really? What did he say?"

"Oh, I don't know."

"And now you're disappointed?"

She smiled at him. "Good-night," she said again, and quietly closed the door.

Michel lay down on the bed with his head pillowed on his arms. He felt like a moment's respite before unpacking, but he fell asleep at once. Hélène came in again, intending to say something more, and saw him lying there. She went over to the bed and looked down at him. Then she covered him with a blanket, blew out the candles, and tiptoed from the room.

The next morning Michel inspected the hospital with Paul. The scene was a familiar one: a dark, damp, dirty building in which scores of sick people lay on the floor in their own filth with no one to nurse them.

Michel took no more than a brief look round – one glance sufficed. It was always the same old story. The majority would die, but he might be able to save a fair number. He had given Paul a scented handkerchief to hold over his mouth and nose, or he would never have endured the frightful stench.

"Well?"

"It's the plague, right enough. What treatment have they received up to now?"

"None. The physician died too, and we couldn't persuade another to come here. They're all afraid of catching the disease themselves."

"The hospital must be demolished," Michel said when they were outside in the street again. "Everything must be burnt. We shall need another building – one that admits the air and sunlight. Clean clothing and a supply of fresh water, too, for washing. I shall also require some assistants."

"How many?"

"Ten, at least. I propose to examine every inhabitant and fight the disease before it takes hold. Everyone will be given prophylactic medicine. I shall train the assistants myself. The medicine we must manufacture ourselves. For that I shall need suitable premises, including a room where I can examine people."

"You're really willing to help us?"

"That's why I'm here."

Paul embraced Michel. "God bless you," he said. "You shall have all you need."

Paul was as good as his word. He obtained some premises where Michel could work and a building where the sick could be housed. The old hospital was demolished the very next day, just as Michel had asked. He was impressed by the speed and quiet

determination with which his brother organized everything. He himself was always on the move between the
hospital, his consulting room, and the dispensary where
the medicines were made. He also obtained the helpers
he wanted, one of them being Hélène. Initially reluctant
to let his wife work with the others, Paul had given way
when he saw how badly Michel needed every extra pair
of hands. Hélène dried and ground herbs while others
stirred the paste and rolled the pills.

One day Michel entered the dispensary with some
men bearing baskets of flower heads. The women took
the baskets from them and proceeded to pluck off the
petals, which they tossed into a large sieve suspended
above the fire. Hélène looked over at Michel, who was
on his way out again. Wiping her hands on her apron,
she hurried after him.

Michel crossed the courtyard and headed for the new
hospital, as he did every day at this hour. Regular visits
were important, he knew. The patients looked forward
to them and counted the hours till he came because
his presence lent their long days and nights a sense of
purpose.

Hélène ran down the steps and called his name. He
turned and walked back to her.

"I was thinking," she said. "If we employed a
few more people we could manufacture pills for the
whole district. We could even deliver them to Aix.
Not only would we be helping the sick, we could
earn enough money to pay our workers a decent
wage. We can't expect them to work for love indefi-
nitely. Consciences are soon salved, and then what?
I've had another idea, too. When everyone is better
we could turn to making perfumes. What do you
think?"

"Let's talk about it this evening, shall we?" said Michel, eager to get to the hospital.

"Michel?"

"Yes?"

"I'm so happy you're here."

"Really?" He smiled, a trifle embarrassed.

"You . . ." She hesitated. "You make my life worthwhile — mine and that of the others who work with us. They all say so." She slowly backed away with her arms behind her, nodding and smiling. Then, without warning, she darted forward and flung her arms around his neck. "We're all in love with you, didn't you know?" She kissed him full on the lips, ran back up the steps, and vanished into the dispensary. Michel stood staring after her, but at last he turned and hurried off in the direction of the hospital.

The windows of the big, bright sick-room stood open. The bedridden were being washed by Michel's assistants, men by men and women by women. Michel himself was seated on the edge of an old crone's bed. She was telling her beads while he felt her pulse, the state of which evidently satisfied him.

"You spend so much time with us, doctor," she said. "Aren't you afraid of the contagion?"

He stroked her hair. "No."

"I pray for you every day."

"Thank you, my dear." Smiling, he rose and moved on to the next bed.

The waiting-room was crowded that evening. He nodded to his patients, went straight to his consulting room, and settled himself at the desk. The nurse brought him a glass of elderberry juice. He thanked her and drank it down in one.

"Very well, let's begin."

The nurse summoned the first patient, a beautiful woman in her late twenties. Strangely aloof in manner, she was very tall and slender. Her dark hair was combed back severely and gathered on her neck, and her sumptuous gown of rose brocade, lavishly embroidered with gold thread, made her pale skin look still paler and her dark eyes still darker.

Michel yawned. "Forgive me, madame, I haven't slept for two nights. Please sit down." He gestured to the chair in front of his desk. "I must ask you a few questions." He produced a sheet of paper and took the quill from the ink well. "Your name?"

"Anna Gemelle."

He wrote it down. "Age?"

"Twenty-seven."

"I'll examine you now." He indicated a screen in the corner. "Please undress."

"Completely?"

"If you would."

She nodded, went behind the screen, and proceeded to undress. Michel propped his head on his hands.

"Are you married?"

"Widowed."

He looked surprised. She was still so young. "Widowed," he repeated, noting it down. "Do you have any children?"

"None."

"Who shares your home?"

Now it was her turn to look surprised.

Michel noticed her expression and laughed. "It

wasn't curiosity that made me ask. I wished to gauge the risk of infection, nothing more."

"Ask away. I live alone, except for a cook, a chambermaid, and a coachman."

"Three others, in other words. Please send them to see me too."

"They're waiting outside."

"Good."

Anna emerged from behind the screen. All she wore now was a short undergarment.

Michel rose and went over to her. "Please turn round." The nurse, who had been hovering discreetly in the background throughout, pushed the screen a little to one side. She attended every examination at Michel's request. He wanted no recurrence of the foolishness at Agen and had no time to squander on bored, disillusioned women eager to see how far they could get with him. He sounded Anna's back, listened to her breathing and heartbeat, palpated her spine, and did all that was needful to gain an initial impression of his patient's condition. At length he nodded to the nurse and told Anna to turn round again.

She did so, with the nurse holding a towel over her nakedness. Michel stood facing her. She was as tall as he, even in her bare feet. They looked into each other's eyes, Michel with professional interest, Anna with some curiosity, rather amused by his earnest demeanour. He felt her neck, examined her throat, nose and ears, rotated her head, felt her armpits and breasts. Last of all, having first emitted a discreet little cough to warn her, he examined the telltale glands in her groin. She flinched a little as he did so.

"You may get dressed again."

The nurse pushed the screen back in front of her.

Michel washed his hands thoroughly in a basin of water and dried them on a towel. The nurse took the basin and emptied it into a large pail.

"You're perfectly well, but I shall give you some prophylactic drops to be on the safe side. Please take them regularly before every meal, thirty a time. They'll increase your resistance."

The nurse took a small bottle from the shelf and put in on the desk. Michel added some more particulars to his list. He rubbed his eyes.

Anna had been watching him over the top of the screen. "You should get some sleep," she said.

"I shall sleep when this epidemic is over. For a whole week on end."

"And when will it be over?"

"I can't be sure." He looked at the nurse. "Are there many more outside?"

"Thirty."

"Thirty, eh? We'll soon have examined eight hundred townsfolk. How many people live here, anyway?"

Anna, still tying her hair back, came out from behind the screen. "I'd like to help you," she said.

"Really? What skills do you have?"

"None worth mentioning." She laughed. "But I can learn."

"Go to see my sister-in-law Hélène, the mayor's wife."

"I know her."

"Hélène will tell you what to do." He smiled. "Thank you. We need all the help we can get."

Michel worked until very late. It was almost midnight before the waiting-room emptied. He retired to his consulting room and shut the door.

Moments later Anna entered the waiting-room carrying a basket with a colourful ribbon wound around the handle and tied in a bow. She knocked on the door of the consulting room and went in. It was deserted. She surveyed the room with an inquisitive air. Just as she was putting the basket on the desk she heard a noise in the small adjoining room. Going to the door, which was ajar, she peered in.

Michel was standing with his back to her, stark naked. Suspended from the ceiling overhead was a water cask, and dangling from the cask a length of string. He tugged at the string, a sluice opened, and a hundred tiny jets of water cascaded down on him. Anna watched him for a moment, then beat a tactful retreat.

Michel dried himself off, swathed his naked body in a voluminous towel, and went to his desk. Catching sight of the basket, he lifted the little lid. Inside reposed a roast chicken, a bottle of wine, and some fruit. He went to the door and scanned the waiting-room, but there was no one there. With a shrug, he sat down at his desk and tucked in heartily.

The next day, as Michel was crossing the courtyard on his way to the hospital, two of his volunteers emerged carrying a dead body between them. He crossed himself and ran up the steps to the sick-room, where he saw Anna bending over a woman patient. She was gently dabbing the sweat from her brow with a cloth soaked in vinegar.

Michel went over to her. "And you said you were no good at anything. You do that very well."

"Don't make fun of me."

"I'm not, truly I'm not. I'm glad you're here."

All at once, through the window, he caught sight of some leaping flames. He hurried to the window in time to see that the volunteers had lit a bonfire and were about to burn the corpse. He called to them to stop it at once and ran out into the courtyard.

"Who told you to burn the dead here?" he shouted. "I won't have it, I've told you a hundred times. I won't have the dead cremated here, where all my patients can see them and smell the stench and picture themselves in their place. How do you expect them to recover, or don't you care?"

"Of course."

"Then why do it?"

The men shuffled their feet and said nothing.

"You knew it was against my orders?"

"Well, yes."

"The dead must be burned outside town." Michel shook his head and laid his hands on the volunteers' shoulders. "Forgive me, I'm on edge. Many thanks for your help, but it really does the patients no good to see such sights, do you understand?"

They nodded sheepishly.

"Very well," said Michel, and returned to the sick-room.

Anna was standing at the window. She had been watching him all the time.

That night he dozed off in his chair while at supper with Paul and Hélène.

"It's amazing how he heartens people and persuades them to help," said Hélène.

"He must have many sins to atone for."

"You're a cynic, Paul."

"Or perhaps he aspires to sainthood."

"Few saints have cured as many as he has." Hélène rose, laid a hand on Michel's shoulder, and softly called his name.

"Let him sleep awhile longer," said Paul.

"Yes, but not here."

Michel woke up. "Yes, what is it? Oh, forgive me, I must have dozed off. The meal was delicious, thank you."

"But you've scarcely eaten a thing."

"I'll eat later." He got to his feet.

"Surely you're not going out again?"

"Only for a while – only to the dispensary."

"You ought to get some rest."

Michel made for the door. "I can't leave those women working on their own," he said.

"I'll come with you," Hélène called, following him out.

Paul shook his head and went on eating in solitary state.

Hélène ran after Michel as he hurried down the street.

"Michel, wait!"

He paused to let her catch him up. They were standing in the shadow of an overhanging roof.

"Michel, I only wanted to tell you . . . Yesterday, when I . . . I was a little . . . I don't know how to say it . . ."

He stroked her cheek. "You've no need to say anything, Hélène."

"But I want to – I want to tell you that I . . . I'm . . . I've . . . Michel, please! Please don't make me beg like this." Her voice sank to a whisper. "I'll do anything you want."

He took her in his arms and kissed her. She returned his kisses, strained against him, fondled him. He buried his face in her hair, kissed her throat, her breast, her mouth, the nape of her neck, clasped her to him. "It's so long," he said falteringly, "so long since I was last with a woman. Hélène, I . . ."

"Don't speak." She kissed him passionately. He ran his tongue over her face, explored the hollows of her ears, her nostrils, drove his teeth into her shoulder. Lifting her up, he gripped her buttocks and thrust her against the wall. She pulled up her skirt and wound her legs about his hips, clung to his neck. "Michel," she moaned, "Michel . . ."

And then, from one moment to the next, he released her and stepped back. "It's no use, I can't. You're my brother's wife. It's no use."

He turned on his heel and hurried across the street.

Hélène watched him go, not only frustrated but bitterly offended. She smoothed her gown and tidied her dishevelled hair.

Michel had reached the dispensary and was standing outside, breathing fast. He ran his fingers through his hair. The whole situation was impossible. He had half a mind to leave at once, tonight, but he couldn't abandon his patients. How would he ever again look Hélène in the eye – or Paul, for that matter? He must talk to her, reason with her, make her understand. She must forget all about it. Nothing had happened, nothing at all. He shook his head fiercely, like a dog emerging from a pond, and went into the dispensary.

One or two women were still at work there, Anna among them. She was standing beside the cauldron, stirring the herbal paste with a big wooden ladle.

She glanced round when he came in, but only for a moment. Then she concentrated on her work again. He went over and watched her briefly, then nodded and passed on. Anna glanced at him again as he made his way over to the long table, where the other women were moulding the paste into pills.

"We've almost succeeded," he said, proceeding to help them. "Those who are still alive will survive. There have been no new cases for several days."

"We'd all be dead but for you," said one of the women.

Michel shrugged his shoulders.

"It's true," said another. "You're always so modest, doctor. Make a wish – any wish, and we'll do our best to fulfil it. We know how much we owe you."

"And now get off home," said a third. "Go to bed, you're tired out. Get some sleep or you'll collapse on us. We can manage."

Anna appeared while Michel was examining a man in his consulting room the next day.

"You look pale," he told her. He gave the man a nod. "You can get dressed, there's nothing wrong with you. And send your wife to see me." The man thanked him and went out. He washed his hands and turned to Anna. "You're not getting enough sleep. However, I think it'll soon be over. Our work has been worthwhile."

She nodded. Then she said softly, "I'm ill."

He went to her, felt her pulse, looked closely into her eyes, examined her throat. "You're not ill, you're exhausted. You really must get some sleep. You've been working night after night."

"But I ache all over, body and soul. I never knew

what pain was until now – it's beyond endurance. I've been widowed nine years, but now I know that any wound can be healed by the passage of time." She gazed into his eyes. "I'm ill because I haven't seen you for two whole days."

He stared at her, at a loss for words.

"Cure me, I beg you!" She stretched out her hands imploringly, then sank to the floor in a faint.

He picked her up, laid her on a couch, and loosened her bodice. Fetching a little bottle from the shelf, he removed the stopper and held it under her nose, gently slapping her cheeks with his free hand. The nurse inserted a cushion under her legs. Anna's eyelashes began to flutter.

"How do you feel?"

She nodded and sat up. "A trifle dizzy, nothing more."

"Lie back, then. Take your time."

She shook her head and struggled to her feet. "Forget what I said just now."

"How can I?"

"Please, it was all nonsense – I was overwrought. Lack of sleep, the sight of all that disease and death – it's enough to cloud the most lucid intelligence. Forgive me, I'm neglecting my work."

She left the room. Michel stared after her in a daze until the nurse broke in on his reverie by asking if she should summon the next patient.

"Yes," he said, sitting down at his desk. "Yes, by all means."

The nurse returned with a middle-aged man and showed him to the chair in front of the desk.

Michel took his quill from the ink well. "Name?" he asked, without looking at the man.

"Robert Serault."

Michel continued to stare into space with his quill poised. "Age?"

"Fifty-seven."

"Married?" Michel didn't wait for a reply. "I'll examine you now." He indicated the screen. "Kindly get undressed." All at once he rose. "Excuse me," he said, and hurried from the room.

Anna, standing at the press, was extracting the juice from some hibiscus leaves while Hélène stirred the cauldron of paste with the wooden ladle. Michel entered the dispensary, looked around for Anna, and went straight over to her. Hélène started to say something as he passed her, but she might have been invisible: he had eyes for Anna alone. She stared after him resentfully.

"Madame . . ." he said.

But Anna's only response was to turn away and rush out into the street with Michel in hot pursuit. Hélène went over to the window and looked out.

She saw Anna hurry across the street, threading her way through passers-by, porters, wagons laden with merchandise. The town had come to life again, the street rang with the cries of hawkers and stallholders extolling their wares. Michel looked around desperately. He caught a man by the sleeve. "Where does Madame Gemelle live?" he asked. Without waiting for an answer, he accosted a woman. "Madame Gemelle – where does she live?"

The woman pointed to a house on the other side of the street. "Over there," she said. "The white house."

Hélène, who had now emerged from the dispensary, saw Michel run across the street and hammer impatiently on the door. It was opened by a maidservant.

"I wish to see Madame Gemelle. My name is – "

"I know who you are, monsieur, but Madame is not at home."

"But she is!" he said fiercely, pointing down the passage.

"I'm sorry, monsieur."

"Anna!" he shouted.

The girl made to close the door, but he pushed past her.

Anna, who had been standing in the hallway, turned and ran up the stairs. Michel followed, taking them two at a time. She ran along the landing.

"Anna, please wait!" he called. "Please, I implore you!"

She disappeared into her bedroom and slammed the door behind her. He tried to open it, but she had braced herself against it from the inside.

"Go away!" she called. "Please! Please go away!"

He threw his weight against the door. Being stronger and heavier, he gradually forced it open. Anna stood facing him, out of breath and hair in disarray. She retreated step by step until her back was to the window. Trembling all over, she sought refuge behind the heavy curtain. He gently drew it aside. Only inches apart now, they exchanged a lingering look, then hungrily embraced each other.

The maidservant appeared in the doorway. Oblivious of everything and everyone else in the world, Michel and Anna were making love on the broad window-seat. Very quietly, the girl withdrew and closed the door behind her.

They married two days later, Paul and Hélène acting as their witnesses. Hélène had dressed in black for the occasion. She embraced Anna and congratulated her, then did the same to Michel, but with a difference: "I curse you," she hissed in his ear.

Michel and Anna emerged from the church with their guests to find the square in front of it crowded with townsfolk, all of them eager to be present at their famous physician's wedding. A man sidled up to Michel and handed him a book.

"Please accept this gift, monsieur. It's a Bible."

"Thank you," said Michel, leafing through it. "Why, it's translated from the Latin."

The man smiled. "Why shouldn't the word of God be understood by all, whatever their native tongue? Are monks and priests and the Pope alone to know what God desires to tell us?"

"But that's heresy."

"Yes, according to the Catholic Church. But is it heresy to proclaim the word of God? To couch it in language that all can read and understand? To aspire to a Church that obeys the word of God and eschews corruption and crime? If that's heresy, I am indeed a heretic and proud to be one, for I serve the word of the Lord alone."

"You must be a Lutheran."

"I'm a man of God. I and my fellows are building a new Church – one in which there's no place for images or idols. We're building a new world."

Michel shook his head. "I want none of this, not now, not today. Please leave me in peace, for today at least."

From one moment to the next, the townsfolk who had just been applauding their physician became transformed into a raging mob. They stormed the church, tore paintings from the altars, smashed statues with sledgehammers, trampled reliquaries underfoot, looted the holy of holies. They carried the church's treasures out into the square and set them ablaze. Men dug diamonds, rubies and emeralds out of sacred images, women fought over lengths of brocade. One rioter emerged from the church carrying a brightly painted figure of the Virgin in porcelain. He raised it above his head and hurled it to the cobblestones, reducing it to a thousand fragments. The stained glass windows were being shattered by volleys of stones. The man who had given Michel the Bible gripped him by the arm, his eyes alight with fanaticism. "Anyone who seeks to build a new world," he snarled, "must first destroy the old!"

The interior of the church had caught fire. Everyone still inside fled in panic. Michel looked up at the sky, which was growing dark, and walked down the steps to the square. It was now deserted save for three little children who stood staring at him wide-eyed. A few drops of rain fell, black as ink. And then the heavens opened. A dark deluge descended on the children and streamed down their bodies. The air reeked of sulphur. Dense black smoke belched from some tall chimneys on the other side of the square, coating everything in greasy soot. Weird signs – unfamiliar words and pictures defined by tubes filled with unearthly light – flickered through the noxious fog. A wailing sound drew nearer, flashing blue lights appeared, a convoy of metallic monsters swept past, one with many ladders stacked on its roof. An evil-smelling mist rose from the gutters. The square was littered with cylindrical cans of metal and flimsy bags composed of some thin, smooth substance resembling paper.

"Michel, what's the matter?" It was Anna's voice. She shook him. "Michel!"

"What?"

"Michel, it's me, Anna, your wife. What's the matter with you?"

"Anna, yes. I don't know, it's nothing. Shall we go? The cook will scold us if our wedding breakfast is burnt to a cinder."

"Is everything all right?" she asked anxiously. "You really startled me. It was if you'd seen something terrible."

"No." He kissed her cheek. "It's just the excitement. Come."

He took her arm and they walked down the steps, flanked by a waving, cheering crowd. His free hand, he found, was still holding the Bible.

The festivities went on late into the night. Michel was so happy that he ended by joining in with a will, telling himself that his recent visions were merely a symptom of overwork. He always felt exhausted when an epidemic was over, always dreamed of defeat when victory had long ago been won. He drank wine, danced with his wife, and, when they at last retired to bed, slept happily in her arms.

The next morning a wagon drew up outside Anna's house. Jean, accompanied by two sturdy porters, had come to deliver the boxes of books that had lain in Paul's cellar for so many years. He asked Michel where he and his men should stow them.

"First, Jean," Michel said, "would you care to join our household? You would be more than welcome."

"You're very kind, monsieur, but I've written to ask my master if he'll take me back. I should prefer to end my days in his service."

"I must write to him too. He'll be wondering why he hasn't heard from me for so long."

"He already knows. I told him you'd been working day and night for weeks on end."

Michael nodded. "I see."

"And where shall we put the boxes?"

"Take them to the garden behind the house."

"The garden?" Jean eyed him doubtfully.

"Yes, the garden. I'll deal with them in due course."

Jean beckoned to the porters and gave them their instructions. When all the boxes had been carried along the passage and out into the garden behind the house, he and Michel bade each other an affectionate farewell.

Michel and Anna stood looking at the stack of boxes.

"Aren't you going to unpack them?" she asked.

He shook his head.

"But you can't just leave them here," she protested. "What's in them, anyway?"

He levered a lid off. "Wine," he said, and proceeded to unpack the boxes after all. He had the bottles of wine taken to the cellar and tossed all the books into a heap. When he came to the last book in the last box, he leafed through it briefly, then sent it to join the rest. Taking a pitcher of oil, he emptied it over the heap and set fire to it. Flames shot into the air — flames of a strange, preternatural brightness. Anna shaded her eyes with her hand, she was so dazzled. Michel watched the fire until everything had been reduced to ashes. The flames dwindled and died.

"I'm so happy," he said.

"I don't understand. Why did you burn all those books?"

"I love you."

She laughed. "That's no answer."

He took her in his arms. "Yes, it is. I love you and I'm happy. I want to spend the rest of my life with you, here in Salon. I want to practise as a physician and raise a big family with you. I want to lead a normal life."

"Just a normal life, nothing more?"

"Nothing. I'm so happy to have you."

"But what has that to do with those books?"

"Forget about the books, Anna. I love you. Nothing else matters."

She shook her head. "You're in a strange mood today. Did you have a bad dream in the night?"

"No, that's just it – that's why I'm so happy. It's over at last, now I'm with you." He took her hand. "Come, let's go for a ride."

"Don't you intend to work?"

"Yes, later. Now I want to go riding with you. The weather's so beautiful. Who knows how many more such fine days we can look forward to this year?"

They rode out of the town, through woods, across fields and meadows, until they came to a little inn beside a lake, where they stopped for a meal. Then they rode back. Although it was dark by the time they reached Salon, Michel insisted on making a brief detour. He rode to the church where he and Anna had got married, dismounted, and helped her off her horse.

"You mean to go in?"

"Yes."

"Now?"

"Yes, now. I want to thank God for having brought us together."

He put his arm around her and led her into the

church, where they knelt and prayed before the high altar. Having lit two candles, they returned to their horses.

"Nothing will ever part us," he said. "Nothing and no one, do you hear?"

She stroked his cheek. "What's the matter with you?"

"I love you, Anna. You've saved me."

"Saved you?" She laughed. "I'm glad you think so, but your language is a trifle high-flown."

He helped her on to her horse and was about to mount up himself when a voice hailed him from the shadowy doorway of the church: a man's voice, though its owner could not be seen.

"Michel?" said the voice.

"Yes?"

"I must have a word with you."

Michel made for the church door. "I won't be a moment," he told Anna.

The man withdrew still further into the shadows. Michel still couldn't make out his face.

"Why did you burn those books?" The man tapped Michel on the forehead. "You really thought you could rid yourself of them so easily?" He gave a harsh laugh. "They're all inside your head, you fool!"

"Michel," Anna called, "what is it?" Her horse shied suddenly. It snorted and whinnied, eager to be off. She tightened her grip on the reins and spoke to it in soothing tones.

The man said, "For what you did this day, posterity will hold you accursed."

"Leave me be."

"Michel?" Anna called again. "Who is it?" Her horse was almost uncontrollable now. She dismounted, patted the beast, held its head and blew gently into its nostrils to quieten it.

Michel turned to go, but the man seized his arm and held him back. He lit a candle and held it up in front of his face. Michel recognized the mysterious figure at last, and the sight made his blood run cold. The man was himself – he was face to face with his second self!

The figure gave a mocking laugh. "Yes, I'm you. Do you truly believe you can escape yourself and forget everything, your duty above all? That was laid upon you by God." The man that was himself seized him by the collar and drew him so close that he could feel his own breath on his cheek. "It's a sin to disobey the Almighty's command." He pointed heavenward, then gave Michel a push that sent him staggering back into the massive wooden door of the church. "Do your duty, or a terrible misfortune will befall you."

Michel leaned against the door, pale as death.

Anna, who had tethered her restive horse, came over to him. "Michel, what happened? You're so pale – why, you're trembling. Who was with you just now?"

"There's a curse on me, Anna," he whispered, putting his arms around her. "Forgive me, please forgive me." He gave a sob. "Why should God punish me so?"

There was a turret at one end of Anna's house, and it was there, in the attic chamber at the very top, that Michel installed his work-room.

One day not long after the incident outside the church, he was seated on an iron stool with his bare feet immersed in the basin of water in which the stool reposed. A burning candle had been placed on another stool near the basin so that its flame was reflected in the surface. Michel took a small spoonful of red powder from the table beside him, put it to his lips, and allowed the contents to dissolve on his tongue. Then, having replaced the spoon, he took a divining-rod from the table and held it over the basin of water. Every movement he made was deliberate in the extreme, as if part of some predetermined plan. Abruptly, the rod twisted in his hands.

Anna was standing outside the door, listening. Suddenly she heard him cry out. "NO!" he shouted, "NO! NO!" She peered through the keyhole but could see nothing. She called to him but got no answer. She tried the handle but the door was locked. She knocked – she pounded the panels with her fists.

Michel, looking very pale, opened the door at last. "Please leave me, Anna," he said. "I need to be alone. Don't worry, I beg you."

She started to say something, but he shut the door again. After lingering for a moment, she slowly descended the stairs.

Michel did not reappear until breakfast-time the next morning. He sat down at the table looking exhausted. Anna rose and went to him. Kneeling down beside him, she took his hands in hers and kissed them.

"What in God's name is the matter with you, Michel? Why shut yourself away like that? What do you do in there?"

He shook his head, picked up a glass of milk and sipped it in silence.

"You've got to tell me!"

"Don't ask."

"Please, Michel! Tell me how I can help you – you need help, I know."

"Have any patients arrived yet?"

"Yes. I'll tell them to come back tomorrow."

"No, don't do that." He got up and made for the door. "Tell them I'll be with them directly. I'm only going to change my shirt."

Anna followed him. "You don't trust me," she said sadly.

He took her in his arms. "I love you, Anna. I need you. I need your love, your strength, your intelligence, but please don't pester me. Don't ask any more questions."

"I'm frightened, Michel."

"I'm frightened too."

Hélène, stripped to the waist, was being examined by Michel in the consulting room. He was sounding her back while the nurse stood there with a towel, ready to cover her breasts when she turned to face him.

"It's a long time since you paid us a visit," she said petulantly.

"Please take a deep breath and hold it."

She breathed in while Michel listened.

"Why have you stopped coming?"

"Please turn round."

Hélène turned round. The nurse raised the towel and Michel continued his examination. He inspected Hélène's throat, cupping her neck in his hands and holding her chin down with both thumbs.

"You haven't answered me."

"You saw all those people in the waiting-room. That should be answer enough."

He took a divining-rod from his desk and measured

how far it was from her body when it first twisted in his hands. Then he gave her an egg to hold and repeated the procedure. This time the distance was appreciably greater.

"You must be sure to eat fewer eggs, less meat, and more vegetables. All that albumen does your blood no good. You're perfectly well in other respects." He replaced the divining-rod on the desk and washed his hands.

"Do you have to wash your hands when you touch me?" Hélène demanded caustically.

"I wash my hands after every examination."

She started to get dressed. "You see no patients in the evenings or on Sundays. You could visit us then."

"Then, Hélène, I'm tired. I work hard all the week."

"You do look pale, I must admit." She went over to him and put out her hand as if to fondle his cheek.

"No, Hélène, please don't."

She hesitated, summoning up her courage. "May we talk in private for a moment?"

"Now?"

"Yes, now."

"But the waiting-room is full."

"Please."

Michel nodded to the nurse, who left the room.

"I've been sleeping badly of late," Hélène said.

"In that case you should try to discover if you're sleeping above an underground stream. I could find out for you, if you like. You may have to change the position of your bed."

"I often go walking alone at nights. I often pass the house in which you live these days."

He laughed. "That's a complicated way of putting it, Hélène. It's my home now."

"I see a light at the top of the turret every night. It was still burning at three this morning."

"What does your husband say to your roaming the streets alone in the small hours?"

"What do you do up there at night, Michel?"

"I read."

"I think we must be the only two people in Salon awake at that hour, Michel. Sometimes I stand for many minutes on end below your turret, looking up at that lighted window. I'd so much like to know what you do up there."

"I told you, I read." He laughed. "As a rule, though, I fall asleep over my book and the candle burns until it goes out." He slipped his arm through hers and escorted her to the door, anxious to bring their conversation to an end.

"Are you so eager to be rid of me?"

"Give my love to Paul. We really must see each other soon."

Hélène's eyes suddenly filled with tears. "Sometimes I wish the plague would return. Then we could work together as we did in the old days. Do you remember what we said when the plague was still raging? Once it was defeated, we said, we would only make nice things – perfumes and cosmetics and preserves – and sell them all over France. Do you remember?"

He nodded.

"Well, why don't we do that now?"

"I've no time for such things. Why not do it yourself?"

She gazed into his eyes. "You coaxed me out of my kitchen, Michel. You can't send me back there now."

"Don't you read any books these days?"

"You're evading the issue. I won't stand for it!"

"But you were always reading once upon a time. Why not now?"

"How can I? I'm not the same person." She pointed to her bosom. "There's someone inside there, Michel. He's devouring me alive." She looked him in the eye. "It's you."

Michel put his arms around her. "Listen, Hélène . . . I'm married – happily married. We're going to have a child, and my work keeps me busy day and night. I'm – "

She cut him short. "You think you can simply toss me aside? I won't stand for it, I tell you, so be warned!"

With that, she threw off his embrace and hurried out of the room.

"You're imagining things, Anna. What can she do to harm me?"

Anna, thoroughly perturbed by the news of Hélène's threat, looked at Michel across the supper table.

"How should I know what goes on in the head of that lovesick creature?"

"She's an unhappy, over-emotional woman, that's all. She'll see sense in the end." Michel laid his napkin aside, took another sip of wine, and rose.

"*I* could think of any number of ways to harm you."

"What, for instance?" He sat down again.

"If I couldn't have you? I might. . ." She hesitated for a moment. "Well, I might kill you."

He laughed and got to his feet again. "Then I'm doubly glad I married you."

"It's no laughing matter, Michel. Be careful."

"Careful in what way, exactly?"

She shrugged.

"You see," he said, "you don't know either. I can hardly take her to bed." He laughed again. "Or can I?"

She laughed too. "Don't you dare!"

He took her in his arms and kissed her tenderly. "Perhaps we should invite them to a meal, Hélène and brother Paul. How would next Sunday do? I could show her the turret – after I've tidied away all my clutter, of course."

Anna shook her head. "There's no placating a woman disappointed in love."

A candle was burning in the turret chamber late that night. Michel, seated once more on the iron stool in the basin of water, gazed with trancelike fixity at the reflection of the candle flame as it danced on the surface. Oily streaks appeared in the water, writhing and merging. Beside Michel stood a table bearing some sheets of paper and an ink well. He was writing swiftly, without pausing for thought, as if some text were being dictated to him by an inner voice. The table and the floor were already littered with closely-written pages. He completed yet another sheet, brushed it off the table, and continued to write.

Hélène was standing outside the house, looking up at the turret window. Anna, concealed behind a curtain at a window on the first floor, was watching her intently.

Michel entered the kitchen carrying a sheaf of closely-written pages and sat down at the breakfast table. When Anna came in, as she did a moment later, he put out his hand and drew her to him. She perched on his lap and stroked his hair.

"You need a shave," she said.

He rested his head against her breast.

"She spent the whole night loitering under your window again."

"Perhaps you could have a word with her."

"With pleasure, but what would I say?"

"Tell her to leave us in peace."

"That wouldn't do much good. Maybe ... I don't know. I'll think of something."

Michel took a pear from the fruit basket and a large carving knife from the drawer. He put the pear on the table so that part of it overhung the edge and placed the bread basket immediately beneath it. Raising his arm, he brought the knife down on the pear in one quick movement, slicing off the top. It dropped neatly into the basket.

Anna looked puzzled. "What are you doing?"

He picked up the bread basket and put it on the table, retrieved the piece of pear and held it up by the stalk. "That's how they'll cut off the king's head. With a knife-machine. In Paris." He dipped his finger in a pitcher of water and traced the outlines of the contraption on the table. "The blade will descend on his neck from above and the head will fall into a basket. They'll storm the Bastille and release all the prisoners. Mob rule, streets running with blood. And then they'll start killing each other with the knife-machine, one after another. Thousands will die in that manner. I saw it all so clearly. Revolution, turmoil, utter chaos. The queen, too, will die."

Anna laughed. "And when will all this happen?"

"Two hundred years from now."

"What!" She stared at him incredulously.

"I see things more and more clearly now. Scaliger

was right: the visions become quite distinct when I take the proper dose." He picked up the sheaf of paper and held it out. "Can you read this scrawl?"

Anna glanced at it and nodded.

"Then do me a favour and copy it out."

"But why?"

"When God entrusted me with this terrible gift, he did not mean me to keep it to myself."

She looked aghast. "You mean to publish these things?"

"I must warn people. If they persist in their ways they'll destroy everything – the countryside, the whole earth, themselves – with the aid of machines and bombs so terrible that they surpass the imagination. Frightful wars will break out. France will seek to conquer the world and come to grief in Russia. Germany will do likewise, and will likewise come grief in Russia. Men will perish in their millions. The Church, too, is doomed. Everything will go up in flames. The light of the sun will be extinguished and all will be engulfed in darkness. The earth will freeze, the oceans turn to fields of ice. But the age that will dawn in time to come, far, far in the future, will be more blissful than any that has gone before."

"If you publish such predictions," Anna said in a low voice, "they'll put you to death."

He shrugged. "Is that any reason to conceal the truth?"

She pointed to the sheaf of paper. "Burn it," she said firmly.

"I can't."

"But if everything is destined to happen as you say, how can it benefit people to know? It would only alarm them."

"I do not write these things for simple folk, only for a handful of initiates."

"But anyone will be able to read them."

"I shall encode my prophecies, so that only those with the key to the code will understand them. I need only wait for one of them to come true in the foreseeable future. Then I shall be believed."

"When will that be?"

"I don't know."

She smiled despite herself. "If you know everything, you ought to know that."

Their maidservant entered the kitchen followed by old Raoul. Michel rose and embraced him warmly.

"Raoul! How glad I am to see you here at last." He turned to Anna. "This is Raoul, my old friend and assistant. Raoul, meet my wife Anna."

Raoul chuckled. "And I was looking forward to dying in peace!"

"Let others do the dying. You're still sorely needed, or I wouldn't have summoned you here to help me with my practice. Ah, Raoul, how quickly time passes! Eat, drink, and tell me what you've been doing all these years."

"There's not much to tell. Still, now that I'm back with you, I may come to life once more. They were tedious, all those years without you."

"Then don't complain if I ask you to burn the midnight oil again."

"Of course I'll complain, and complain like the devil!" Raoul cackled. "What is there left for an old man to do, if he can't carp and grumble?"

The fence that would enclose the pasture was half completed. Paul and a handful of men were hard at work driving posts and nailing rails into place. Hélène came walking across the field towards them carrying a basket.

"I've brought you something to eat."

"The others too?"

"There's plenty for all of you."

Paul removed the cloth that covered the basket to reveal a substantial midday meal: a brace of cold roast fowl, some thick slices of venison, a big loaf of bread, cheese, fruit, and wine. He called to his men to come and get their food. He himself took half a chicken from the basket and went over to a nearby tree. Seated with his back against the trunk, he proceeded to eat voraciously. Hélène poured him a mug of wine and sat down beside him. The others, having helped themselves, sprawled on the grass some distance away.

"The men are working well," Paul said with his mouth full. "We'll be finished by nightfall. Tomorrow we can drive the cattle to pasture."

"Your brother's in league with the Devil, and all you can think of is your cattle."

"Don't start that again!"

"He sits in that turret, night after night, until dawn. He never sleeps, never tires."

"He's a good physician, and we all owe him a debt of gratitude. What he does at night is none of our business."

"If that doesn't give you cause for concern, you should at least be angry at the way he treats me. He behaves in an impudent manner – he makes lewd remarks whenever he sets eyes on me."

Paul lost his temper. "Enough of this nonsense! Do you think I haven't seen *you* making eyes at *him*?

You cavorted around him like a bitch in heat, and he spurned you. Do think I don't know why he never comes to see us any more? Because he has no wish to embarrass himself or me, that's why! Leave the poor man in peace."

He got up and strode over to the others.

Hélène watched him go, flushed with anger, before heading back across the fields to Salon. Half-way there she caught sight of Anna waiting for her. She was tempted to make a detour, then told herself not to be silly and walked straight up to her.

"So it's you," she said. "Don't tell me you're here by chance."

"I'm not. Your cook said I'd find you here. This scheme of yours for manufacturing perfumes – Michel told me you've talked it over with him. I think it's an excellent plan. We should put it into practice. What do you say?"

"What does *he* say? Surely he doesn't agree?"

"He'll help us, naturally, and once we've learned how to make those things. . ." Anna broke off. "Or doesn't the idea appeal to you?"

"Yes, of course. By all means."

"He'll be delighted, just as I am. Come to our house tomorrow and we'll discuss the whole matter."

The water changed colour as Michel added various essences, creating oily streaks on the surface. He bent lower over the basin and added one more drop from a phial. All at once the appearance of the water changed again. There was a sudden glint of gold, and the will-o'-the-wisp colours took on shape and substance. They resolved themselves into a multitude of variegated banners fluttering in the breeze. Sunlight glittered on the visor of a golden helmet. A horse reared up, a lance transfixed the helmet and pierced the eye beneath. A cry rent the air. A man fell from his horse: the king. Many people clustered around him, among them the wielder of the lance. Standing apart was a woman clearly recognizable as the queen, Catherine de Médicis. She had a hint of a smile on her lips and was holding a book in her hand. Clasping the book to her breast, she sauntered over to the figure on the ground. The others respectfully stood aside to let her pass. Another woman came running up: Diane de Portier, the king's much older mistress. She hurled herself on him, stroked his cheek. The queen stood looking down at the pair for a moment, then beckoned. Two men hurried forward with a litter, placed the king upon it, and carried him to a tent. Diane started to follow, but the queen smilingly laid a hand on her arm and restrained her. Controlling herself with an effort, Diane bowed low and curtsied to the queen. Her time was up, and she knew it. The queen slowly turned and, still smiling to herself, set off for the tent to which her husband had been taken . . .

Michel leapt to his feet. Gathering up a mass of handwritten sheets, he ran downstairs to the bedroom. Anna was already asleep with little César, now one year old, snuggled up beside her. Michel shook her by the shoulder.

"Anna! Anna, wake up!"

She stirred, yawned. "What time is it?" she asked.

"The king is going to die!"

She rubbed her eyes sleepily. "What king?"

"Our king – King Henry II. I even know the day and manner of his death. He'll be killed while jousting at a tournament, pierced through the helmet and eye by his opponent's lance. *That* will be the proof that my predictions come true. I can publish them at last!"

Anna was wide awake now. "Are you out of your mind? The Church and the king will crush you like a beetle!"

"But not the queen."

"Come, let's go downstairs, you'll wake the child. I was so relieved when he went off to sleep at last."

She got out of bed and wrapped herself in a coat. Together they went downstairs to the kitchen. Michel cut himself a slice of bread, fetched some ham and olives from the larder, and poured himself a glass of wine. He was hungry and in the highest of spirits.

"Catherine is much given to consulting soothsayers, I know," he said. "Her court is swarming with Italian charlatans who cheat and fleece her, but she's a shrewd woman none the less, and when the king dies, well . . . I think she may welcome the death of a husband who has humiliated her by flaunting Diane de Portier in public throughout their marriage."

"Is it really true that the Portier woman was his wet-nurse?"

"Yes, and she still suckles him, even now."

"Amazing that any woman could retain the king's affections for so many years."

"She must know all his weaknesses. No person is dearer to a man than a woman who condones all his failings."

"You speak from experience, do you?"

He laughed and took her in his arms. "I do indeed."

"But what if the queen is deposed? Take care, you may be gambling on the wrong horse."

"Catherine is clever. She'll conduct the affairs of

state on her young son's behalf. I couldn't have a better protector, believe me. And now, please get dressed and copy these out for me."

He handed her the handwritten sheets, kissed her, and prepared to go upstairs again.

"I've spoken with Hélène," Anna said, helping herself to a slice of ham.

"And?"

"She thinks it a wonderful idea, our making perfumes and preserves together – provided you help us."

"You shouldn't waste your time on such nonsense. I need you. We've so much work to do."

Anna looked at the pages he had written and gave a little start. "These are poems," she called, but Michel had already left the room.

A week had gone by – a week in which Michel had worked day and night to produce the pages which Anna had copied out and delivered to the print-shop. That was where they were now. The printer removed a sheet from the press, glanced at it, and laid it flat on a large table.

Michel inspected it briefly and nodded. "How many more pages do you have to set?" he asked.

"Six."

"I see. And how long will that take?"

"A week, or thereabouts."

Michel turned to Anna. "Stay here and read the proofs. Every letter, every word must be as I wrote it down."

The printer indicated the sheet on the table. "These poems, did you write them in earnest, or are they merely works of art?"

"Since when have works of art not been seriously intended?"

"You know what I mean."

Michel put his hands on the man's shoulders and looked him straight in the eye. "No one must see this book before the queen has read it. No one, do you hear? Only one copy will leave here, and that will be for the queen's eyes alone. If it finds its way into the wrong hands too soon, we're lost. You and I both."

"I feared as much."

"Then act accordingly."

Michel left the print-shop and went to the dispensary where medicines had been manufactured at the time of the plague. He had rearranged and re-equipped it in the last few days. Hélène was in the act of pouring boiled water through a filter into a glass bottle. The table was heaped with flowers of many kinds and the walls were lined with shelves on which stood flasks of alcohol and essential oils. A still had been set up beside the stove. Michel took a small flask from a shelf. Using a pipette, he added a few drops of essential oil and gently shook the flask to mix its contents. Then he dipped a thin strip of paper in the fluid, sniffed it, and gave a broad smile. He handed the strip to Hélène, who had been watching him closely throughout.

She took the strip of paper and sniffed it too.

"Mm. . ."

"Good?"

"Very good."

"Let's set to work, then."

It was early morning at the Château de Blois, where the royal court was in residence. Catherine de Médicis strode swiftly along the corridor that led to the king's apartments. The two sentries on duty bowed low, opened the big double doors, and stood aside.

Catherine entered the royal antechamber. A lord-in-waiting stepped forward and made his obeisance.

"His Majesty is still asleep, I fear."

"Then I'll wake him."

"His Majesty is not alone."

"Who's with him? Diane?" She gave a mirthless laugh and opened the door of the bedchamber.

Henry, seated in a bathtub with a book in his hand, was having his back gently sponged by Diane. Catherine paused in the doorway, watching the scene with a wry smile. As soon as the king saw her he climbed out of the tub and donned a dressing-gown. Then, casually tossing the book he had been reading on to the pillows, he lay down on his bed. Diane went and sat beside him. He put his head on her lap, opened her peignoir, and began to stroke her thighs. At length he pointed to the book.

"Is that your latest reading matter, madame?"

Catherine saw that it was the book she had been searching for all the previous evening – the book sent her by Michel de Nostradame. "How did you come by it?" she demanded.

"You must have mislaid it. A servant found the volume, assumed that it was mine, and brought it to me last night. I knew at once that it must belong to you – no one else at court reads such things. That was why I meant to send for you, because I can well conceive of your distress at losing it. Very interesting." He took the book, opened it at random, and read aloud. " 'Two lions at a tourney will contend, and there the elder beast must meet his end. Though safe within its golden cage, his eye will be put out, and he will surely die.' And so on and so forth." He tossed the book aside again.

"If it interests you so much," said Catherine, "you may keep the book a little longer."

"I don't understand how you can waste your time on such nonsense. Mine is far too precious to me." Still caressing his mistress, Henry looked up into her face. "What do you make of such prophecies, my love?"

Diane picked up the book, read a word or two, and threw it on the floor. "The style is crude and vulgar. It would be no pleasure to read."

Catherine smiled. "I've invited the man who wrote it to visit me."

"Then he has done what he set out to do," the king retorted. "Don't give him too much money. He's a swindler, like all those Italians in your stable. They do nothing but cheat you."

Still smiling, Catherine retrieved the book from the floor and prepared to withdraw.

The king was fondling Diane's breasts. She buried her fingers in his hair and addressed the queen over his head.

"I was speaking of you to His Majesty just before you came. I told him it was time he paid another visit to your bed. I've spoken with your physician. Tonight might be a propitious time, being so soon before you ovulate. Would that suit you?"

Catherine looked at the king, who was now nuzzling Diane's breast.

"At about ten?" Diane pursued. "We shall be at cards till then. Or would you be too tired at that hour?"

"Not at all, ten will be perfectly convenient."

Catherine continued to smile. She stood there proudly, determined not to let them humiliate her.

"Good. In that case, I shall deliver the king to your door at ten."

Catherine nodded and left the room, but not before Diane had added an afterthought.

"Perhaps you should first take one of those mud baths you detest so much. We don't want His Majesty to overtax himself too often, do we?"

The coachman's whip cracked, the horses redoubled their efforts, the carriage rocked and swayed as it sped through the forest. Eventually it pulled up outside an inn. Two ostlers unhitched the weary beasts and harnessed up a fresh team. The landlord came out, passed Michel a basket of food through the carriage window and handed the coachman a sausage and a flask of water. Everything proceeded very quickly, and the carriage was on its way again within minutes.

They reached Blois the next morning. The door of the château was opened by a footman who bowed to Michel, then hesitated.

"Monsieur, forgive me, but may I ask you a question?"

Michel nodded.

"Countess Beauveau has lost her lapdog. She pines for it all day long, and I was wondering, since you're a famous soothsayer. . ." He broke off, struck by Michel's look of astonishment. "News travels fast here at court, monsieur. Anyone ignorant of the latest gossip can pack his bags."

"You'll find him in rue Royale," Michel said. "At the butcher's shop."

He ascended the grand staircase, and another footman escorted him straight to the queen, who received
him in her laboratory.

Catherine sniffed the perfume Michel had brought
her as a gift. He stood beside her, surveying the room,
which was bigger than his own dispensary. One wall
was covered in cabbalistic signs, another bore a number
of horoscopes.

"So you also make perfumes?" said Catherine.

"My wife manufactures them as a pastime, Majesty,
together with my sister-in-law."

"I've read your book, but much of it escapes me.
You know why I summoned you?"

He bowed low.

"Don't stand on ceremony, I wish to speak with
you as a colleague. I've been working for years with
Ruggiero. You know him?"

"No."

"An Italian, and reputed to be the best astrologer
living. We shall see. Ruggiero is versed in the occult
sciences. You have predicted the king's death and
many other dreadful things. Have you no fear of the
Inquisition?"

"Only you have seen my book till now. I've released
no other copies."

She laughed. "And you think I'll protect you?"

"Will you?"

"That remains to be seen." She pointed to the
horoscopes on the wall. "My enemies. Everything you
see here serves one purpose only: to destroy them —
to destroy anyone who stands in my way. As I see it,
any means to that end is permissible. Don't look so
shocked, doctor. I'm not mad, I'm merely a poor, weak
woman, and the king is merely a foolish, helpless victim

in the clutches of that. . ." She drew a deep breath. ". .
.that creature. You see? I'm being quite open with you.
He'll soon be dead, you predict. Good! High time too,
before the entire kingdom goes to rack and ruin. I shall
assume the regency on behalf of the eldest of my young
sons. It will not be easy to steer a middle course between
Catholics and Reformers, between Spain, England, and
the Netherlands. France is at her last gasp. It's simply
our good fortune that none of our enemies has grasped
the truth. I shall be dependent on my own cunning
and strength of purpose. I expect no assistance from
anyone. One of my few advantages is that no one
thinks me capable of ruling this country, or even of
wishing to do so. Another is that my enemies are so
divided among themselves. I'm uninterested in any one
political clique or brand of religious faith. I abominate
the struggle between Catholics and Protestants. It's
merely a struggle for power, not that either party
knows what to do with that power. I'm interested
only in France, a strong and independent France. That
may sound strange, coming from the lips of an Italian,
but I happen to be the queen of France. God has willed
it thus. I shall discharge my bounden duty, therefore,
and no one on earth will prevent me from doing so.
Will you assist me?"

"If I can." Michel was impressed by the woman. She
was so unlike all that was known and said of her. Her
thoughts were as lucid as her manner of expressing
them. She knew what she wanted, and what she wanted
made sense.

"You sound uncertain," she said.

He hesitated.

"What are you thinking?"

"I'm no politician."

"I need no politician, I need someone who understands life, who knows human beings, their weaknesses and spiritual abysses. You shall accompany me on my way and tell me when I'm in error. Whether or not I act on your advice is my affair. Will you do that?"

Michel nodded.

"Good. I want to know all that you know. And now I shall introduce you to Ruggiero. It would interest me to hear what you think of him."

She went to a secret door, opened it, and led the way into another laboratory, where Ruggiero was engaged on an experiment. Catherine touched him on the sleeve.

"Ruggiero, I should like you to make the acquaintance of Doctor de Nostradame."

Diane was sitting in the nude for François Clouet, painter to the king. Henry looked on from an armchair while Ruggiero, standing beside the window in a deferential pose, sipped a glass of wine.

"Well," said the king, "what shall we do now?"

Diane rose, swathed herself in a silken peignoir, and gave Clouet a nod. "We'll resume tomorrow."

Clouet deposited his brush in a jar, bowed, and hurried from the room.

Diane took a carafe from the table and poured herself a glass of wine. "That man Clouet," she said, sipping it, "has painted me so often, he should soon be able to manage without me."

"He paints you only because I ask him," said Henry. "I so much enjoy watching."

She stroked his head, then turned to Ruggiero. "This Doctor de Nostradame," she said, " – kill him."

Henry raised his eyebrows. "You think it's necessary?"

"Kill him today," she told Ruggiero. "His Majesty
will receive him in audience this afternoon. Wine will
be served. Procure some lethal concoction from that
witch's kitchen of yours and insinuate it into his glass."

She signed to Ruggiero to withdraw. He bowed low,
deposited his glass on a small table, and backed out of
the room.

The king reached for her hand. "Why do you take
that charlatan so seriously?"

"I've read his book."

"How? The queen took it with her."

"You remember when I glanced at it briefly? I made
a note of the printer's name and sent for a copy." She
laughed. "He wouldn't release one at first – he had
to be persuaded. Nostradame is a cunning fox. He
doesn't intend to publish until he has obtained the
queen's blessing."

"I still fail to see why you take him seriously."

"I take anyone seriously who predicts your death."
She looked at the half-finished painting and wrinkled
her nose. "I'm growing fat."

Henry came up behind her. He put his arms around
her waist and kissed her on the neck. "You grow
lovelier each day."

That afternoon Michel waited for the king in the
audience chamber with several ladies and gentlemen
of the court. Ruggiero was standing at the back of the
room, studying his shoes with downcast eyes. Before
long the doors were flung wide and Henry entered with
Diane on his arm, followed by Catherine. He went up
to Michel.

"So you're the prophet whose book has already caused such a stir, even though no copies are to be had. You're an astute man of business, monsieur, but I fear you'll get no custom from me. Quite unlike my wife, I've no time for such rubbish."

He walked on. Michel, not having expected such a brusque reception, turned pale and inclined his head.

Henry retraced his steps. "For all that, even I was astonished to hear what people are saying. It seems a servant found Countess Beauveau's stray dog in rue Royale, just as you prophesied. Remarkable."

"Your pardon, Majesty, but that was no prophecy."

"I'm sure it wasn't. A conjuring trick? Would you care to tell me how it was done?" He laughed. "Forgive me, I know that no magician ever divulges his secrets, or he would soon be out of work."

He beckoned to a footman, who approached bearing a tray on which stood a number of glasses. The king glanced at them, took one, and handed it to Michel. He picked up a glass himself and took a sip. "Your health, Doctor."

Diane watched with bated breath as Michel raised his glass and drank.

Henry nodded. "You have predicted my death, I'm told. Do you consider that a courteous thing to do? Don't trouble to answer, I shall pay you back by making a prophecy of my own." He levelled his finger at Michel. "You, monsieur, are going to die."

Everyone looked startled.

"What do you say now?" Henry laughed heartily. "Am I not as good a prophet as you? Or do you claim to be immortal? All of us here will die in God's good time."

There was general laughter at this, and Diane softly clapped her hands. Catherine smiled. She found her husband's sally inane, but its underlying note of menace was not lost on her. He had meant it as a threat, even if he was now preening himself and happily accepting compliments on his little witticism from the flatterers around him.

Henry readdressed himself to Michel. "I had a reason for wishing to see you, monsieur. Your marvellous work during the plague more than atones for all those scribblings of yours." He turned to Catherine. "What do you say, my dear? I propose to appoint Monsieur de Nostradame physician to the court." And to Michel, "The queen would prefer to appoint you prophet to the court, but for that she will have to wait until she holds the reins of government."

He nodded briefly to Michel and walked on with Diane at his heels.

Catherine hurried over to Michel. "Come to my laboratory at once," she whispered. She glanced at the king, who had paused beside Ruggiero and was asking him something. Ruggiero's reply seemed to reassure him, because he nodded and continued on his way. Ruggiero gave Michel a sidelong, searching look.

Michel could hardly stand by the time he entered the laboratory with Catherine, his stomach cramps were so severe. Pale as death and sweating profusely, he tore at his collar with trembling fingers, coughing and retching. He pointed to a jar of powder and whispered, "Quickly! One gram of that, together with three drops of alcohol in a gill of water."

Catherine weighed out the powder and emptied it into a flask, looked around for the alcohol but failed to find it. Michel pointed feebly to a phial on a shelf. Catherine extracted some alcohol with a pipette and added three drops to the flask. She asked if she should summon Ruggiero, but he shook his head. He made his way along the shelves, clinging to them to prevent himself from falling, and pointed to various phials. Past speaking now, he clutched his stomach. His face was twisted with pain. Catherine took the phials he indicated and added as much of their contents to the flask as he signified by holding up his thumb and forefinger. At last he snatched the vessel from her, shook it, and drank it down in one. The flask fell to the floor and smashed. Dark foam oozed from his lips. Then he lost consciousness. Catherine caught him just in time to prevent him from striking his head on the edge of a shelf. Unable to support his weight, she carefully lowered him to the floor, bent over him and felt for his pulse, but to no avail. Panic-stricken, she took a mirror from the table and held it to his mouth and nose. The film of mist on the glass was so faint as to be almost invisible. He was still breathing, but only just.

Michel's eyes were closed and his face was whiter than the pillows beneath his head. Suddenly his eyelids fluttered and opened. Catherine, seated beside the bed, took his hand.

"How do you feel? You've slept for two whole days. I was very concerned."

Michel tried to sit up, but he was too weak. He sank back against the pillows.

"You're not to get up yet," Catherine told him. She smiled. "How is it, Monsieur Prophet, that you failed to discover they planned to kill you?"

"I know when I shall die, and that day has yet to dawn. I should like to go home."

"But if you know when you'll die, you can remain here awhile longer with an easy mind."

He smiled feebly. "Although the stars never lie, how can I be sure that I always read them aright? If I misconstrued their message I should have no opportunity to regret my error."

She stood up. "I want you to meet my children. I shall order you some strong broth. Then you must sleep. I shall introduce you to my young ones tomorrow."

A footman entered bearing a tray with numerous letters on it. All were addressed to Michel. Catherine took the tray and put it down on a small table beside the bed. He looked at her inquiringly. Who would have written to him? He knew no one here.

"They're invitations." She opened a few of the letters and showed them to him. "There, what did I tell you? Invitations, all of them. Word of that business with the dog has spread. Remain here. You could become a wealthy man."

Catherine was pushing Michel down a long passage in a wheelchair.

"How do you feel today?"

"Unwell."

"But you look much better than you did yesterday."

"It's these clothes. They constrict me, take my breath away, compress my body, congest the blood, paralyse the muscles. I don't understand how courtiers can wear such garments."

She laughed. "Then why don't you wear the clothes you always wear?"

"My shabby old coat? When I'm a guest of the queen?"

"The queen sent for you, not your coat."

He was still chuckling when she wheeled him into the royal nursery.

Mounted on wooden horses, the two wooden knights confronted each other with lances levelled. François and Élisabeth stood beside the miniature tilt-yard, awaiting the signal. Mary, seated on a tall chair, flourished a flag in the air. Swiftly, the other two children proceeded to wind the cranks that operated the toy. The knights glided towards each other along rails. One of them drove his lance into the other's wooden head and thrust him off his horse. François threw up his hands and yelled with delight: he had won yet again. Élisabeth was furious. She picked up her vanquished knight and hurled him at her brother, who ducked. The knight landed at the feet of Catherine, who was just wheeling Michel into the room.

"This is the famous Doctor de Nostradame of whom I told you, monsieur," she said to François. And, to Michel, "My eldest son François, future king of France."

"I bid you welcome to our nursery, monsieur," François said solemnly. "May I present my future consort, Mary Queen of Scots?"

Mary giggled. François glared at her so sternly that she stopped laughing at once. Then François himself started giggling, and Mary had to join in.

Michel gave a little bow from his wheelchair. "I'm profoundly honoured that you should receive me, monsieur."

Catherine pointed to the girl. "My eldest daughter,

Élisabeth, and the Duc d'Alençon." She indicated a baby whom a nurse had just brought in and deposited on a downy blanket on the floor.

"He cannot walk yet," said François.

"Like me," Michel replied. He rose with an effort, knelt down beside the baby, and put a rattle in its hand, then very gently shook the baby's hand to and fro. The rattle made a funny noise, the baby beamed with pleasure and kicked its little legs in the air.

There was a humming-top on the blanket, and musical instruments lay scattered everywhere: bells, cymbals, drums, rattles, flageolets. Michel started the top humming and struck a cymbal, François beat a drum, Élisabeth shook a rattle, and Mary rang a pair of bells. They all played as they pleased, with cacophonous results. Then another two children came in, both armed with wooden swords. Catherine pointed to each in turn.

"Charles, my second son, and the Duc d'Orléans."

The newcomers promptly seized an instrument apiece. All the children were playing at once now, loudly and exuberantly. Catherine herself became infected by their high spirits. She picked up a flageolet and trilled a piercing accompaniment. Pandemonium reigned. The children hopped and skipped around the room, beside themselves with glee.

Then, all at once, the merry, chaotic din became overlaid with a bass ostinato in a minor key. A muffled drum began to beat, trumpets set up mournful chorus, a harp twanged as if someone had drawn a file across the strings. And voices? Where were they coming from? They seemed to be moaning and wailing in an unseen void. Michel looked round, bewildered. A new sound invaded his head: a shrill, high-pitched, relentless whine. He saw blood on the sword in Charles's hand. And then he caught sight of more blood running down the wall. There was blood all over the floor. A tidal wave of blood surged into the nursery. The children's faces and clothing were spattered with it. Blood everywhere – the whole room was awash with blood. He rose to his feet, clinging to the arms of his wheelchair, only to sink back again. He put a hand over his eyes to blot out the fearful scenes he was witnessing.

The children had stopped playing. They gathered round, gazing at him apprehensively. Their mother's friend had suddenly become a source of disquiet.

"Are you ill, monsieur?" François inquired.

They were walking through the gardens of the château, Catherine with her arm through his.

"I want to know the truth," she said. She came to a halt and looked him in the eye. "Whether I like it or not."

Michel hesitated.

"Is it so terrible?" she asked. "So terrible that you won't come out with it? What does Seneca say? 'Minor concerns speak out, infinite concerns keep silent.'"

He sighed. Then he said, "Much blood will be spilt over your children."

"That's inevitable. We live in bloodthirsty times."

He drew a deep breath. Should he tell her what he had seen? To what end? Why should he upset the woman? What was to come would come. She would have time enough to accustom herself to the horrors that lay in store.

"Please," she said, "I must know. That was our

agreement. You were to tell me all you know, don't you remember?"

Michel nodded. "Each of your sons," he said, "will become king of France. But you yourself will outlive them all."

She stared at him in horror, let go of his arm and walked on alone for a little way. He slowly followed her. She had recovered her composure by the time he caught her up. She paused and waited for him.

"Are you sure of this?"

He shrugged. "Yes," he said. What else could he say?

They walked on in silence. Some gardeners busy trimming a hedge stopped work and bowed low as Catherine passed by, but she had eyes for no one. "There's no worse fate than to outlive one's children," she said after a while. "Very well, I shall prepare myself for terrible times to come." Then, as if nothing untoward had occurred, she linked arms with Michel and said, quite cheerfully, "You must now decide whether to spend your future in the salons of bored ladies, predicting the whereabouts of their stray lapdogs and pussycats, or – "

He laughed and made a dismissive gesture. "No, no, certainly not."

"But you'd earn a great deal of money, and your perfume would very soon make you the darling of high society. Doesn't that tempt you?" She smiled at him. "What's more, you would never be far from my side. Is even that no inducement?"

"It's not for me to decide what I should do. I have a task that was set me by God."

"So you mean to go home?"

"As soon as ever I can. Besides," he added with a

smile, "my wife is expecting our second child, and I should like to be there for the birth."

"Then you must leave at once. Very well, go, but you must promise to send me everything you write. I'll read it before it goes on sale. Do you promise?"

"I shall esteem it an honour."

"None of that courtier's nonsense, please! The matters we discuss are too serious for empty platitudes. What do you have in mind?"

"I shall resume my work. I shall absorb the visions every night and then verify them."

"You don't trust your own intuitions?"

"Yes, but I want to be absolutely sure of them and purge them of all subjective influences. I re-examine each of my prophecies. Till now the stars have always confirmed the accuracy of what I see in my trances."

"When will your next book appear?"

"Very soon. It will deal with the century to come. Then, if God wills it so, I shall look still further into the future."

Catherine embraced him. "My poor friend, I wish you all the strength in the world."

Michel travelled home by way of Agen in order to pay a call on Scaliger. Scaliger was an old man now, and who knew when he might have another opportunity? He got to Agen late one afternoon. The door of the carriage was opened by Jean, whom he warmly embraced before going inside the house.

There were some pots of paint on the floor of the chamber that had once housed the secret library, and an artist was busy adorning the whitewashed wall with a pretty landscape. Michel stood waiting in the middle of the room in which he had worked for so many years.

Scaliger appeared at last, but he uttered no word of welcome. Instead, trembling with indignation, he held up the book in his hand. It was Michel's book of prophecies.

"This was foolish of you," he said angrily, "foolish and conceited. And dangerous!" He flung the book down on the floor. "How could you publish such a thing?"

The painter gave a little bow and hurriedly withdrew.

"Answer me, Michel! You've put us all in jeopardy. Why don't you speak? Defend yourself. I want to know what made you take such a step."

"I had to do it."

"You *had* to?"

"Night after night I sit on my stool with the divining-rod poised above the water, and then, in the silence, a flame springs up. My room is filled with a divine glow, Julius, and I feel a thread reaching into my soul – a thread connecting me to the future, which then reveals itself to me. Everything within me is directed by God's inscrutable omnipotence. It is he that imbues me with the spirit of prophecy, not bacchantic frenzy or lymphatic delirium. All that I see comes from him and is confirmed by the stars. I see the most dreadful things: murder, rape, torture, catastrophes of boundless magnitude, terrible wars waged with weapons of which we still have no conception. Men will fight with ships that travel under water. They will swoop from the skies with undreamed-of velocity, dispensing fire, poisonous gases, and lethal vapours undetectable by the human eye. They will destroy everything. Themselves too, in the end."

"Will no one survive?"

"That I have yet to discover. Every night brings me something new. My present visions are of the twentieth century."

"Four hundred years hence . . ." Scaliger shook his head wonderingly.

Just then Madame Scaliger came in. She embraced Michel and asked if they were coming to table.

Scaliger looked at Michel. "Are you hungry?"

Michel shook his head.

"Then please leave us to talk in peace," the old man told his wife. "We have so little time together."

Madame Scaliger nodded, embraced Michel again, and quickly left the room.

"The twentieth century," said Michel, "will be especially terrible. Three frightful wars will encompass the whole world, nor will they be the last. A few nations will become inordinately rich while multitudes starve to death. Others will be afflicted with diseases beside which our plague will seem innocuous. New philosophies will arise, complete with baneful promises of salvation. They will make people wretched and stir them up against each other."

Michel, watched with rapt attention by Scaliger, had raised his left hand as if drawing strength from the cosmos itself. He shut his eyes. Then, abruptly, he uttered a single word: "Hadrie."

"What is Hadrie?"

"Hadrie will be the twentieth century's most monstrous leader of all. He and his sect will inflict boundless misery on the world. Many Jews will be killed – more than ever before. With poisonous gases."

He took a thick brush from a pot of red paint, went over to the wall, and paused for a moment. Then, with sudden certitude, he daubed a big crooked cross over the artist's pastel landscape. He stepped back and stared at the swastika in surprise.

"What's that?" Scaliger asked.

"I don't know."

Thin rivulets of red paint were trickling down the wall.

"Yes I do," Michel said. "It's a symbol of death."

They walked down to the lake and sat on the bench where Michel had often sat with Marie in former years.

"Our descendants will fly high into the sky," Michel went on, "in huge aerial ships built of metal. First they'll voyage to the moon, then further out into the universe. Men will set foot on Mars and Jupiter."

"And then?"

"I've yet to discover. Every night I delve deeper into the future. It often seems to me that I've glimpsed the Apocalypse, the end of everything: leaping flames, terrible earthquakes, raging waters far and wide. And polluted blood." He looked at Scaliger. "It's a punishment, believe me, an unending affliction. It goes on and on, growing steadily worse as the centuries unfold. The periods during which the human race recovers are never anything but brief. They merely enable it to gather the strength to commit fresh atrocities."

"My poor friend! Is there nothing beyond all those disasters, that terrible darkness? Is there no hope at all?"

Michel shrugged. A momentary silence fell. "I used to sit here with Marie," he said. "Twenty years ago."

Scaliger put his arm around Michel's shoulders. He wanted so much to comfort him, but he knew it was impossible. He felt infinitely sorry for his former pupil.

*   *   *

Michel, kneeling beside the graves of Marie and the children, prayed while Scaliger lingered in the background with a package under his arm. Michel rose and came over to him, then turned for a final look.

"I shall never see their graves again," he said as they slowly left the churchyard. "Thank you, Julius, for tending them so well."

They set off along a path through the fields.

"I long debated whether or not to publish my prophecies," Michel said at length.

"And why did you?"

"I even thought it wrong to soothsay – wrong with an eye to the future. The evil people who commit all the atrocities I see may simply feel strengthened and justified in perpetrating their misdeeds by what I write, believing that all is preordained and thus inevitable."

"And is everything really preordained?"

"I'm not entirely sure. In any case, I have encoded everything and couched it in oracular language to give such people no excuse. Only he that possesses the true key to them will understand my *Centuries*, and he will be chosen as I was chosen. I propose to write that man a letter."

"When will he come?"

"At the end of the twentieth century, I think. I shall tell him that the works of God are absolute and his mysteries unfathomable. All prophetic inspiration has its origin and impetus in God the Creator himself. That is how the truth reveals itself, not by way of cold intelligence or magical speculation. Magic is abominable – it clouds the mind. The one exception is true astrology. That is the touchstone with which to test all revelations; it distinguishes between truth and mere fancy. I have disguised all but a few of my prophecies. Those will be readily verifiable by anyone, so the world will see that I know and speak the truth. I have obeyed the injunction of our one, true Saviour: 'Give not that which is holy unto the dogs, neither cast ye your pearls before swine, lest they trample them under their feet, and turn again and rend you.' "

"But Michel, what can be done if all is as inevitable as your visions imply? Are we to put our hands in our laps and abandon all hope?"

"It may be, though I cannot tell for sure, that those who grasp my meaning will be able to alter the course of their destiny. Perhaps my visions are only of the worst that can possibly happen. If human beings grow wiser and more sensible, things may turn out differently."

Scaliger sighed. "Human beings have never been wise or sensible. The worst has always happened. No new weapon of destruction has ever remained unused."

"Then the world will become a terrible place, desolate and deserted, just as my visions have always foretold."

They looked out across the broad plain. All was quiet and peaceful. "I shall die soon," Scaliger said. Michel looked into his eyes and felt his pulse. "Your gall-bladder and kidneys don't function as well as they did, but in other respects . . ."

"We shall not see each other again."

Michel regretfully concurred. Scaliger took his arm, and they walked on. "When I heard you were coming," said the old man, "I was so angry, I had no wish to receive you."

Michel smiled. "But you did for all that. Why?"

"Because you're the only person to whom I can

entrust this." Scaliger indicated the package in his hand. "There was one thing I never showed you in the old days. You shall have it now."

Michel took the package, which was carefully wrapped and sealed. "What is it?"

"The greatest secret in the world: the Revelation of St John the Divine."

"But I know the book. Everyone knows it."

"This is the original in his own hand. Uncensored and unabridged."

Michel laid the flat of his hand on the package as if trying to gauge the nature of its contents. "Well, what does it say?"

Scaliger looked at him. "I've never read it. I could never summon up the strength to do so."

Anna had already given birth to their second child, a girl, by the time Michel finally reached home. Mother and daughter were both in fine fettle. Anna had made little of the birth, which was an easy one. One life generated another, she felt, and that was that. The rest was love and upbringing. Her view of the matter was wholly practical. Whenever she wanted to tease Michel she used to say that she was responsible for love and he for upbringing, so the children would never become a bone of contention between them.

One day some years later, when she was making a fair copy of another of his texts, he came downstairs from the turret chamber and walked past her in a daze. She jumped up and followed him.

Going out into the garden, he gathered some dry wood into a heap and placed the book Scaliger had given him on top. Then he doused the whole bonfire with oil and lit it. The flames shot up in no time, bright and dazzling. Anna shaded her face with her hand and Michel screwed up his eyes, the glow was so intense. Although the wood was quickly reduced to ashes, the book lay in their midst unscathed.

Anna pointed to it. "What in God's name is that?"

Michel retrieved the book from the ashes. It was not even warm. "The Revelation of St John," he whispered.

She crossed herself.

Michel deliberated briefly, then went over to one of the two wells in the garden and dropped the book down it. The same afternoon he had the well filled in and the stone parapet demolished. Finally, he scattered grass seed on the trodden earth. His son César, now nearly ten years old, watched him with a puzzled expression.

"Why did you have the well filled in, Father?" he asked. "It gave good water."

"We'll sink a new one," Michel told him. "The old one was running dry."

"But is there more water in the garden?"

"Of course." Michel fetched a divining-rod and made his way to another corner of the garden. The rod soon flexed in his hands. He circled the spot, measuring the depth, quantity, and exact source of the water. "There's plenty of good water here," he said, "and only twelve feet down. Bring me a stick. This is where we'll sink the new well."

César brought a stick and embedded it in the turf at the point Michel indicated with his foot. "I wish I could do that too," he sighed.

Michel put the divining-rod in the boy's hands and showed him how to hold it. "Now try. That's right, but a little higher. Hold it quite loosely, so that it can flex, and keep it horizontal all the time. Off you go."

César circled the spot, but the rod remained immobile. He turned to his father with a disappointed air.

"It didn't work."

Michel stroked his head. "It takes time to acquire the knack," he said consolingly. "Don't despair, practice makes perfect." He corrected the boy's position. "Hold it quite loosely. Yes, that's it. Now try again."

Anna, who had been watching from a window, came running out of the house. Angrily, she snatched the rod from César's hands.

"Come inside at once."

"But I was just learning how to – "

"I don't care!" She snapped the rod in half. "That's a trick you'll never learn."

The boy stared at her, thoroughly disconcerted. He had never seen his mother so furious.

"Come now." She took him by the hand and led him into the house.

Michel watched them go with a smile, then followed them inside. Anna had sat down at the kitchen table and was already hard at work on another fair copy. She was still angry, he could tell. He came up behind her.

"Where's César?"

She continued to write without looking up. "In his room."

"Why so angry?"

She laid the quill aside. "I don't want you teaching him such things – I want him to be happy. I see how much strength it takes out of you. César is not as robust as you – it would kill him. Leave the boy in peace!"

"You copy out all I write, but you can't have read any of it."

"What makes you think so?"

"Have you at least read the dedication?"

"Yes, and it angered me beyond belief."

"That was because you misinterpreted it."

She seized a sheet and held it up. Her hand was trembling. "'To my son César' – that was what you wrote."

"Yes, my spiritual offspring: the César who will appear at some future time. I wrote it so that he will interpret my verses correctly and find the key to the whole work contained in them – so that he fully understands them. His power will be immense, and I pray to God he wields it aright and refrains from misusing his knowledge."

"When will he be born, this 'son' of yours?"

"Five hundred years from now, perhaps."

César had stolen into the room unobserved. He gazed at Michel wide-eyed. "Will people read your book in five hundred years' time?"

Anna couldn't help laughing. "That remains to be seen."

"But will you live as long as that?" César demanded.

Michel took the boy in his arms and kissed him, then drew Anna close. "Never fear," he told her. "Our son has many gifts. He's sensitive and intelligent. He'll be a fine scholar, but he lacks the divine spark."

"Are you sure?" She laughed. "I couldn't endure another man in the family as tiresome as you."

Michel had been waiting a long time for the big package the courier had brought from Naples. Anna asked what it contained.

"Raw material for our perfumes," he told her as he paid the courier generously for his trouble.

The man grinned. "All the townsfolk are going mad with love, they're so intoxicated by the sweet scents issuing from your laboratory when they pass it."

Michel took the package to the laboratory, where Hélène and some other women were manufacturing perfumes. One of them was applying a thick layer of ox and pig's fat to a sheet of glass in a wooden frame. Another was laying petals on a similar sheet of prepared glass, one by one, so that the grease would absorb their scent. A third woman was sluicing the fat off yet another sheet of glass to conserve the precious essential oils derived from jasmine and tuberoses.

Michel put the package on a table and opened it with care. There was a wooden casket inside.

Hélène wiped her hands on a cloth, pinned her hair up, and went over to him. "How bold of you to venture in here without your wife," she said. "What's that?"

He shook his head at her. "You never give up, do you?" Carefully opening the casket, he unwrapped its contents: five potato-sized glands covered in hair. Hélène recoiled in horror and held her nose.

"My God, what a stench! What are they?"

"Rutting glands taken from musk-deer. They live in the Himalayan highlands."

"What are we to make out of the revolting things?"

"A new perfume."

"What! It might put the Evil One to flight, but it would never inflame anyone's senses."

He laughed, holding the glands at arm's length, for he was just as revolted by the disgusting smell. "They contain a secret substance that drives the hinds wild. Very small quantities of it added to our perfume will render it heavy and sensual." He laughed again. "If a woman smells of it, every man will be after her like a rutting musk-deer after the hinds."

Hélène took one of the glands and examined it closely. "Perhaps I should eat one raw this minute. What do you think, Michel?" She stroked his cheek.

"Please don't, Hélène," he said, faintly irritated. He took the gland from her, put it back with the others, and handed the casket to one of the women. "Take it to the store-room, but keep it well away from the flowers. Their scent would be ruined."

"When do we start using them?" Hélène asked.

"Tomorrow. I've been thinking, Hélène, and you're right. We manufacture perfumes, so why not other things as well? Let's make sweet-smelling soaps and incense candles. Cosmetics, too, and fruit preserves. Let's make nothing but good things that gladden people's hearts!"

It was July 1st, 1559, and the tournament was in full swing. A sea of banners fluttered above the lists, countless spectators occupied the stands. Catherine was seated in a box with Michel de Nostradame's new book beside her. She picked it up and clasped it to her breast. In the next box sat Diane de Portier. King Henry and Count Gabriel de Lorges Montgomery, commander of his Scottish Guard, were waiting to joust for a third time. Their horses' heads were adorned with magnificent plumes, their flanks protected by heavy, brightly-coloured blankets. Pages handed Henry and Montgomery their lances. A fanfare rang out. Diane looked across at Catherine, saw the book in her hand, and suddenly remembered. She jumped up and hurried down to the lists.

"Henry!" she called, running up to the king.

"What is it?" He donned his golden helmet.

"Don't do it, please!"

"Why not?"

"Please! The prophecy. The tournament, the lance, the golden helmet, the third contest – his description tallies in every detail."

The king laughed. "Anyone would think you as foolish as that crazy wife of mine."

"Please, I beg you."

"Don't make a laughing-stock of yourself. Out of my way!"

He raised his arm. Montgomery, at the other end of the lists, did likewise: both contestants were ready. Another fanfare rang out.

Tensely, Catherine rose to her feet. She saw the king order Diane to leave the lists and resume her seat. His mistress made one last attempt to dissuade him, but in vain. She returned to the box, her face a mask of apprehension.

She glanced at Catherine, who merely gave a faint smile and transferred her attention to the lists.

The riders broke into a gallop, lowering their lances as the distance between them diminished. Sunlight glittered on the king's golden helmet, the tip of Montgomery's lance. Henry spurred his horse into an even faster gallop, confident of victory. Montgomery's eyes narrowed as he aimed his lance at the king's chest. Foam flew from the horses' muzzles, the spectators leapt to their feet. Montgomery, the king, the two lances – they were very close now. And then Montgomery's lance crashed into Henry's breastplate, glanced off it, transfixed his helmet, pierced his eye. Blood spurted through the golden grille. Henry tumbled off his horse. A chorus of horrified cries filled the air. Catherine closed her eyes, beside herself with happiness.

Diane ran down to the lists. Many people had gathered round the king, who was lying motionless on the ground. She knelt beside him, held his hand, rested her tearful face on his breastplate. He was quite unconscious.

Everyone stood aside as Catherine slowly made her way over to him. She looked down at Diane, touched her on the shoulder. Diane looked up, saw her faint smile, and understood. She rose and curtsied low. Her great days were over, and she knew it.

Utterly calm and composed, Catherine bent over the king and nodded to herself. It had happened just as the book had foretold: the lance had pierced the grille of her husband's golden helmet and embedded itself deep in his eye. Blood was trickling through the visor and seeping into the sand. Catherine turned and beckoned to some men, who hurried up with a litter. The king was placed on it and carried to a tent. Catherine slowly followed. Diane made to do likewise, but one look from Catherine – one cold, imperious, regal, dismissive glance – deterred her. Never having seen the queen like that before, Diane was suddenly conscious of her enemy's inner strength. All those years of dissimulation, and now this aura of authority, this serene self-assurance. Catherine had been waiting a long time for this moment, and she was enjoying it – quietly but unmistakably enjoying it, yet no one present reproached her for doing so. For the first time, she stood before them as the true queen of France.

Diane watched the king being borne away, then left the lists – alone.

Montgomery hurried after Catherine, too distressed

to speak. She paused and turned to him. "No blame attaches to you, Count," she said, so quietly than no one but Montgomery could hear. "I cannot, however, guarantee your safety. You had better leave here today – preferably for England. I shall confiscate your property." He looked aghast, but she smiled. "Confiscate it," she added, "and send it all to England, together with a small reward. Now go."

Montgomery bowed low as she turned and disappeared into the tent.

Henry died on July 10th. Young François was crowned king in his stead and Catherine assumed the regency on his behalf. The prophecy had been fulfilled.

Michel was hard at work on the new perfume. Hélène, his sole assistant in this venture, watched tensely as the crucial moment drew near. He filled a pipette with some highly dilute essence of musk and added a few drops to a flask containing cypress oil, Florentine orris-root, carnation, calamus oil, coriander, and rose oil. That done, he gently swirled contents of the flask to mix them thoroughly.

He had conducted many experiments beforehand, repeatedly varying the proportions and composition of his mixtures. He had tried and abandoned lavender and lilies, cinnamon and ambergris. Pome-citron and bigarade, saffron and ginger, almond kernels and yew root, box and beech – he had distilled their essences and mixed them all in different quantities. Why? Because the one, inimitable, bitter-sweet scent which would be neither too light nor too heavy, which would titillate the senses but did not overstimulate them, which possessed body as well as soul, which a person could sense without being aware of it – a subtle sublimate of that kind was obtainable only by balancing various essences against each other with the utmost precision.

Michel had told Hélène that, when composing a perfume, he favoured the procedure adopted by the artist Zeusi of Heraclea, who, when he wished to paint a girl, always used a number of models. He would take the nose from one, the mouth from another, the cheeks from a third, the breasts from a fourth, the hips from a fifth, the thighs and ankles from a sixth. He summoned as many models to his studio as would furnish the details he required, so that at last, when he had put them all together like a patchwork quilt, he was confronted by the girl that had existed in his imagination from the first – one that surpassed even Helen of Troy in beauty. It was just the same, Michel said, with perfumes. Roses smelled wonderful by themselves, as did cinnamon and ambergris and violets, but they could not befuddle and intoxicate the senses on their own; they lacked the sensuality of the spirit.

He slowly swirled the contents of the flask once more. They were now at a temperature that would enable the scent to diffuse itself fully.

"Well, what are you waiting for?" Hélène said impatiently. "Get on with it."

He took a thin stick with a tuft of lamb's-wool wound around the end, dipped it in the fluid and held it to her nose. She sniffed. She took the stick from him and sniffed again, inhaling more deeply. Then she dabbed a little of the perfume on the inside of her wrist to see how it smelled when in contact with her skin. She allowed it to evaporate for a moment or two before taking another sniff. Finally, she closed her eyes with a look of rapture.

"Incredible!" she said. "It's beyond belief. To think those evil-smelling things could produce such a magical scent."

Taking a scrap of silk, she dipped it carefully in the perfume and dabbed herself with it: behind the ears, on the throat, on the wrists. Then she held out her arm for Michel to smell, watching him closely as he did so.

"Well?"

He nodded and laughed. "We shall sell a great deal of it."

She looked disappointed. "Is that all?"

"Why else are we making it?"

Hélène glared at him furiously. Without warning, she snatched the flask from him and hurled it to the floor. The glass shattered, the perfume went trickling over the flagstones.

He stared at her aghast. She clasped his head in her hands and kissed him fiercely on the mouth, forced him down on the table and tried to crush his body beneath hers. In an extremity of passion, she breathed endearments in his ear, some fond and foolish, some coarse and obscene.

Michel managed to extricate himself. He slapped her face and made for the door, but she was too quick for him. Reaching the door first, she locked it and dropped the key down the front of her dress. "Come and get it!" she cried, darting round to the far side of the table. "Come and get it!" With a wild laugh she fished out the key and dangled it in the air.

Michel found the whole situation too ridiculous for words. "Be reasonable, Hélène," he pleaded. "Give me that key."

"Come and get it!"

"Please, Hélène. This is absurd."

She shook her head. Suddenly, Michel vaulted on to the table. It took her by surprise – she hadn't expected any such move. Looking down at her, he was suddenly reminded of the way Sophie, too, had darted around the table and snatched his edition of Ovid. She had held the book in the air just as Hélène was doing with the key, and he had leapt at her and embraced and fondled her. No! he told himself. No, no, no!

He jumped down off the table and advanced on her. Hélène backed away until she was brought up short by the wall and could retreat no further. Having wrested the key from her hand, he strode to the door and unlocked it. She watched him go with a look of consternation. Then, on a sudden impulse, she stooped and picked up a sliver of glass from the broken flask. "Look!" she cried, and slashed her wrist in one quick movement.

She laughed hysterically as blood spurted from the wound. Michel dashed to the table, picked up a cloth lying there, and hurriedly applied a tourniquet. She offered no resistance, he uttered not a word. Once he had stopped the bleeding and bandaged her up, he turned to go.

Supporting herself on one hand, she leaned against the table and gazed after him. Tears were streaming down her cheeks, not that he saw them. He had hurried off without a backward glance.

Anna was at home, correcting the latest batch of printer's proofs. Michel had lately written down the recipes for his fruit preserves with a view to publishing them. He had also completed a book of predictions for the following year. The printer couldn't cope with the demand for Michel's books, which had been selling like hot cakes since King Henry's death. Michel was now planning a book on how to beautify and rejuvenate the body; on the sweet-smelling pomades, salves and oils to be used for that purpose; on what was required to clean one's teeth and prevent them from going rotten; and on ways of keeping one's breath sweet when they had already done so. There was a market for such books. The children were growing up fast, and educating them was an expensive business. The practice now brought in too little on its own, but the books were proving a lucrative source of income.

Michel looked over Anna's shoulder, chewing a mouthful of bread and ham. He said nothing of what had just happened in the laboratory, not wishing to upset her.

At length he went upstairs to his turret chamber, but he was still too agitated to work. He paced nervously up and down, then walked to the window. Hélène was standing in the street below, looking up at him. He shook his head, sat down on the stool, and debated what to do. He went over to the window again, but Hélène had disappeared. He stood there irresolutely for a while, then weighed out some powder and scattered it on the water in the basin. Settling himself on the stool, he picked up a divining-rod. What he had to do was far more important than worrying about the erotic paroxysms of a sister-in-law who pursued him like a bitch in heat.

Meanwhile, Hélène was on her way to the church. She walked up to the great wooden door, breathing heavily, and, after a moment's hesitation, knocked. There was no response. Weakened by loss of blood and in pain from her wound, she was incapable of knocking hard enough. She stooped, picked up a stone, and hammered on the door until it was finally opened by a monk. She hurried inside, and the monk closed the door behind her.

The terrible visions had returned. In the depths of his trance, Michel saw buildings collapse, shattered by bombs, engulfed in flames and smoke, overwhelmed by walls of water. Whole cities were devastated, whole tracts of land poisoned and polluted. A monstrous mushroom cloud sprang up and loomed over all. And then the earth disintegrated: the planet itself exploded into a ball of fire. The end had come at last.

But in the starry sky, already far removed from this catastrophe, Michel saw an enormous aerial ship speeding away from the place where the earth had formerly been. It was flying to another planet beyond which, with preternatural brilliance, an unfamiliar sun was rising. The ship's speed decreased. Jets of fire spurted from tubes in the stern as it altered course and headed for the planet. Closeted within it, helmeted figures attired in strange, bulky clothing peered anxiously at innumerable instruments, some resembling the face of a clock, others like rectangular sheets of glass with greenish images flickering behind them. One of the men gave an order. The ship tilted until its stern was pointing at the surface of the planet, which was now very near. More jets of fire issued from the tubes in the stern, and the aerial vessel's speed decreased still further.

Moments later it landed in a lush meadow on the shores of a lake set in the midst of a broad, verdant valley. A door in the side opened, and seven of the crew emerged. All of them, men and women alike, were wearing the same bulky garments and glass-visored helmets. The leader made his way cautiously down a ladder to the ground. The others slowly followed. They stood there in the meadow, consulting some instruments they had brought with them from the ship. Tensely watched by the rest, the leader proceeded to loosen the safety devices that secured his helmet to his costume. The woman beside him made a last attempt to dissuade him, but he smilingly shook his head and removed the helmet altogether. Bare-headed now, he drew the fresh air deep into his lungs. It was warm and aromatic. He laughed aloud and flung his helmet away. The others, too, removed their helmets and breathed freely. They embraced each other in delight and walked down to the lakeside. The leader bent, scooped up some water in the hollow of his glove, and drank. It was good. Now they all removed their protective clothing. More of the crew emerged from the ship and ran down to the water's edge, stripping off their outlandish garments as they went. They drank, splashed each other playfully, even plunged into the lake and swam. Animals joined them, warily at first, but it was not long before they began to graze and drink without fear.

Though still in the depths of his trance, Michel was smiling. This was no vain illusion. There was hope after all: he had glimpsed the paradise that awaited mankind when the earth had ceased to exist. People, human beings like himself, would survive to see that paradise and dwell there.

And then the door of the turret chamber burst open. Soldiers of the Inquisition rushed in, followed by the inquisitor himself and Hélène. She stood on the threshold with her bandaged hand extended and her forefinger levelled at Michel, whose trance persisted. "There he is!" she cried triumphantly. "He's in league with the Devil, just as I said!" In her excitement she tore at the bandage with her teeth, ripped it off her wrist, and furiously scratched the wound beneath.

Anna came running up the stairs and pushed past the soldiers. The inquisitor was grasping Michel by the shoulder. She wrenched his hand away.

"Don't wake him now, please! It could spell his death!"

The men seized Anna and dragged her out of the room. The inquisitor gestured to a soldier, who went over and shook Michel roughly.

"Michel de Nostradame," said the inquisitor. "I arrest you in the name of the Holy Inquisition."

But Michel heard nothing, nor was he aware that two soldiers had picked him up by the arms and legs and carried him down to the street. His face still wore the same blissful smile.

They had taken Michel to a cellar in the house of the Holy Inquisition and imprisoned him in a high-backed wooden armchair. There was an iron band around his head, his arms were shackled behind his back, his ankles chained to the legs of the chair. His face was streaming with blood, his shirt torn, his body a mass of cuts and abrasions. They had thrashed him with rods and chains, laid him down on a bed of nails, scalded him with boiling water – tried every means of inducing him to confess. Now he had fainted yet again.

The inquisitor was seated in an armchair richly upholstered in red velvet. Beside him stood a table, and on it lay Michel's book of prophecies. Hélène was lurking behind a column in a corner of the cellar, watching the scene with feverish eyes.

The inquisitor was growing dissatisfied with the progress of his interrogation. He signalled to a soldier, who roused Michel by throwing a bucketful of water into his face. Then he rose, he made his way around the table, and halted just in front of the prisoner.

"Your books, Michel de Nostradame," he said softly, looking into Michel's eyes, "were written by the Devil. That much we already know for sure, whether or not you admit it. All that concerns us now is your immortal soul. Unburden it. The Almighty may yet have mercy on you if you confess your sin and sincerely repent of it. Recant!"

Michel's lips shaped a single word: "No."

The inquisitor hit him in the face.

"We shall see," he said. "We have time and ingenuity in abundance. Michel de Nostradame, you stand accused of having allied yourself with the forces of darkness; of having so bewitched Count Montgomery that he slew Henry, King of France, just as you predicted years earlier." He took the book from the table and held it up. "And for what reason?" he bellowed. "So that people would buy your scribblings! So that they would believe and follow you!" His voice dropped again. "But we, monsieur, are unimpressed by such sorcery. You are charged with the most heinous crime of all: blasphemy. Do you confess your guilt?"

Michel did not hear. He had lost consciousness again.

"Answer me!" the inquisitor yelled. He took hold of Michel's cheek in one clawlike hand and squeezed it cruelly. "Answer me!" he repeated. "Do you confess your guilt?"

He picked up a bucket of water and flung it in Michel's face. In response to an unspoken command, two soldiers released him from the chair and dragged him over to a wall, where they chained him up and put an iron band studded with spikes around his neck. Although the band was as yet loose enough not to embed the spikes too deeply in his flesh, blood began to trickle down his chest. Next, the soldiers inserted his hands in iron gloves fitted with screws that enabled each finger to be broken in turn. Michel cried out in agony as they proceeded to tighten them. Then his head fell forward on his chest. The inquisitor grabbed him by the hair, yanked his head back, and banged it against the stone wall. His face was only inches from Michel's.

"Do you confess your guilt?"

Michel smiled. "My eyes have seen paradise – it does exist. A blissful age will ensue on all the horrors of this world. Humanity is destined to survive."

The soldiers tightened the screws in the gloves and the ring of spikes around his neck.

"You can kill me," he whispered, "but the truth will live for evermore."

Furiously, the inquisitor lashed him across the face with a thin whip of plaited wire. "Retract your lies!" he yelled. And, to the soldiers, "Why so half-hearted?" He laid about them, too, with his whip. "Are you sparing the man because he brought your children into the world? What makes you so sure they're not the Devil's bastards?" He grabbed Michel by the throat. "I want a confession, do you hear!"

"The Devil is in him!" Hélène screamed wildly. "Kill him! Kill him!"

"Confess your guilt!" the inquisitor roared.

"Why should he, when he's innocent?"

Everyone, the inquisitor first and foremost, turned to see who had dared to say such a thing.

Catherine de Médicis, Queen of France, was descending the cellar steps.

"Release him," she commanded.

The inquisitor arrogantly shook his head. He neither bowed nor uttered a word of greeting. "This court is fulfilling the will of God, and of his representative on earth, His Holiness the Pope. It derives its authority from the Almighty himself. That being so, any interference in the affairs of the Holy Inquisition, from whatever source, is a crime against – "

Catherine smilingly cut him short. "Would you care to stake your life on obtaining the confession of which you spoke?"

The inquisitor was taken aback. He hesitated for a moment, then made a deep obeisance.

Michel was surrounded by his numerous children: César, Michel, André, Madeleine, Anne, and Diane. They were all seated at the big kitchen table. Michel's neck and hands were bandaged, but he had recovered with surprising speed. At present he was explaining the solar system. Anna came in carrying a tray laden with glasses of fresh orange juice. She handed them round.

"This is the sun," Michel said, taking a big red apple from the fruit basket. "And that's the earth." He deposited a cherry on the table some distance from the apple.

César took another cherry, ate it, and spat the stone out on the table close to the first cherry.

"And that, César," said Anna, "is very bad manners."

"But Mama," César protested, "it's the moon." He pushed the stone even closer to the cherry.

"Have a care," said Michel. "The moon exerts a great influence on us. It moves the sea, and it can also make Mama lose her temper in no time."

Anna laughed. "That's not true."

Michel laughed too. "Oh, but it is." He picked up the cherry and popped it into his mouth.

Soldiers were standing guard in front of Michel's house. A stir ran through the crowd that had gathered outside as a carriage came into view, preceded and followed by detachments of mounted soldiers. It pulled up outside the house and Catherine alighted. She looked about her. One or two onlookers waved. A few faint cheers rang out. Then the first hats flew into the air and the cheers redoubled in volume. Catherine acknowledged them before walking quickly up the steps and into the house.

Michel started to rise when Catherine entered, but she stopped him with a gesture. Anna and the girls curtsied, the boys bowed. Catherine surveyed the family with a hint of emotion. She beckoned to César, who glanced uncertainly at his father. Michel gave him a reassuring nod, so he went over to the queen. She bent down and put her hands on his shoulders.

"You must promise me something, César," she said. "Never be concerned about your father again. No one will ever harm him, not while I'm alive. Do you promise?"

César nodded shyly.

Catherine straightened up and patted his head, then turned to Michel and asked how he was. She sat down at the table.

César held up the apple. "This is the sun," he said.

Catherine relieved him of it and took a big bite. "Very good," she said. "Now the sun is shining inside my belly."

The children rocked with laughter.

"Monsieur de Nostradame," Catherine said, "Not for the first time, I've come to seek your advice."

PART SIX

The Last Day

The weather was being more than usually kind to Salon in the summer of 1566. It had rained sufficiently in June, and the farmers were expecting a good harvest. On July 1st Michel took the entire family to the church in which he had married Anna, and they prayed together. The sun was shining when they came out. Michel was slightly afflicted with gout nowadays, and he had worked the whole night long, but he was in high spirits none the less. He took Anna's arm and asked if she would care to come for a stroll across the fields outside town, to the hill that afforded such a splendid view of the countryside.

Anna looked concerned. "Won't it be too much for you?"

"Alphonse can fetch us in the trap," he said.

She nodded and sent the children home, eager to be alone with him. It was arranged that Alphonse should come for them in an hour's time.

"I've made my will," Michel said suddenly, when

they were taking their ease on a bench at the top of the hill.

"Why speak of it now?"

He put his hand on hers. "You've no need to worry about the future – I wanted you to know that. There's more than enough for you all. The perfumes are selling well. So are the recipes, and the books will continue to bring in money for some time to come."

"I don't like it when you talk in that fashion."

"My work is at an end. I penned my last quatrain this morning. My predictions extend as far as the year 3797. In church just now I thanked God for giving me the strength to complete my work."

She beamed. "You'll never know how happy and relieved I am. Now you can rest and enjoy life. We shall have a little more time to ourselves at last."

"Do you think that young Rodolphe is really the right husband for our Madeleine?" Michel asked.

"He comes of good stock."

"If you approve, she shall marry him. In any case, you'll have to make all such decisions yourself from now on."

"Don't talk like that! Why are you so gloomy today?"

"I'm not gloomy, Anna. On the contrary, I'm very happy."

"Everything will look better tomorrow."

"Tomorrow morning, my dear, you'll find me lying between my bed and the little bench in front of it."

She flung her arms around his neck. "Please, please don't say such things!"

"Why not? Every life has to end sooner or later." He gazed at her fondly. "I love you, Anna. I love you just as I did that very first day, when you came to me to be examined."

She couldn't repress a smile. "I've never forgotten how you coughed to warn me before you touched me below the waist."

He smiled too. "I coughed because I was confused and embarrassed. I'd examined many women in my time, all of whom had confronted me naked. But when you came in I hardly dared to touch you for fear you would feel how my hand was trembling with desire. Ah, Anna, we've had a good life together in spite of everything."

She started to cry. Michel gently brushed the tears from her cheek. "Don't weep," he said, "or I really will become gloomy."

Alphonse drove up and helped Michel into the trap. Anna got in beside him and spread a rug over his knees. He took her hand.

Alphonse cracked his whip and the horse ambled off. He wheeled the trap and drove back down the hill towards the town. The sun was setting behind the mountains.

The coffin was walled up in the Franciscan Minorites' church at Salon, on the left of the west door. Anna had her husband's epitaph composed and set out after the manner of Titus Livius, the Roman historian:

Here lie the remains of Michael Nostradamus, whose wellnigh divine pen, esteemed by all, was worthy to write and acquaint mankind with events that would occur throughout the globe under the influence of the stars. He died at Salon de Craux in Provence on July 2nd in the year 1566, aged 62 years, 6 months, and 17 days.

Posterity, disturb not his
repose. Anna Pontia Ge-
mella wishes her hus-
band eternal
bliss.

Epilogue

Early one morning in October of the year 1791, three men bearing pickaxes, crowbars and sledgehammers approached the ruins of the Franciscan Minorites' church, which had been destroyed by marauding Revolutionary soldiers. One of them was a blacksmith, another a carpenter, the third a farmer. They had spent the entire night drinking to get their courage up. Their plan had first been conceived a long time ago, and they now proposed to carry it out. They stood in silence for a moment, looking at the plaque that concealed the coffin.

"This is it," said the blacksmith, whose idea it had been in the first place. "He's inside that wall there."

"Why didn't he have himself buried like anyone else?" demanded the carpenter.

"Maybe he didn't want people treading on him," the blacksmith quipped.

The carpenter bent over the plaque, which was already weather-worn. "What does it say?"

"Posterity, disturb not his repose," the blacksmith

read laboriously. "Anna Pontia Gemella wishes her husband eternal bliss."

The farmer was feeling uneasy. He shivered, even though warm sunlight was already streaming into the ruined church. "Should we really open the coffin?" he said doubtfully.

The blacksmith nodded. "That's why we're here. We've talked about doing it long enough, now let's do it. I'll wager that coffin contains the secret key to his prophecies. Just imagine if we find it!" He nudged the farmer and guffawed. "Then there'll be a new inscription: In October of the year 1791, Bernard Pelletier found the key to the secrets of Nostradamus and so became the most powerful man in the world!"

"I don't know," said the farmer. "I'm scared."

"Of what?" The blacksmith dug him in the ribs again. "Do you reckon he's going to bite you?" He took a hefty swig at his bottle, handed it to the carpenter, spat on his hands, and attacked the wall with a sledgehammer. The others picked up their tools and followed suit.

"He foretold his own death to the day," the farmer muttered. "On July 1st, 1566, he said they'd find him dead the next morning, lying on the floor between his bed and the bench in front of it. And that's the way it turned out."

"It's an old wives' tale," said the carpenter, shaking his head.

"What are you doing here, then?" the farmer demanded.

The carpenter laughed. "You never can tell," he said.

They battered away at the wall, levering out the larger stones and tossing them aside. At last they came to the coffin. None of them spoke. They cleared away the rest of the masonry and there it was, a stone coffin vertically embedded in the wall.

"Should we really do it?" said the carpenter, whose Dutch courage was also wearing off.

Even the blacksmith was uncertain whether to open the coffin. He merely shrugged. In the end it was the farmer who took a crowbar and prized the lid off.

The skeleton of Michel de Nostradame stood facing them for a moment, but only for a moment. Then it tottered, collapsed, and fell to bits. The three men sprang back in alarm.

On top of the heap of bones, illuminated by a single shaft of sunlight, lay an amulet. Slowly and hesitantly, the men edged closer to the ruined skeleton. The blacksmith bent down. The amulet bore an inscription. He peered at it and turned pale.

"What's the matter?" asked the carpenter.

The blacksmith was trembling now. Bereft of speech, he merely pointed to the amulet. The farmer bent over it. "What does it say?" he asked.

"It says," the blacksmith replied in a low, awestruck voice, "'My coffin will be opened in October of the year 1791.'"

They shrank back in terror, staring at each other. Then, as one man, they turned tail and fled. The jumble of white bones continued to lie at the foot of the coffin, the amulet glinted in the sunlight.

NOSTRADAMUS

A NOTE ON THE AUTHOR

Knut Boeser, Ph. D., born 1944, studied general and comparative literature in Berlin and Paris. Thereafter he pursued a free-lance writer's career in Berlin and Vienna. Having been chief dramatic adviser and, subsequently, director of Berlin's Renaissance-Theater, he was later appointed chief dramatic adviser to the Staatliche Schauspielbühnen, also of Berlin. Knut Boeser has published books on Max Reinhardt, Erwin Piscator, and Oscar Panizza. He now divides his time between Berlin and Traunkirchen, writing stage plays, screenplays, essays, and prose works.

Knut Boeser also wrote the screenplay of the movie, *Nostradamus*.